Lorna Gray was born in 1980 in Bedfordshire. Her relationship with the glorious countryside of the Cotswolds began many years ago when she first moved to Cirencester. She has been exploring the area through her love of history, adventure and romance ever since.

This is Lorna's fourth post-WWII mystery. Her three previous novels are *In the Shadow of Winter* (2015), *The War Widow* (2018) and *The Antique Dealer's Daughter* (2018). She lives in the Cotswolds with her husband.

🐦 @MsLornaGray
📷 @MsLornaGray
📘 /MsLornaGray
mslornagray.co.uk

Mrs P's Book
of Secrets

Lorna Gray

OneMoreChapter

One More Chapter
a division of HarperCollins*Publishers* Ltd
1 London Bridge Street
London SE1 9GF

www.harpercollins.co.uk

First published in Great Britain by HarperCollins*Publishers* 2019

Copyright © Lorna Gray 2019

Cover design by HarperCollins*Publishers* Ltd 2019
Cover images © Shutterstock.com

Lorna Gray asserts the moral right to be identified as the author
of this work.

A catalogue copy of this book is available from the British
Library.

ISBN 978-0-00-836825-8

For all the people who have contributed to
the making of this book

Chapter 1

December 1946, Moreton-in-Marsh

My grandmother and mother performed a rather unusual war service. Through the medium of regular séances, they worked – and still do work – to guide the wandering souls of poor lost soldiers out of the filthy quagmire of war.

There were some, they say, who found the shock of their violent end so sudden and so disorientating that it bewildered their soul. The living senses might have made the switch from the roar of bombs to the silence of the hereafter, but the shadow of the men they had been would sometimes remain there still. Detached from the nightmare of the battlefield, but bound to it; staggered and confused.

The process of reaching them called for no miasma, no rattling tables. My grandmother and her little gathering of fellow spiritualists simply treasured the serious belief that they were extending a kindly hand to those rudderless souls, before steering them first towards acceptance, and secondly into peace.

When my husband was killed, I refused flatly to let them do it.

I couldn't bear to think of his soul being stranded in those dismal terms. And not because I was selfish, or enjoyed the kind of superior cynicism that masquerades as lucid reason. Everyone has their own way of dealing with loss. But for me it felt as if real selfishness would dwell in that sort of calling out of his name. I would never stand by while they did it without me, but if I joined them and some part of it worked, my husband might learn the truth from me – that I didn't want to let him go.

Because, real or not, it would never feel like whispering a tender farewell to him across the divide. It would be like calling him back.

It would feel like I was telling him flatly that I can grasp him wherever he is, and that I mean to shackle him to me, when surely, of all things, I have to trust in the deeper workings of my heart and believe he has already found his release.

So, for now, I keep to life and leave my husband well alone.

I was first carried home to this place by that feeling eight weeks ago. This was the time, after all, when our newfound peace was stumbling towards its second Christmas in all the monotony of rationing. And in the spirit of the year's end and the time of darkness and so on, it has lately seemed to me that nowhere was a better light shining for me than in my uncle's little book printing business in the north Cotswolds town of Moreton-in-Marsh.

I was enjoying the process of reacquainting myself with his

busy little first floor office, above the street front shop and the narrow printworks in the outbuildings behind. My uncle wasn't staid, but his building was.

The rooms for Kershaw and Kathay Book Press Ltd ought to have belonged to a legal office or an academic's study. Every surface was made of dark wood, and quiet studiousness had taken root in the dry corners behind the cabinets.

There were three of us working up here on the first floor. Robert Underhill was my uncle's second-in-command, and he had the office that ran in a narrow line along the end wall from front to back. He also had possession of one of the fireplaces and the first of the windows that overlooked the street. For the few hours when the winter's day outside grew bright enough to have any effect, white lines showed in the warped gaps between the wooden panels that divided his space from mine.

My uncle's office occupied the other two windows at the front of the building. My desk was set in the square area behind. My view was of those closed office doors and the thin glass of the screen that stopped the draught from the stairs.

At present this small reception area also contained a member of the public by the name of Miss Prichard who was beaming at me through the unflattering glare of my electric lamp.

Miss Prichard hadn't come to see me. She had come to thrust her manuscript under the nose of Mr Underhill, only he was out – as he had often been during this last week or so – and my uncle was shut up in his office muttering vagaries on the telephone.

She and her felt hat were sitting in my guest chair, looking every inch the aged housekeeper she was claiming to be with a story to tell about an old doctor who had employed her to keep house for him in the 1920s. I believe she took it as a sign of our seriousness as a publisher that she was being interviewed by the woman who answered the telephone and wrote Uncle George's letters.

'It's very thrilling,' she confessed, 'to be in here at last. I suppose the editors are terribly busy.' She kept running her eyes across the closed doors as though waiting for someone important to bustle out, proving that only by sheer luck and cunning had a small author such as her found a way in.

I thought that it was at times like these that my real job began.

I had been taken on because my aunt had retired. Aunt Mabel's hands had grown too arthritic and I was stepping in to fill the gap. I had been told that my aunt was the chief tea-maker – to ensure I understood the limitations of what the family company could do for me, presumably – but I was already learning that I was performing a fundamentally larger role in this business.

I was lending prestige to our two editors, Uncle George and Robert Underhill, because it transpired that new authors of the sort who would pay for the services of Kershaw and Kathay Book Press Ltd really liked to feel the weight of the towering intellects couched behind those enticingly unwelcome closed doors.

There was a sort of tradition in it, I suppose. I imagine it matched their general idea of the marvellously grand publishing houses of the capital city, only on a more intimate, old-time scale.

Those London publishing houses weren't very like us really, though. Uncle George didn't have their degree of clout with the government agency in charge of paper supplies. Instead, he worked to produce the smaller treasures of the literary world – the unusual memoirs, the local histories and the unsung gem of a novel – all bound in sturdy little hardbacks about the size of a Victorian pocket book. Needless to say, there wasn't a lot of money in it.

And also needless to say, the process of submitting a manuscript to us was actually managed without anyone being required to negotiate their way past me; when I wasn't the gatekeeper, and rudeness was hardly my uncle's forte, and Mr Underhill barely spoke at all.

Miss Prichard was smiling at me again as she set down her teacup on its saucer. 'I did catch your name correctly, didn't I? Mrs Peuse?'

'You did. Mrs Lucinda Peuse. It isn't a terribly nice name, is it? The staff here call me Mrs P. The lady who runs the shop downstairs started it, and then the abbreviation caught on like wildfire.'

'Well,' Miss Prichard replied comfortably, 'I suppose it's easier than a surname which might stray close to sounding like "peas" in the local accent, or "puce", when I gather it simply ought to sound like "pews"?'

'Precisely.'

My family called me Lucy.

My visitor was getting up to leave. Then the door from the stairs opened with a waft of damp air as a man of about thirty stepped in and moved quietly past us with only an idle eye for my visitor. The door for Mr Underhill's office was pressed shut behind him. Miss Prichard turned back to me. Her eyes briefly widened to silently enquire whether this pleasantly built stranger had indeed been the great editor himself. I smiled and tipped my head. It created the right impression.

I told her, 'Thank you for coming. I'll pass on my notes and your papers to Mr Underhill or Mr Kathay later today. Either way, I'm sure you'll hear from us soon.'

She let herself out. And I, in the moment of hearing her footfalls creak down to the turn and away into the small shop below, felt again the odd stillness that sometimes followed in the wake of any bustle in this building.

Anything that happened here by day passed away behind a closed door or into another room, and always the tired wooden floorboards added their solemn voices to the distant tale. They stayed with me at night too because there was another door in the wall between the stairs and my uncle's office. It led to the attic where my bedroom lay.

My night-times were spent nestling in the space beyond the office kitchen and a storeroom that housed an awful lot of unsold books.

'That was Doctor Bates' landlady, wasn't it?'

Mr Underhill's question made me jump.

I found that I had left my seat but paused in the act of moving past my desk. I had hesitated with my fingertips just touching the base of my lamp. It was as if the severe pool of light had become my anchor in the midst of that curious sense of being very much alone after the woman had left.

I turned my head. He couldn't have been aware of the silence of this place because it didn't dwell behind his office door. Clouds were streaking across the sky outside his window but, even so, daylight was streaming in and brightening the floor beside his desk.

I told him, smiling, 'Landlady to a doctor may be a fair description of her business, but appearances are deceptive. I vaguely remember the doctor who had the practice before the fellow who sold it to Doctor Bates. About twenty years ago he was the town's greatest claim to fame. I think he found his way to developing a new vaccine. By the time I knew him he was a crabbed old man and adored her, so if the lady's book even begins to stray into their little tale of rich and poor, it'll be pretty inflammatory stuff.'

I was speaking with one of those cheery undertones that didn't really mean to convey anything except perhaps my relief at being interrupted. Only then his mouth merely mustered something far short of his usual brief smile, before he asked me to join him in his office.

His reaction surprised me, actually. It wasn't normal for him to embarrass me by making it seem as if I had been attempting to gossip about the lady's unmarried state, and it wasn't normal either for him to summon me to his desk.

Over the past two months since I had joined this office, we'd exchanged pleasantries about the weather or some future publication or other that he was editing, but very little more. My unbound cheeriness shocked him sometimes, I knew, but I could usually tell when that had happened because he'd retreat to his desk – which was, admittedly, just as he was doing at present – and I'd settle into collecting up whatever papers I had for him before moving to follow.

Usually, I was glad of it. Quiet reserve was what I was used to from him. It kept us safely clear of that other extreme of the office workplace – the one where my little slips into unchained friendliness would have been exploited as an excuse to be over familiar, as only a higher ranking male in business might. But he had never preyed on any mistakes of mine.

So I suppose what I'm trying to say is that in the main I found his uncomplicated style of company wonderfully restful. Whereas this moment was different, because it was unlike him to make me uncomfortable.

None of this was remotely exciting enough for Amy Briar who ran the bookshop below us. She couldn't understand him at all.

She had told me that he had been one of those poor unfortunate men who had gone over in the first wave and been captured almost on the spot. He'd been a prisoner of war until the cessation of hostilities in '45. Amy couldn't comprehend why any man would choose, after all those years of incarceration, to settle in this small town business when he might have seized freedom with both hands and claimed every excitement with it.

I remember thinking simply: what a waste war had made of five years of life.

Today, as I handed Miss Prichard's manuscript to him across his desk, I was realising that at least part of the embarrassment I was feeling came from knowing that it was eleven o'clock and my uncle's second-in-command had barely stepped into the office. And he had immediately approached me with a question about our work, only to catch me staring into the shadows when I ought to have been busy too.

There had been a subtle touch of hesitation in his interruption, like concern when I didn't want it. Now he made everything worse by accepting the manuscript from my hand and remarking, 'Hearing you say all that about Miss Prichard's memoir, it seems to me as if you and I ought to be trading jobs. My experience in publishing only runs to about nine months, whereas yours runs to years. Don't you mind settling for taking the messages?'

His eyes briefly lifted from the manuscript in his hand. He really was different today.

This was the change that had been brewing over the course of all his little absences of late – a harder energy which ran itself back into stillness through a pattern of asking me more about myself than was the norm.

I thought he did it whenever something had unsettled his peace of mind. This time, though, I couldn't help stiffening to say in a clipped sort of voice, 'That's an oddly challenging question, Mr Underhill.'

Then I caught the sound of my own defensiveness. It

made me add more cheerfully, 'It isn't that I mind, exactly, that you might occasionally require more from me than a harmless chat about the weather. But didn't you know that you aren't supposed to draw attention to the smallness of my role?'

Because he was right in a way – I was an experienced editor. I'd spent a good portion of my own war years working on the staff of the regional ministry office. I'd won one of those under-reported roles that basically required me to ensure that all information leaflets and posters and National Savings campaigns were adjusted to be relevant to the local population. So, thanks to me, a Mrs Whatsit from Ham Cottage had known that in the event of invasion, her emergency food distribution point would be the such-and-such building in Stratford-upon-Avon.

Then, as it happened, the German tanks hadn't invaded. The leaflets had been made redundant and so had I. And, with that in mind, this unsolicited comment on my new role here was a bit like that question mark which hangs over the way people talk about the cleaning ladies and the servers. Dignity was a very delicate thing.

In my case, and the case of an awful lot of women like me, everyone knew how much we'd slaved for the great machine of war when we'd filled the void left by the departing men. They knew too how we were being cheerfully relegated once more to the role of underling now that peace had brought the survivors home again. And yet absolutely no one except a few restless youths ever dared to actually comment on it. Because who amongst us knew what complaint to make, when we were all poor and those war-shaken men had to have the chance to feel that normality was re-emerging somehow?

So, I suppose the real issue here was that I had already grasped that there was a considerable difference between Robert's career prospects and mine. I even had a plan for what I would do if it ran into my future. I just never would have expected this particular demobbed soldier to humble me by asking me about it.

Particularly when we both knew that Uncle George didn't have the work for three editors. Or the money. And it had been an act of generosity that my uncle had even been able to do this much for me.

With a head full of concerns of my own about what was the matter with this man today, I couldn't help retorting then with uncharacteristic coolness, 'Anyway, it isn't so much a case of whether or not I mind noting down the messages for you, Mr Underhill. It's simply that I set quite a high value on having the funds to buy food this side of Christmas, that's all.'

I shouldn't have said that. It turned out that not only was I struggling to deal with the sudden sense of my inequality here, but I also knew even less about his present mood than I thought. Because his head lifted from the manuscript again and I found that I had surprised him.

He hadn't expected to offend me. And his expression didn't match the usual blankness that came in whenever I said something unguarded in this quiet office. This way of studying me was steadier. Aside from his reaction to the barb in my words, I thought it pretty clear that he had noticed that my

11

mercenary summary of my motives was a lie. Normally I spoke by smiling.

I didn't even have the chance to answer that look by telling him something truthful, because there was a clatter of the other office door opening and then Uncle George was there in the doorway.

The older man bustled in with a question for his second-in-command. He didn't notice the closeness of my position to the corner of Robert's desk, with the editor himself standing in the small space just beyond.

Uncle George didn't notice the speed of my self-conscious retreat to the cabinet by the door either. He was about as opposite a stamp of man to Robert as possible. George Kathay was the intellectual who fitted books and these quiet rooms but was also jolly and comfortable and long overdue for retirement. He had looked the same in all the years I had known him: willowy and wispy-haired and amiable, dressed in neat but old-fashioned brown suits made of wool.

'Good morning, Mr Kathay,' said Robert. He had moved when I had moved, but more smoothly.

He had passed further behind his desk to set the manuscript down, and now he was checking his watch to confirm that it was indeed still morning. Just.

My uncle didn't have time for the preliminaries today. 'Morning, Lucy. Rob. I'd hoped you'd be back sooner than this. What news have you got for me?'

Robert's reply was brief. 'Mixed'

'Ah.'

There was an odd little pause in the wake of that when it struck me that they were speaking in code. Then my uncle seemed to suddenly consider my presence more seriously. In fact, he began to look like a man who was about to ask me to go and make the tea.

And that part really surprised me, because I was already making my discreet exit from the room. I mean to say that I always made the tea; it's just that it was unlike my uncle to use it as a means of bustling me out of the way.

Today, however, Uncle George gave me the strange experience of learning that after weeks of complacently enjoying the process of finding my feet, I might have been wrong for imagining that we were all friends here, each bearing a different share of the work. Because the rank of editors above the lower staff really did exist. And these two men had private business to discuss.

It gave me a very peculiar feeling then to slip away to my desk.

My dim corner was screened from Robert's desk by the partition between us, so he couldn't have seen my flush. I thought they might simply shut the door and exclude me that way. But then the younger man made the span of the floor-boards between my seat and that open threshold so much narrower when he said with unexpected mildness, 'Can you give me five minutes to gather together a few things, Mr Kathay, and then I'll come along to your office?'

He made it seem as if they were merely about to have one of their ordinary weekly consultations. But it was too late. Uncle George was fidgeting into the open doorway, and then he announced as if it were news the other editor needed to hear, 'Lucy is our borrowed daughter, you know.'

Now I truly was concerned. Because I thought I knew what my uncle was about to say next, and yet I was certain that if Robert had managed to grasp my professional qualifications, he must surely have gleaned this little detail.

All the same, my uncle made it worse by rushing into saying, 'Lucy is a farmer's daughter who dislikes the mess of a farmyard. My brother-in-law's family have a place beyond Worcester with an awful lot of sheep. And cows. Or crops. Actually, I think it's just sheep and crops, isn't it Lucy? She's agreeing.'

He added that last part for Robert's benefit since the younger man couldn't see my uncertain nod.

I was staring. Because these rapid words were designed to convey affection and an awful lot of care. Uncle George was acting as if I had stalked out and he needed to make amends, only I hadn't stalked anywhere. And now he was gripping that doorframe and earnestly explaining to the younger man by the desk, 'My wife and I were childless and growing old before our time, and Lucy wasn't keen on farming. So when Lucy was about four, her parents sort of loaned the girl to us. And then—'

'And then it just sort of stuck, Mr Underhill.' I raised my voice so that it carried into the other room.

I had to stop this. It was all wrong that I should discover the tension I'd noted in Robert present in my uncle too. And I certainly couldn't bear to hear this story of my childhood being told on these terms; as if my uncle needed to worry himself into an apology, when I didn't need to be offended by this.

So perhaps I even intervened for Robert's sake, because he had been a part of this too, and I thought he might recognise the gesture behind my abrupt return to plain honesty.

I added in that same clear voice, 'This life stuck so completely, Mr Underhill, that some twenty-two years later when my job dried up and things got a little frayed about the edges, my idea of running for home carried me here.'

My uncle beamed at me.

Then he shuffled away to his office. He didn't hear the way I felt compelled to add my own small aside to the secrets of this place by murmuring to myself, 'Of course my real motive was that Aunt Mabel bakes like a dream and we *are* four weeks from Christmas ...'

'Mrs P?'

Robert was calling me back into his room. He hadn't heard that last part either. He was being distracted by the effort of remembering whatever it was that he and I had been speaking about before my uncle had begun to lecture him on my origins.

At least his voice was closer to his usual harmless tone. He was searching through the papers on his desk when I approached near enough for him to say, 'Did she ask any particular questions, by the way?'

'Who?' I asked blankly.

'Miss Prichard. What were you talking about as I climbed the stairs?'

It turned out that his idea of what had passed between us

was different from mine. He wanted to discuss Miss Prichard and the submission of her manuscript.

While he eased a pen out from beneath a stack of notes, I told him, 'She wanted me to give her some examples of similar titles we'd produced. She had heard about the Willerson archive, naturally. Everybody has. She asked how soon she might expect to be able to get her hands on a copy. She wondered if it might be out for Christmas.'

On any other day, a comment like that would have been guaranteed to draw a laugh.

The Willerson archive was a collection of photographs belonging to the family of a dead airman by the name of Gilbert Willerson. He had documented his non-operational life, his happy days spent on leave, the dances, the encounters with people in the town and his friends. Now his family wanted to publish the collection as a memorial to his death and, to be honest, the whole project was one big complication for us.

Gilbert Willerson's fearsome last act with one of the training planes from our very own airfield had enthralled the national press. This was a man who, not to put too fine a point on it, had long been exploited for the purposes of propaganda. For my uncle, any attempt to publish even our small portion of the man's private photographs was a tricky dance around the Official Secrets Act. It meant that Uncle George was having to negotiate with the various Ministry departments which might have an opinion on whether we should be prohibited from publishing at all. Robert had the unenviable job of pulling the pictures into some kind of logical order to give a sense of narrative. It was safe to say we were months away from making the print run that would be our largest title yet.

Today, however, Robert neither shuddered nor gave the customary rueful smile.

He merely paused in the midst of testing whether his pen worked while the distant sound of a rather wet sneeze carried through the floorboards from the shop beneath our feet. I saw him give an unconscious grimace, then he asked, 'And was that the moment when she decided her manuscript should be submitted to me?'

'She didn't decide that. I did.' I couldn't help the impatience that was beginning to creep in. I wasn't so nervous of his questions any more; just bemused.

'So she wasn't sent to us by her tenant, Doctor Bates?'

'Not that she told me. And I should say,' I couldn't help adding, 'that if you could hear our conversation as you climbed the stairs, you already know this.'

Suddenly, he proved he could still smile after all. 'I couldn't really hear a word,' he said, 'but it's a fair point.'

Then he changed the subject.

He tipped his head towards his desk and said in a lighter tone, 'I saw your note about the Jacqueline Dunn book, by the way.'

Oh heavens, I thought. At last I understood why I was finding that every fresh turn today seemed designed to remind me of my place – because here was proof of my absolute inability to keep within the bounds of my job.

'I'm so sorry,' I said in a very different spirit of sincerity. 'I thought I was doing the right thing. I sent out the proof copy on Monday.'

I added shamefacedly, 'You weren't here, but you and I had discussed last week how the author had to approve it in a matter of days if the print room people were going to have even half a chance of binding the books before Christmas. Uncle George couldn't say where you were; I didn't know when you would be back, and I thought that if you were going to be keeping the same uncertain hours this week as you had at the end of last week, you might not come in to the office in time to get it into the post. Today is Wednesday, so she must have it by now. I really am so sorry. I suppose you needed to check it before it went. Should I—?'

While I worked myself into a tangle, he seized the opportunity to say, 'Why should you apologise? Under the circumstances, I don't think you could have done anything else. I was simply going to say thank you.'

He implied that I'd misunderstood him completely this time.

He made my hands still, where previously my fingers had been tying themselves in knots. I heard myself ask with a rather too eager quickening into confidence, 'Do you really think so? Are you sure? Because it's a marvellous story and we don't publish much in the line of children's histories so I couldn't help taking a quick look, only ...'

I made the mistake of forgetting every one of the difficulties of the past minutes. I leaned in to confide with a brief twist of a teasing smile, 'Only, do you know if she really means to spell Ashbrook with only one "o"?'

Of course it was a really terrible moment to make a joke out of the quality of his author's spelling. I saw his expression change in the way that it always did whenever I slipped into revealing my usual unguarded self, and it was worse today because of the shadow that had come in with his late arrival.

Instantly, I was apologising and retreating back a step to the doorway.

'I'm sorry,' I was saying more formally. 'I'm talking when I ought to be serious, and I know you don't like it. I should let you get to your meeting with my uncle, with Mr Kathay, I mean, and—'

'Mrs P.' He said it flatly to interrupt the flow.

He waited until I stalled and turned my head to look at him. Then he asked with absolute incredulity, 'Why on earth should you think that I mind the way that you *talk?*'

I floundered on the threshold. I was dumbstruck, really.

This was like that moment earlier when he had caught me staring by my desk. He tripped me headlong out of worrying about the people of this office, into acknowledging the reality that sometimes they cared for me in my turn.

He stated firmly into the silence I left, 'I don't mind.'

I believe the full depth of my stupefaction embarrassed him.

The turn of his head towards the papers in his hand was a means of curbing the feeling.

And yet, even though this was finally closer to what I considered normal for him, he also proved that something really was wrong here. Because the act was also my dismissal.

After that, it was with very mixed feelings of my own that I returned to my desk for the final time that morning. Robert wasn't merely the man who had pipped me by a matter of months to the editor's job. He was also the reason why I was making a home in the creaking attic above the office.

My aunt and uncle's house stood on the other end of the High Street. They had a room to let in the outbuilding behind their kitchen. In days of old, the room had been home to a pair of junior clerks from the town gasworks. They had been a harmless addition to the household when I had been a small girl. These days, the tenant was Robert and Aunt Mabel didn't think it would be terribly seemly for me to return to my childhood roost in their second floor bedroom, when I was a widow of only twenty-six and they had an unmarried man living on the property.

My aunt didn't, however, need to worry too much about the impropriety of crowding both me and Robert into the small space of her home for the next couple of days. Her houseguest left the office after lunch on Thursday, and on Friday, when I received the call to go and help her bake the Christmas cake, he wasn't at home at all.

Chapter 2

One of the main hazards from living above my own desk was that I hadn't actually stepped out of doors that Friday until I set off for an evening at my aunt and uncle's house. It meant that I wasn't remotely prepared for the force of the wind. Or the darkness that had descended abruptly at about four o'clock and had refused to shift since.

Moreton-in-Marsh was particularly poorly lit anyway. The main thoroughfare was exceptionally wide so that the shops and hotels opposite were a distant line screened by ranks of bleak pollarded trees. Behind me, the heavy doors that barred the passage to the printworks were rattling ominously against their lock. Very little else was moving, except I caught the distant shrill of a train whistle about five minutes later when I ran up a steep set of steps at the northern end of the High Street to let myself into my old childhood home.

Aunt Mabel always baked her cake on the first weekend in advent. This was a ritual. She was supposed to follow this by tipping in a teaspoon of brandy weekly until the moment it was iced. Instead, my aunt basically waved the sherry bottle at it whenever she remembered, and Uncle George could drink whatever was left. This was another Christmas ritual.

Now Aunt Mabel was muttering about eggs while Uncle George skulked in the long passage of the hallway to help me as I struggled out of my coat. I might describe the rows they had at times like these as loving but that would have been a lie. They did love each other very much, it was simply that they forgot when it came to crucial things like the cake.

The problem this time was that they had miscounted the number of eggs they had accumulated through hoarding their ration and my aunt hated to bake with the powdered stuff. It was fortunate, therefore, that I had thought to save the solitary egg which constituted my own ration this week.

My aunt was hunting for the baking powder. She was flushing in a happy sort of way as she got me to reach a tin down from the top shelves in the cupboards. Then she was distracted in the midst of giving me my instructions for the margarine.

She turned her head towards the hallway. 'Was that the front door?'

I said with a smile, 'I think Uncle George is trying to make amends by taking on the job of putting out the empty bottle for the milkman.'

A murmur carried along the length of the hall as he spoke to someone outside, before the door rattled shut again.

My attention was firmly drawn back to the task at hand by the sensation of a mixing bowl being placed before me. I knew which duties were mine of course. We had performed this little dance about the kitchen table since I had first moved here aged four.

Aunt Mabel was frowning at the weighing scales with the bag of flour held ready and asking me, 'Are you keeping warm enough in that attic of yours? And are you taking that advent calendar? George found it today when he was looking for the box of decorations and thought you'd like to see it. I haven't filled it.'

The item in question was a relic from my childhood. It was made of twenty four small matchboxes set in pairs so that twelve tiny cardboard drawers could be opened on each side. The end of each drawer had been numbered very carefully by hand. In my younger years the drawers had been filled with treats and puzzles but they had been left empty for a long time now.

In truth, it was the sort of object that inspired that bittersweet sense of all those happy childhood Christmases. That sort of naivety could never be regained. I suppose it really ought to have found a new generation to enthral only there wasn't one, and yet, somehow, the sight of it wasn't as melancholy as all that.

I set the calendar aside for the sake of more practical things such as opening the tin of baking powder for my aunt, and then she asked tentatively, 'Lucy?'

'Mmm?'

'Will you answer my question?'

'I'm snug, thank you. The attic is perfectly warm. Like toast.'

'But?'

I gave in. 'All right. But I do have to ask ... Did the floor joists always creak?'

She laughed. 'Like a sinking ship.'

My aunt had a fabulous laugh. Her style of loveliness was the homely sort which dressed in neat blue frocks and chose yellow and brown patterned wallpaper for the stairs and hallway to match the lampshades which had little tassels dangling from them.

The only part of her that was out of place these days was the unhappy curling of those beautiful fingers. They took up the sieve and I watched her with a parody of the fascination that as a child had made me covet this duty, and made her smile.

She made me smile in my turn when she remarked far too knowingly, 'If you're worrying about noises in the attic, I suppose you've noticed the bang that goes off like a gunshot on the step at the turn every once in a while? It always caught me unawares when I used to work late there sometimes. I swear it would get worse whenever dusk descended.'

I countered, 'Don't forget the pane of glass in the third window. It's near my bed and it's loose and it makes a scratching noise like fingernails. Only you don't have to worry, dear Aunt,' I confided quickly because she was beginning to look concerned.

I knew it mattered to her that I was living alone there. 'I've been making a habit of learning all the daytime noises so that I can cross them off at night. It's becoming quite comforting now. Like growing up here and getting used to the way the rain thrummed on the roof, you know?'

I was teasing her and preparing to be tutted at because as a child I had made an extraordinary amount of fuss about that rain – it was the one of the many variants of a joke we shared about the squeamishness of a girl born on my father's farm. But she didn't quite react in the cheerful way I had thought she would.

She set the sieve down beside me, dusted off her hands and then startled me completely by saying in a tone entirely removed from any cosy childhood memory, 'I'm sorry. I must just pop into the garden room to see Rob. He came in just now and put his head around the door, but he only stayed for a moment because we were talking and he didn't like to interrupt. I expect George has gone along the hall to tell him that I'm keeping his supper warm.'

She added distractedly, 'Rob's had a long day running back and forth on the train. We probably ought to have let him move in above the office and made you come home properly but, well, to be honest I think Rob's better off where he is. You don't mind, do you?'

'Mr Underhill is home? *Now?*' Then, 'He overheard all that nonsense about the attic?'

She didn't notice my dismay for the simple reason that she had already passed out into the hall.

I was standing in a silent kitchen that suddenly seemed strangely large and starkly lit. The ingredients of an unfinished cake were in my hands and I was feeling rather too much like the adopted girl who had come home after a short stay away to find a new and prettier child already installed in her place.

On an adult note though, there was something truly anxious about the hasty way my aunt had abandoned her obsession with Christmas. It matched the preoccupation my uncle had shown a few days ago when he had drawn Robert aside for their private meeting. They had excluded me and left behind a distracted edge of doubt that time too, and I couldn't understand why.

So it was with a very peculiar degree of concern for these people who had all my love that I respected their privacy and avoided listening too intently to the distant whisper of voices.

Instead, I finished the cake and set it in the oven. Then I climbed the stairs to my old childhood bedroom.

Chapter 3

I had, naturally, been back to this house many times since I had left at the bright age of nineteen for my wartime employment. I had also been here many times in the past two months for various dinners and Sunday lunch, so it was uncanny really that it had never before occurred to me to notice how hard it had been to establish whether they ever shared their other mealtimes with Robert.

Or why, when my aunt's murmurings about propriety could hardly have applied to dinner, he never joined them when I was there.

The thought accompanied me upstairs. It followed me into the room that had become my haven after exchanging life on the family farm for an aunt and uncle I had barely even known.

This evening, I had come up here to rediscover the oddments and trinkets I had treasured in the years since, which might now make excellent fillings for the drawers of that old advent calendar. Only, when it came to the point of finding all these bits and pieces, I didn't even have the exercise of rummaging under my old bed frame.

Most of the larger furniture had gone and it wasn't because, as might be inferred from the pattern of my homecoming, my aunt had also given Robert the contents of my room.

My bedroom was largely empty because the ironwork of my bedstead had been turned into a Spitfire sometime in '41 and the mattress was in my new attic hideaway. I thought I could guess too who had helped my uncle to move it from one house to the other. I deduced this solely on the basis that my uncle couldn't have done it alone and yet no one had mentioned the part played by the man who was presently occupying my aunt's garden room.

I wondered what Robert had thought when he had seen the bare attic floorboards of my current sleeping quarters above the office, with the storeroom of books and a mattress denuded of its bed frame. And how much it related to what he thought he knew about me.

Disconcertingly, I believe I caught the same thought there on his face when I tripped down the last of the stairs to the floor below to abruptly encounter him as he came out of the short passage from the bathroom.

He knew where I had been. I was looking thoroughly at home by now and flushing slightly pink because it had been strenuous searching through the boxes of my things and I had some of those childhood treasures piled into the crook of one arm. They spoke loudly of belonging to this house, both in the past and in the present.

He had been washing the grime of a winter's day from his face and had found that my aunt had whisked his towel away to the laundry. He had shed his suit jacket, and was stumbling

28

in rolled shirtsleeves to the linen cupboard when I stepped down onto the narrow landing and saved him the job.

His hair was wet and so was his skin when I handed him the towel. The space here was tiny. My aunt was quite right to keep me in the attic above the office. There truly wouldn't have been room here for us both.

'Thank you,' he said as I slid away along the wall.

He made me pause in the midst of making for the next flight of stairs. I turned my head. 'It's nothing,' I said.

His voice had held a firmer hint of certainty than I was used to when compared to the man who often looked taken aback if I surprised him in the office.

It was, in fact, like a continuation of that moment when he had corrected me for saying that he didn't like me to talk – unexpectedly decisive.

And I was flushing because it really had been a rapid search through drawers and boxes upstairs, and his few words of thanks cut a little deeper when I lingered before making for the next set of stairs. There was a different kind of steadiness in the way he met my eye. Quite simply, he was at home here too.

And now that I had finally been permitted to meet the man out of hours, I could see that my aunt had been right to fuss and worry about his supper. Not even weariness could alter the posture this man had, or the way that he moved, but he certainly was tired. And for him I believe this quiet exchange was one of those gentler moments that are seized like an intense release after a test.

Wherever he had been on that train, it hadn't been pleasant

for him. Whereas this; in these few peaceful seconds, this was better.

I didn't tell any of this to Amy Briar. It was Monday and we were in her shop and she had a theory about our Mr Underhill. It was fuelled, I might say, by the doctor who was Miss Prichard's tenant and Amy's friend and here with us in time for the morning cup of tea.

She was saying regretfully, 'I had a cold last week.'

Doctor Bates understood her point even if I didn't. He was nodding seriously from the other side of the counter that kept customers away from the foot of the stairs.

Beside me, the curve of Amy's mouth moved as she added with a meaningful nod, 'I was ill last week and he was barely here. I'm better today and he's upstairs.'

'Don't be silly.' My retort came swiftly.

I surprised the doctor. He often stopped in during the brief respite between his round of home visits and his lunchtime surgery. Today, his grave tones ought to have befitted a man who was old and wispy-haired. In fact, the doctor was in his late thirties and his hair was sandy and he was one of those thoroughly self-assured people who had been demobbed from his military service and seamlessly bought his stake in the town practice as if he had never spent time away.

Now he asked me with mock seriousness, 'You don't believe that our Mr Underhill was afraid of catching the office cold and put himself into quarantine? So what's your explanation?'

Ignoring my memory of the way Robert had grimaced

when Amy had sneezed last week, I protested rather too keenly, 'I'm certain that Mr Underhill wasn't hiding in his bedroom, at the very least. He went away overnight. And my uncle – Mr Kathay I mean – knew about it, so he must have been working on a job, mustn't he?'

And that was when I realised that I'd just shared the way my aunt and uncle were guarding Robert's absences, and I must have done it to prod Amy into showing that she knew where he was going.

Only of course she couldn't tell me anything, and I was thoroughly ashamed of myself because the morning was running on and I shouldn't be down here speaking about Robert like this when my mind was still swimming with the vividly living memory of the way the man had looked on Friday night.

That had been an abrupt encounter with thought laid bare, and now he was upstairs and working quietly in his office, while we were skulking down here and discussing a different kind of man who might have spent weeks creeping away from his desk because my uncle's shopkeeper had shown the merest hint of ill health.

I didn't want this conversation. I tried to curb it. 'Anyway,' I said brightly, 'what about my advent calendar? I only really came down just now because today is the second day of December and I spent the weekend filling these drawers. I had imagined that Miss Briar would like to be the first person to bring our advent calendar up to speed.'

As it was, this was another decision I would rapidly come

to regret. Amy obediently drew out a drawer, discovered a neatly rolled length of very pretty ribbon and set it to one side without really looking at it. Then she seamlessly resumed the discussion about her concern for Mr Underhill.

And it really was concern. She was a universally caring woman who seemed as if she and her country tweeds had worked for my uncle since the dawn of time. She hadn't. Amy was like the doctor and only about ten years old than me. I hadn't known either of them as a child.

'Watch him,' she told me seriously. 'Next time someone sneezes, you watch him. I have a theory about our Mr Underhill. You know he trained as a doctor, don't you? Before the war, I mean?'

'He never qualified,' corrected Doctor Bates. 'He and some of his fellow students got caught up in all that excited talk about duty and service, and abandoned their medical college when the first call went out for volunteers.'

He didn't mean that as a compliment. He meant to imply that the decision counted as lunatic when Robert might have qualified and postponed his war duty, or might even have never served abroad at all.

Amy added thoughtfully, 'Actually, it must drive the man mad, really, mustn't it, to think that after all that enthusiasm and training, he had one brief battle in northern France and was a prisoner for the rest anyway.'

'I served in the European War too, you know,' remarked the doctor a shade plaintively when he realised how his comments had been interpreted. 'I'm not suggesting that qualified doctors didn't serve at all. I staffed a field hospital behind the front line, wherever that line should have been at the time.'

'You were already qualified?' I hadn't meant to say that. I had meant to slip away to resume my work. Then I realised what I'd asked. I drew back and added quickly, 'I'm sorry. I don't mean to pry into your war service.'

Just as I had never asked Robert about his life as a POW, it wasn't really the done thing to push returning soldiers into speaking about their experiences, any more than anyone dared ask me about my husband. People offered whatever they were willing to share and we were all content to leave it at that.

Doctor Bates, to do him credit, though, didn't look remotely shaken by my question. He didn't look proud either. He simply looked tougher all of a sudden. Less like a Cotswold teddy bear and more like a man who had experienced some of the harder corners of the world when he said, 'I qualified in '36. I got my name on a brass plate the year Mr Underhill began his training. In fact, he and I both studied at the same university hospital in Birmingham, although I'd already left by the time Underhill joined my old college.'

Amy leaned in to rest her folded arms upon the glass countertop. Beneath her, ranks of pens and other writing tools glittered as a shining island in a sea of yet more old and blackened wood. 'You knew him back then?'

The doctor shook his head, 'He wasn't a native of this town. There was no earthly reason for our paths to cross either before or after his studies, until Underhill moved here and took up his job with Mr Kathay. But you might be interested to know that these days I'm still very much in contact with my old lecturer, and he mentioned Underhill's name only last week. In fact, the story the old fellow told was quite enlightening. Mrs P, has your uncle ever mentioned—'

'Mr Underhill,' Amy interrupted with renewed energy, 'was drafted as a medic.'

She didn't notice the way Doctor Bates was staring at her. I didn't think he was used to being interrupted. Which was silly really because she did it to the rest of us all of the time.

Amy added, 'Mr Underhill spent his war begging the guards for plasters and aspirin so that he might treat the many ailments of his fellow inmates. I believe that these days the poor man feels he's seen enough sickness and runs away.'

'Do you know this? Or are you surmising?' This was said sharply, by Doctor Bates.

Suddenly, he wasn't looking so much like a man who had been offended by her lack of interest in his university life. Instead, he was paying far more attention than he had before.

Amy's bracelet clattered on the glass countertop as she moved. Beneath the cuffs of jacket and blouse, a thin gleam caught the dim light. She closed her hand over it, muffling it as she told her friend, 'It's just a guess, but the evidence is there in the way he kept away from me last week, wouldn't you say? You must have seen plenty of signs of mental damage in the returning men.'

They didn't notice my quiet movement as I slid my advent calendar from the counter and retreated for the stairs. She was telling the doctor earnestly, 'I don't mean to blame Mr Underhill if he can't bear to see people with winter colds. I mean he might justifiably have a real horror of illness now. That might be what brought him to us.'

'Really?' The light from the wall lamp caught the side of the doctor's face as he stirred. He was being framed by the dark ranks of every title we had ever published, while the golden lettering of each book's embossed spine ran away like fine threads into the gloom of the shop. He asked, 'What do *you* know about Underhill's arrival here?'

Amy replied, 'The first time I set eyes on him was when he wandered in one morning in the early spring with Mr Kathay, who took him upstairs and sat him down with a cup of tea. I can't help wondering whether we'd find it was illness he was running away from that time too. The war can take people like that you know. It can leave them rootless. It can make them fragile.'

She added softly, 'And Mr Underhill's got that handsome look that goes a bit drawn down to a fine art, if you know what I mean? He looks like a man who ought to have gone back to doctoring and finished his studies. The trouble is, he definitely doesn't fit that life any more. For all we know, he mightn't quite fit this one either.'

I saw her fidget as she confided with renewed energy, 'He might be going away for days on end because he's building up the courage to escape us. One of these days I think we might find he's gone and he won't come back.'

'And yet,' the doctor added like it was his job to be the voice of reason, 'let's not get too carried away with this dire portrait of a man shaken by war.'

I thought I caught a sideways glance from him. I didn't

think that he was saying this for her sake. He was saying it for mine. He was a man who liked everything to be orderly and he must have abruptly noticed that I was retreating step by step up the stairs.

I don't know what my expression was showing, but it was as if Doctor Bates didn't want me to leave like this when he observed calmly, 'If Mr Underhill is truly afraid of illness, he might simply be aware that the slightest hint of a temperature is enough to bring out his more difficult memories in the form of some awfully vivid dreams.'

'What do you mean?' I asked, puzzled.

The doctor replied kindly, 'Mr Underhill may simply be a man for whom a short illness will mean a hard battle with some utterly troubled nights. It's a common enough problem, believe me, for men who have experienced war. And if the man actually *caught* an illness of some kind, the ensuing mental fatigue might certainly be enough to keep him away from his work for a few days. But,' he added as an afterthought, 'I believe, Mrs P, you said that he went away on a job last week?'

He seemed to be expecting me to answer this. He barely even blinked.

But Amy had noticed a detail that I had missed. I saw her head turn on its neck and her remark was a quick, 'You're speaking with a remarkable degree of authority there. Do you mean to say that Mr Underhill is your *patient?*'

Outside the shop door, a car went past with its headlights blazing. In here, the amber cast on our faces made us all look rather too eager to learn how a man might have recently

36

visited his doctor to talk about the influence of illness upon his state of mind.

And now I was angry with them. And with myself too, because I had let them follow this course and I knew that the doctor's tactful refusal to answer Amy's question would change how I saw Robert now. It merged with my uncle's troubled looks and my aunt's eagerness to settle their house-guest down to his supper last week.

I knew that when Robert and I spoke next, I wouldn't be able to avoid searching his face for signs of disturbed sleep.

In the next moment, Doctor Bates abruptly moved on from dissecting Robert's health to remark in quite a different tone, 'I understand it was you, Mrs P, who saw my esteemed land-lady the other day. What did you think of her book?'

I couldn't help remembering the expression I'd found on Robert's face on that day too. I lingered on the staircase and said quite shortly, 'I haven't read it, Doctor. I handed it on to the editor and he'll write back to her in due course with his thoughts.'

I was standing on the stairs, clutching the advent calendar and suddenly thinking how utterly trivial this little relic from my childhood history was in the face of a stiff discussion of the consequences from our recent past. I didn't know whether either of my companions had noticed how reluctant I was to add the information that I'd given the manuscript to Robert. I asked instead, 'Has Miss Prichard been worrying about it?'

'No, no.' There was a quick glimmer of a smile. 'Consider this just the idle questions of a busybody who is wondering what kind of offer you intend to make his vulnerable old landlady.'

He left a silence that was clearly meant as another invitation to fill the void. And perhaps it was just a reflection of the way I was feeling now but I vaguely resented the implication in his tone. I was suddenly very conscious that he wasn't just the visiting friend of our shopkeeper, but a customer; or the tenant of one.

I was representing my uncle's business when I said carefully, 'I can't really discuss the terms we might offer Miss Prichard. But rest assured, Kershaw and Kathay Book Press works very hard to make sure every one of our authors feels that it is money well-spent.'

'So you do intend to make her contribute to the costs then? I was hoping for the opposite. I thought I might claim the triumph of negotiating her first advance.'

His mouth dipped in a manner I believe he took to be charmingly daring. It worked on Amy. She giggled at the care he was showing for his aged landlady.

Whereas I was suddenly thinking very intensely about every word I said. It was conversations such as these that could create an awful lot of trouble if they could be quoted along the lines of, 'Ah, but Mrs P said that the fee was negotiable ...'

And it was always at times like these that I ended by feeling hopelessly small. Particularly when I had to say quite plainly that it would be up to my uncle to set the terms we would offer, and the doctor followed the discovery by remarking airily, 'Not to worry. I imagine my landlady is looking at the wider options, anyway. I believe she may have had interest from another publisher. The one at Abingdon, you know? Nuneham's.'

He said the name like it ought to mean something to me. It didn't. Then I made my excuses and slid away up the darkened stairs.

I was back at my desk when I was joined by my uncle who benignly opened the second drawer on my advent calendar. He found it was a boiled sweet, which he never eats, and then handed me the returned proof copy of the Jacqueline Dunn book.

'Rob asked me to ask whether you would mind lending a hand.'

The door into the other office was firmly shut and the only light coming through the gaps between the panels that divided us from Robert came in thin lines from the electric lamp that stood upon his desk. I was suddenly flushing because it was very quiet up here and I knew from experience that the whispering floorboards in this place liked to tell their own stories.

Uncle George noted the involuntary stray of my eyes to that closed office door and misunderstood, which made it worse.

He was suddenly an angular and kindly man saying anxiously, 'I'm sorry. It's what we said would never happen, isn't it, when we said we could only afford to take you on to manage the correspondence side of things? It's absolutely vital that you don't end up doing Rob's job while being paid for your own. That's why Rob asked me first. He just needs you to read through the comments that the author has pencilled into the margin and then take the lot down to the print room. Will you do that? Please? He's a bit overawed with things today and he's out again tomorrow.'

My uncle gave me a swift apologetic smile that swept everything else away. I knew then that he wasn't purely being made anxious by the difficulty of asking for my help. He was older than my parents by about fifteen years and today he looked it. The flecked browns of his ancient suit and waistcoat weren't easing the effect.

I found myself suddenly concentrating intently upon his face and asking on an impulse, 'Uncle George. Mr Underhill is all right, isn't he? I mean, he isn't ill?'

Surprise checked the nervous juggling of that boiled sweet in my uncle's hand. His mouth twitched into a bland smile. 'No, of course not. Why ever would you ask?'

The reply was a disguise. But not, I thought, entirely dishonest for all that.

It relieved me but left me with a very different kind of worry. I asked with equal earnestness, 'And *you're* all right, are you?'

There was an infinitesimal pause before he turned this into a real lie. 'It's just the Willerson job. It's putting us all under a lot of strain. I spend half my time terrified these days that at some point we'll overwork Rob so much, he'll take the opportunity to go away on one of his trips and never come back.' He gave a silly titter.

Then he collected himself, and said, 'So work your usual magic, would you, Lucy, and brighten our day? There's a dear.'

40

He left me to quietly open the neatly bound little book to find the first of many edits.

At this moment, though, I wasn't concentrating very well. I was being distracted by the shock of hearing my uncle repeat Amy's idea that Robert might be about to leave us.

He'd said it as a joke, but I had never been allowed to glimpse before the full burden of work being carried by his second-in-command. And now I was having to consider whether Uncle George had also just revealed that the greatest secret of all here was, in fact, the worry the older man was bearing himself.

Chapter 4

I had been glowering at the bound proof for about three hours when Robert finally chose to emerge from his office shortly before dusk fell. He was presumably wondering where his afternoon cup of tea had got to. The part that perplexed me was that he was looking perfectly unharrassed, while I was the one who was feeling short of rest.

I should explain that the Jacqueline Dunn book was a dramatized account of an old family by the name of Ashbrook who had owned a large estate in the region for about 200 years. She had authored it with a person called Harriet Clare, and their version of history was about as unconvincing as any children's book I had ever read.

The last of the Ashbrooks had been snuffed out by the Great War. But aside from the authors' intermittent tendency for spelling the worthy family name Ashbrok or Ashrbook, the main mystery here was how Jacqueline or Harriet had ever decided to call their book *The Man who Bred Miniature Giraffes*.

I suppose it was irrelevant to me whether or not there was any substance to this historic tale of diminutive African plains animals being bred in the Cotswolds. As her publisher, the point that I was concerned with – and was really causing my brain to ache – was the fact that Jacqueline's covering letter had lightly explained that she had passed the book to someone else for a final perusal and this person had noted a few minor edits in the margins. Jacqueline's instructions to me were to confirm or discard this new hand's changes before proceeding to print.

My principle difficulty was that this friend had made some pretty enormous alterations to Jacqueline's idea of the English language. And they had also left a number of unfinished comments, so that often all I had were obscure instructions to insert a reference to the dedication in the family chapel. The problem for me was that no one had thought to mention what this dedication actually said.

So when I looked up to find Robert Underhill standing before my desk bearing the loose sheets of what appeared to be another manuscript, I was perhaps less than friendly.

Unperturbed, he handed his papers to me. 'I thought you'd appreciate the chance to see this. Further to the accusations you levelled at me last week about misjudging your visitor Miss Prichard, I have to tell you that you're guilty of forming misconceptions about the lady too.'

I politely waited for him to continue.

'It turns out,' he said, 'that only a portion of Miss Prichard's tale is about her famous doctor. The rest is about her own career, which isn't purely housekeeping. It's also the history of herbology. Miss Prichard is a historian and she's determined to confront the slander cast upon nosegays by a notable brand of soap.'

'Soap,' I repeated flatly.

'Yes. You know the one. It ran an advertisement in all the papers in the spring. Now half the nation is convinced that in the days before modern baths, brides carried bouquets to disguise their body odour. But Miss Prichard absolutely, categorically and unequivocally states that medieval girls knew perfectly well how to use a damp cloth. And she means to prove the real value of herbs and flowers by making reference to any historical texts that give a contemporary record of their uses. She begins by citing Shakespeare's Ophelia.'

He directed my gaze to the quote at the head of the first page. It read: *There's rosemary, that's for remembrance. Pray you, love, remember. And there is pansies, that's for thoughts.*

I will be frank here and admit that I was a little taken aback by this conversation. He had never spoken to me so freely before. I looked at the papers he had handed to me and then I looked up at him, trying not to feel too much like I was staring.

I wasn't being helped by the guilty memory of all that recent gossiping. And all the time I had the echo of my uncle's concerns ringing in my ear – in effect declaring that this man wasn't permanently fixed here.

I wasn't mute after all. I heard myself remarking vaguely, 'Miss Prichard didn't say a word to me about this last week.'

My eyes strayed to the pages of her manuscript again. Perhaps the change in him was because I wasn't being terribly talkative myself. Or frightening him away by smiling.

I gave myself a shake and asked in a crisper tone, 'Will you publish her?'

'Read it,' he said simply. 'She's a woman after your own heart.'

Then, having said something ambiguous like that to me so that my attention flew back to his face, he asked, 'Now, what about the Jacqueline Dunn book?'

I took a breath and pulled myself together. Straightening my shoulders, I found professionalism and a stronger voice. 'All right,' I asked. 'Who's Harriet Clare?'

'Her daughter. At least, I think so. She's aged about eleven anyway, so I presume she's the daughter.' He hesitated, then added, 'I got the impression that Jacqueline lost her husband during the war and had to move to the rotten lodge on the edge of this Ashbrook estate. As I understand it, the grieving daughter was a bit shaken up by the move so they wrote this book together as a way of forging a fresh start and a new bond with the place. She and Harriet uncovered the old story about the giraffes and dived straight in.'

'That's nice,' I said sincerely. Then because of the way he had paused in the middle of that, added, 'Aren't you sure?'

'It's hard to be certain. Jacqueline is a touch too excitable to be clear at times and one can hardly ask about the husband.'

'No,' I agreed.

I didn't mean him to, but he must have detected an undertone in that reply, because after a moment he remarked, 'This has been rather dropped on you, hasn't it? Shall I sit down and we'll go through it?'

I actually laughed at that; quite genuinely all of a sudden. I had to ask him, 'Have you even *read* the edits?'

I was far too far along the path of failure to mind the implication that, if I needed his help, I didn't know my job. I set aside the loose sheets of Miss Prichard's manuscript to tell him exasperatedly, 'I'm supposed to decide whether the giraffes were the Masai or reticulated sort. And I have a sneaking suspicion that this meddling friend is actually Mrs Dunn herself, because, for all the changes this friend made, they don't appear to have noticed any of the misspellings of Ashbrook.'

Robert claimed the chair on the other side of my desk.

I had already handed him the book and pointed out a few of the more choice corrections. After a time his eyebrows rose. To my relief I wasn't sitting there watching him and wondering if he had slept at the weekend. I wasn't even trying to calculate whether his little trips away meant he had found a new haunt. I was examining a set of bus timetables I had collected when I had stepped out for lunch.

He set the bound proof down on the desk and then leaned forwards in his seat to draw my attention. He lightly tapped the cover with his index finger. 'There isn't much time to get this sorted out.'

I told him by way of agreement, 'I've been down to the print room. Mr Lock says that Friday is the latest they can accommodate my edits without running out of time before Christmas, and that's only going to work if Mr Lock's wife will let him come in on Saturday to begin the printing. I've tried to get Mrs Dunn on the telephone. She's out or not answering or something. She's been out all day.'

It was then that I showed him the bus timetables.

After a moment he said, 'I see.'

'There's no time,' I said almost apologetically, 'to wait for the post. What if she's away or it gets delayed? If it goes in the post today, she should get it tomorrow, which is Tuesday. Everything is fine if she makes the final changes swiftly and sends the book straight back to us. But what if she isn't clear? Or isn't there? I really don't want to be responsible for making us miss our publication date.'

'We won't be missing it. She will.'

'All the same ...'

Abruptly he accepted my decision and came just as swiftly to his own. He sat back in his chair. 'Would you like company tomorrow?'

'Don't you remember? You're going out yourself. Uncle George said so.'

He didn't rise to the bait. In fact, he didn't even acknowledge it. 'You'll have a long day. Your journey home will involve a long stop at either Cirencester or Bourton-on-the-Water, depending on which route you take.'

'I can read a timetable, Mr Underhill. And I think I can manage to buy myself a cup of tea somewhere.'

I made him smile very fleetingly. Then the relief of the feeling left again. He tipped his head to signify that he had come to another decision. This one was clearly less easy to voice. Finally, he said, 'Very well, I'll come straight out with it. You won't find it difficult meeting this woman?'

His directness went through me with a cold jolt that felt remarkably like temper. So did the way he was watching my face. This was like the time he had as good as asked me whether I minded making the tea.

48

I believe it was something very restrained that made me accept his question and tell him rather too precisely, 'I'll be fine. Five years as a widow is long enough to achieve some sort of equilibrium, wouldn't you say?'

After a moment, I added more convincingly, 'I suspect that as long as neither of us pretends to know precisely how the other is feeling, there won't be any trouble at all. In my experience, people always presume that everybody deals with bereavement in just the same way. But when it comes to Mrs Dunn's experience of losing her husband, who but her could even begin to imagine how it felt to explain his loss to a child?'

'It's always the same with you, isn't it? Someone else has always got it worse.'

That sudden twist of sympathy stung me. Even more than his usual reserve. I felt entirely caught off guard. And now he was accepting my decision and climbing to his feet. I certainly didn't dare tell him that I ranked him firmly alongside Mrs Dunn on the list of people I couldn't fathom. 'Mr Underhill?'

He paused with his hand on the back of the visitor's chair ready to set it neatly back into its place. 'Yes?'

'Where do you go?'

'I paid a long overdue visit to my parents at the beginning of last week.'

Something about the simply honesty of this answer touched my heart. I suppose I'd never asked him anything so directly before. In fact, I wasn't sure we had ever spoken frankly like this at all.

Then I noticed the precise wording of his reply. It was a

reflection of my careful evasion of his remark about meeting Jacqueline.

Suddenly, I was shaking my head, disbelieving. 'You were visiting your parents when I was fussing about sending out the proof copy of this book about giraffes. But my uncle didn't tell me.'

I faltered as I worked out what it meant for myself. Then I continued in a stronger voice, 'Uncle George didn't tell me where you were, because he still needed to conceal his inability to explain all the rest. So now I have to wonder whether he *won't* tell me where else you've been going?'

I hesitated before adding, 'Or he *can't?*'

'Don't ask me that. Please.'

His plea was softly spoken. And that surprised me too.

I suspect that the harder dawning of doubt was showing there on my face because in the next moment Robert was saying briskly, to end this, 'Anything else? No? Good. And good luck tomorrow.'

It was my turn to sleep badly that night before waking with the wish I could run away.

The attic timbers were full of their usual creaks and bangs and I had to add a new pressure to the dark. It wasn't, however, formed around a certain editor's unexplained absences, or at least not completely.

My night was filled with a disturbingly persistent dream about struggling to fill the advent calendar for a child. And it was horrible because upon waking it gave me the shock of learning that there was a part of my mind that had been bruised by the loss of the family my husband and I would never have.

Irrationally or not, I blamed Robert for making me think like this. I believe I've mentioned before that there was a general policy to refrain from asking a person about their war experiences. This was why. Until this moment it had never troubled me that my brief six weeks of being wildly in love and then nearly as swiftly wildly in grief hadn't produced a child; there had, after all, barely even been time to learn enough about my husband for real friendship.

But all the same, this sense of the smaller legacy of my loss must have been in me all along to have surfaced now. And it must be said that Robert Underhill hadn't actually asked. He had been concerned for my welfare and he had meant it kindly. But it was the faint compliment that had been given in the unguarded moment afterwards that was really meddling with the way I chose to confront what had happened to me during the war.

It made it impossible to consider that tomorrow I would simply be a representative of Kershaw and Kathay Book Press going to meet an author about her book. Because the author was a widow and, therefore, as far as my colleague was concerned – and anybody else who chose to worry about me – I must remember that I was one too.

Chapter 5

In spite of all those unhappy thoughts at three o'clock in the morning, I believe that the distress of a hard experience did sometimes give me the freedom to be clearer about what I really wanted.

It must depend on the scale of the shock, naturally, but last night, once it had been established that I wouldn't sleep until the traces of the nightmare had been shed, I whiled away the hour of wakefulness by beginning the manuscript of Miss Prichard's book. Memory wove its way through every page; through her study of the written record for herbal medicines from centuries before, and through the life she'd led with the old doctor who had been brilliant in his field.

There's rosemary, that's for remembrance – and, in less Shakespearean terms, the herb represented the power to recall lives lost and lives present. It actually possessed certain properties that might help. In bygone years it would have been carried at weddings and set upon the coffin at funerals. It had no influence upon either happiness or sadness, it simply asserted the value of ever having met each other. And the importance of fixing their memory upon your soul.

This morning, when I stepped out to catch the bus to Cirencester at twenty-five minutes past seven, I might have been a childless widow but I was also remembering that I was really enjoying the prospect of a day out.

The day hadn't yet fully dawned. A thin scatter of stallholders for the Tuesday market were grimly laying out wares with the air of people who knew that this was not going to be one of those bright busy days. Any townsfolk who possessed the energy for early morning bustle were climbing onto this bus, including a well-to-do gentleman in suit, raincoat and hat who was, as it turned out, Doctor Bates.

'Mrs P,' he said cheerfully by way of a greeting. He must have picked up this version of my name from Amy, only from him it sounded like 'pea' rather than simply the initial letter.

He settled beside me on a seat that squeaked and received his little paper ticket from the conductor. I watched him fold it into a breast pocket in a way that made me certain he was going to misplace it for his return trip.

Oblivious, Doctor Bates turned to me and asked, 'Off on a pleasure trip?'

I showed him the parcel containing the book.

'Ah,' he said. 'You work hard at both extremes of the day, it seems.'

'Do I?'

'I saw that the lights were on late at the office last night. Your uncle's got you handling a last minute rush before Christmas, has he?'

This was the first time I had ever met the man on my own.

In the two months since I had taken my job, I had stepped down into the shop on perhaps a dozen separate days to find him chatting with Amy. Today, I shook my head in the midst of making my own dealings with the conductor, and said calmly, 'That was a late telephone call with the author I'm visiting today. Everyone else had gone home.'

Yesterday, I had tried several times through the rest of the afternoon and into the evening to reach Jacqueline. At about seven o'clock she had finally answered, so I knew where I was going and that she would be there to meet me. To her credit, she had actually offered to make the journey herself and come to the office. But I hadn't let her. I really was running away.

The bus cemented my escape by rattling into the line of traffic heading south. The windows were steaming up already. Through the fog of too many people breathing in a confined space, Doctor Bates was remarking, 'The place was lit on Saturday too.'

'You really are determined to consider me overworked, aren't you?' I replied. 'You probably saw the lights from the stairs. I had my sister visiting and the stairs are lethal in the dark.'

'Lives locally, does she?'

'No – in Worcester. We like to catch up.' I realised at last that I was in a way blaming this man for that uncomfortable morning I'd spent gossiping about Robert. I made an effort to be more conversational. 'Where are you going today?'

He didn't notice my change of tone at all. Instead he asked, 'Is she an older sister?'

'Rachel is a year younger. She and I shared rooms in Bristol for a few years while she was based there too.'

I actually had three older brothers – two who had survived the war through working very hard in farming, and a third who had simply been very lucky abroad. Rachel had been followed by two even younger siblings, but I didn't give Doctor Bates room to ask that. Given half a chance, the question would come, I was sure of it. It was what I believed everyone did. People who knew my aunt and uncle would discover this little detail about my other family and then, by degrees, move towards weighing and measuring my feelings about the history that had brought me to Moreton.

And they particularly enjoyed discovering that my move to my aunt and uncle's home had coincided with the conception of the child who had followed Rachel. Presumably they suspected, not unreasonably, that the family farmhouse would have been growing a little full.

So, to cut him off at the start, I asked again, 'Which stop are you travelling to today?'

'Stow-on-the-Wold. I like to catch up with family too.' Doctor Bates smiled at me. And then he made it clear that he had never been interested in probing the wholesomeness of my current relationship with my siblings because it turned out that the doctor was perfectly normal and self-centred, and had merely been thinking about his own concerns.

In the next moment he was ducking his head to be heard over the roar of the bus, and saying with a sheepish kind of charm, 'So, I know I shouldn't expect you to tell me, but I can't bear the suspense. What does your Mr Underhill think of my landlady's little story?'

His barefaced determination to oversee his landlady's

project amused me. It suited my mood this morning. Suddenly it was easier to see what Amy liked about this man – and it mattered what she thought because Amy had to be one of the kindest women I knew, even if she didn't value bits of ribbon that came out of advent calendars.

The dim lights that studded the ceiling of this bus were making his hair shine. It was very fair and drooping over his brow to cast a soft shadow across his eye. And the only part that didn't quite suit him was that I couldn't help thinking that eight o'clock – the time of his expected arrival in Stow – would be a very early hour to be bestowing visits upon any family.

I told him flatly, 'I don't know what Mr Underhill thinks, or at least nothing beyond the fact he recommended that I should take a look. But I—'

'He's read it already has he? Or do you do the reading for him?'

I let my eyebrows rise at that, quite pointedly. It made him grin. 'All right,' he conceded, 'If you won't let me examine the balance of work between you, your uncle and this other editor, what can you tell me?'

'That Mr Underhill read the manuscript over the weekend? And now it's my turn?' I offered. And that amused him too.

The doctor had a good smile. It offset the way he was one of those men who was more self-assured than generally suited my tastes. This was because, to be frank, in a north Cotswold town, his sort of cultured good looks tended to run hand in hand with a person exuding a certain degree of wealth and class, and expecting the same from his friends.

In short, Doctor Bates was handsome without my finding him absolutely attractive, which was a terrible thing to admit, really. Although, I didn't imagine the doctor was thinking seriously of me either.

He probably saw a woman with wavy hair and a decent figure, but wearing an office girl's idea of slacks beneath a winter coat and lacking quite the right manner for higher calibre society. And that last thought was where my embarrassment crashed in.

It rushed all of a sudden into my skin, and it came from the disconcerting realisation that I was thinking in this way at all – that I was thinking about my own attractiveness, I mean.

I was acting as though it were natural to see my body as more than a mere count of limbs, when in truth my recent years had been consumed by a numb sort of sexlessness. And I couldn't have entirely said at this moment which extreme I preferred.

Either way, the effort of discovering this part of myself made me thoroughly self-conscious. I was even more thoroughly afraid that this man would notice my blush. He might think it was for his benefit.

And in the space between one uncomfortable heartbeat and the next, the pressure of containing all this tipped me into saying recklessly, 'Actually, I've just got to the part of Miss Prichard's manuscript where she lists the chemical properties of nettles and sets them against a seventeenth century remedy for improving mobility. Miss Prichard is wonderfully scientific really, isn't she?'

'Well, yes. Her book is impressive. But you're speaking to a doctor. I'm better qualified to give an opinion about treatments that have been founded in modern science, not the kind of quackery that stems from potions and lotions and old wives tales.'

His reply was given in a way that made me think he believed we were speaking about a herbal recipe book. Clearly, he hadn't actually read the manuscript.

Now he was worrying if the distant gleam of light from a house ahead was a sign we were approaching his stop. We weren't. The building was merely a farmhouse, grey and sagging.

The farm flashed by and left me to notice belatedly that the doctor was saying in a very different kind of voice, 'So when you make this sort of book, how much does the author get?'

His sudden change of manner helped me to settle my self-conscious flush back to a sensible colour. I asked him, 'How do you mean?'

He had his hat set upon his knee with his fingers gripping its brim. His thumb smoothed a ruffled patch on the felt. 'Well, if for example you sell one book, how much will Miss Prichard get from it?'

It was a common enough question from our new authors or, indeed, their friends so I tried to meet him with equal steadiness. 'It rather depends on where we sell it. If we sell it through our own shop, the costs for us are lower so she'd get marginally more. If it gets sold by another bookshop or if a wholesaler takes a box full or something, they have to take their cut too. And we have to send the books out in the first place. All those costs have to be accounted for.'

This sounded unattractively dry, even to me as the woman who would be typing up the publisher's letter, so I added, 'Our authors do get a very good royalty rate from us though.'

'So what you're saying is that if the book sells for a few shillings, you'll take your fee, the bookseller takes theirs and so will the postman and anyone else who claims to have a stake in it. And after all that, Miss Prichard will have to make do with the penny or so that is left over. Is that right?'

My companion added on a wistful note, 'I'm sure you know what you're doing, Mrs P, but it does seem to me that authors really are the last person to make any money from their books.'

It was remarks such as these which made me wish that more people looked at the books in their hands and tried for a moment to sense all the human lives who had contributed to the task of bringing it to them.

I replied calmly, 'If we're recognising the bookseller and the postman and so on, you might also think of the typesetter, who will lovingly lay out all those lines of text. Or the hands that will direct the binding.' I hesitated. 'I don't know if I should tell you this because it will sound too sentimental, but I think books are a beautiful monument to unity.'

Whereas, by contrast, the bus driver's handling of the road was rattling my teeth, and Doctor Bates had no idea of anybody's united effort.

My neighbour was only saying blankly, 'Are you referring to Mr Lock?'

Then he admitted, 'If I'm honest, I'm really worrying about

the fee your uncle is planning to charge Miss Prichard for the pleasure of seeing her book finished.'

'In that case, I don't know if I should tell you that none of us makes a lot of money out of selling books,' I replied gently. 'It's perfectly true, though.'

'Your uncle seems to be making enough to pay your wages. And for that man Underhill.'

'Because without us, Uncle George couldn't possibly manage all the work himself.' I shouldn't have said that. A painfully defensive note was creeping in as though I too thought it exploitative to expect our authors to pay their way when surely this might all be done simply for the love of books.

I added feebly, 'We're a very small book press, Doctor Bates, and the war hasn't been kind. Even in the years before every supply of paper and ink was rationed – when it wasn't so hard to print enough books to make a title profitable – our reach was never as large as one of the big London publishers. We've always had to ask our authors to bear some of the risk just to make sure the project was viable.'

This wasn't helping. I tried a different tack. 'We all have to charge people. How would you feel if I asked about your decision to buy your way into your present practice? You must have done it, after all, on the principle that you would make a reasonable rate of return?'

It was an utterly foolish thing to say. I made him laugh. Then he countered cheerfully, 'My whole livelihood is about to be adjusted to make things easier for people who have every need of my expertise but no means of paying the fee, just as soon as the new National Health Service comes in.'

It was at times like these that I felt very much the newcomer to this town. I didn't know this man very well and I didn't know how honest I ought to be. Particularly when, to him, I wasn't myself, as such. I was clearly being cast again as Mrs Lucinda Peuse, typist and telephonist and present representative of Kershaw and Kathay Book Press.

I said more sensibly, 'I'm sorry. I'm doing a terrible job of explaining how our style of publishing service is truly very valuable. In no small way, it is testimony to my uncle's commitment to his work that the effects of the war have never made him miss a step. Our authors come to us because we still care to make the special books that mightn't sell in the thousands but still are absolutely valuable to the reading world at large. I think Miss Prichard's manuscript is set to become one of those special books.'

And it was then that I realised that it sounded as though I had just reduced Miss Prichard's effort to the level of frivolous nonsense. Only it wasn't fair because I always seemed humbling myself at the moment and discovering that I didn't know my job. I had thought that the feeling might be because I was a woman and I often seemed to be justifying myself to men. But actually, in this instance, the issue of gender was clearly irrelevant because in the next breath the doctor proved that he wasn't trying to ridicule me. He betrayed his true interest. He was concerned about Robert.

The doctor gave a brief smile that lightly bared his teeth. 'You have to understand that I'm just trying to be a good friend to my landlady. But this Mr Underhill. He isn't even a book man is he? He only joined your uncle's business in the spring. He was going to be a doctor and then he was a prisoner of war. You can't tell me that the Germans ran an extensive library in their camps. So how is a man like that even qualified to tell a person how to write a better book?'

I didn't like to say that I didn't know how Robert had got the job either; that I didn't even know the practicalities of how he had met my uncle.

Instead I replied, 'That is probably why he's so good at it, shouldn't you say? He experienced all that and now he's here. And I can ask you about bookishness since you really are a doctor. Didn't you have to do an awful lot of reading when you were a medical student?'

'Oh,' said Doctor Bates. I saw it pass across his mouth – that urge to pursue his cause, followed swiftly by a certain degree of gratification for the compliment. That mouth conceded, 'Well yes, I did have to read extensively. Great volumes of studies and all sorts of journals and so on. Medicine is a language all in its own right, you know. In fact, I'm sure you do know, Mrs P, because you're observant. But ...'

I caught his sideways glance. Flattery could be applied as a counterattack too it seemed. Then he gave it up. He abruptly looked at the road ahead and used it as a cue to set his hat upon his head.

In a voice that was suddenly brisk and undisguised, he remarked, 'We're coming into Stow. Thank you for answering my questions. Will you tell Mr Underhill that I've advised Miss Prichard to take another look at the offer she might have from Nuneham's? Let's help the old lady along a little at the very least, shall we, you and I?'

'I thought you'd encouraged her to submit her work to us in the first place?' I was thinking of that vague insinuation Robert had made.

But the doctor only said, 'No. She didn't discuss it with me beforehand. So, what about that rival offer – will you tell him what I said?'

The bus was swinging to a fearsome stop in a small town that seemed even colder and greyer than Moreton. And then he was rising to his feet and I was putting out a hand as if to check him, only to have to use it instead as a brace against the rim of the furthermost seat in front of me as the bus lurched towards the kerb.

I was saying quickly, 'Just a moment. Since we're speaking of helping people, can you tell me if I need to worry about the health of my aunt or uncle?'

It was only afterwards that I realised my plea had sounded like a barter for assistance. A trade of his particular knowledge for mine.

Then his answer came, and it was given so crisply that it released me once again, even to the extent of giving me a reproof. The doctor told me with absolute decision, 'I'm bound by certain rules of privacy, Mrs P. I can't discuss my patients, not even with you.'

The bus stopped. I sat back in my seat, disappointed and absurdly conscious of just how much I was worrying about them.

He must have seen. I thought he had stepped away down the bus but then I felt his gaze upon my face. Without straying back into that peculiar territory of obligation, the man beneath the smartly brimmed hat somehow drew my eye and said steadily above the clatter from the departing passengers, 'I can suggest that there are no serious conversations you need to be having with your aunt and uncle on that score, in the immediate future. Will that do?'

My heart jerked once in my chest.

I gave a nod. 'Thank you.'

'And we might meet sometime to discuss the rest, if you like?' He wasn't offering a trade. And it wasn't only a remark on our respective cares for aging people – or the way his concern for his landlady and mine for my aunt and uncle might unite us after all.

But before I could flounder into deciphering what he was offering, he'd allowed himself to be swept at last into the tide of descending passengers.

As he went, his final words were, 'In the meantime, you will tell him about Nuneham's, won't you? Good. Goodbye Mrs P.'

As I say, he didn't really give me time in those last moments to react to the fact that I might have just been courted a little. Realisation would come later, with a useless little flustered bolt of recollection at about half past four in the afternoon as I caught the second of three buses homewards.

Instead, at this moment, while the present bus was pulling away from the stop and rattling on towards Cirencester, I was mainly preoccupied with the other strange things he had said. I was thinking about his parting request to pass on the news about the rival publisher to Robert. And I was thinking about the less obvious detail which had come a few seconds before, when the doctor had made it thoroughly clear that he was duty-bound to safeguard his patients' private records.

He couldn't tell me about my aunt and uncle's health because, as a doctor, he would never discuss his patients.

It was a contradiction of the memory I had of yesterday, when the doctor had felt free enough to hint an awful lot about his views on the health of another man; my uncle's war-damaged second-in-command.

Now I was supposed help the doctor while he negotiated a better offer for his aging landlady. But I thought the doctor's remarks about Nuneham's were more specific than that. He really wanted Robert to hear our rival's name.

Chapter 6

Christmas in Jacqueline Dunn's house was edging its way in more swiftly than it was at my aunt's home. Or in my attic, for that matter. I suppose it was because there were school children here. The window ledges and any high shelves were lined with fir cones and handmade characters from a nativity scene crafted out of old newspaper.

The book was, I understood, meant to fill the main part of Jacqueline's Christmas present list. There was none of the tiptoeing around Mrs Peuse or Mrs P with this woman. She called me Lucy from the start. She was slender, aged about forty-five and swathed in a woollen jumper and slacks as only the terrifically elegant can be. She was living in the solitary gatehouse to an old park estate.

Finding it had been a simple case of deciding which of the innumerable villages on the Fairford road by the name of Ampney something-or-other was the stop I needed. The bus had set me down in a sleety shower by a river bordering the graveyard for a tiny, sinking church. The church had no tower because quite simply it would have capsized into the sodden ground. From there I had to trace the footpath across a narrow bridge and find the ridgetop drive that would have saved me a deal of trouble if only I'd had access to a car. At the tip of this drive was the lodge that housed Jacqueline.

'I have to tell you,' she said brightly, 'that before I can allow you to discuss the edits in my book, you absolutely have to join the ranks of the initiates who appreciate the full truth behind my giraffe story.'

'I do?'

Apparently, I did. These were the parts of her tale that hadn't been deemed suitable for a light children's history and it was hard to get her to even consider how little it mattered what I believed just so long as we got the book finished. She kept getting side-tracked into showing me old photographs of the way the park had been, before the last Ashbrook had been lost to the trenches of the Great War.

Finally, I gave in and asked, 'The name *is* Ashbrook, then?'

I was sitting at her kitchen table and peering at a small black and white print of people in Victorian dress. They were standing on the front steps of a small country house that had been bleached to white by the glare of sunlight. The building was square to afford a good view over the surrounding park-land and its core was probably Tudor, but the house in the photograph consisted of three storeys of tall windows with various trimmings added on through time. The most impressive of these additions was the sweep of pillared and shaded steps to the broad front door.

She was tapping the centre of the image where a few men ranged between fine columns in tall hats and impressive beards. 'That's Walter John Ashbrook. He's the son of Graham

Hanley Ashbrook, the man who wrote "Fevers of Africa". Do you know it?'

It was a common misconception that those of us who work with books must have devoured every work ever written. I was not, however, and never will be sufficiently well read to ever answer a question like that in the affirmative. I shook my head.

Jacqueline wasn't impressed by my ignorance. She told me in an authoritative sort of way, 'Graham Hanley Ashbrook inherited the most enormous Kenya estate. That's where he nearly lost his assistant and closest friend to yellow fever. After the fellow's recovery – which must in itself have been pretty remarkable – our man Graham was inspired to study the survival rate in the local population. He observed that travelling Englishmen tended to succumb almost instantly, whereas born and bred Kenyans had a better chance of pulling through. The study made for some pretty pioneering research into disease resistance. He published his book about it in 1865. These photographs were taken around that time, after Graham Hanley Ashbrook had retired to his English country estate. He was pretty frail by then so it was left to his son Walter John Ashbrook to try to preserve the family's other great legacy.'

She left a suitable pause. Then she added, 'A study of the management and care of the Ashbrook giraffes. This was the park where Graham kept them, naturally.'

'Oh, naturally.'

I was studying the other characters in the photograph. There were three other men, all equally bearded and all of the calibre of clerks or estate managers with a few urchin-like children ranging about in the foreground. It looked like harvest time in a standard English summer and there were no giraffes in sight.

I asked, 'How did you get this information? Your book doesn't make that clear.'

Jacqueline beamed as though I had asked something particularly delightful. 'Shall we walk up to the house? I'll just go and pull on my boots.'

She left me blinking in the sudden peace of her kitchen. It was an angular room of the sort with a low ceiling where no two windows quite faced the same way. There was a short run of steps up to the living room which was narrow and hung with photographs – two boys in the uniform of the very smartest school in Cirencester and a father, who made me wonder suddenly if I'd blundered when I'd asked about her access to the details of the Ashbrook family. They might have come to her through her husband's family.

There was not, I couldn't help observing with a sense of doubt that was at odds with the simple homely clutter of family life, a photograph of the daughter Harriet Clare.

Jacqueline bustled me along the length of the ridgetop drive in what turned into a fierce rainstorm. Great pollarded lime trees towered leafless overhead.

She was wrapped in one of those enormous country jackets that made her look stylish even in a wintry squall. An oilskin hat drooped low over her loose hair. My own hair was twisted up under my hat. It had the sort of stiff brim that cut a deep slant across the eyes and it was a beloved remnant of my Bristol life, but kept irritating me today because it was threatening to fly off if I didn't keep a hand on it. As we walked, my guide was shouting out between breath-stealing gusts the more recent history of the house.

'The last Ashbrook,' she told me, 'met his end in 1916, unmarried and childless. Afterwards the house was passed about between distant heirs male, to stand empty for a few sad, lonely years. Then it was requisitioned at the outbreak of our recent war to house the patients of a London children's hospital.'

'I imagine, then,' I shouted above the wind, 'that it's in a terrible state of repair, now that it's been emptied of evacuees and returned to public ownership. Was that when you bought it?'

'Absolutely. Do you recognise these steps from the photograph?'

We had reached that same flight of white stone steps between pillars from the photograph. I was met by dirty stonework and windows that stared with that blank coldness of decay.

But Jacqueline didn't really care about the appearance of the place. She was interested in the stables which ranged behind.

The yard mirrored the house, in that it was arranged as a square and everything that was older had been retouched to suit Victorian tastes. It was entered by passing beneath a staggeringly grand arch that united the two wings of a coach house. The boundary was set by a sweeping run of roofs with masonry scrolls and small oval windows in delicate brickwork. It was utterly lovely. And private.

She observed reverently, 'It would have been the perfect place to house the secret of a herd of giraffes, wouldn't you say?'

I suspected that it had simply been designed as a means of saving the farm horses from draughts.

Jacqueline made it seem as though we were entering a cathedral when she hauled on a vast sliding door and led me into the coach house. She cautioned on a whisper, 'This is where the workmen are storing their tools, so take care.'

This space was more than a simple chaos of tools. There was rubbish from the house that had been preserved because it was saleable for scrap. There was a shrouded old car acting as a relic from the last time the coach house had been put to its proper use. Beyond this was an impression that here was a tall building that was dry, with excellent light. But it didn't smell of animals.

I had been braced, I think, to scent that strong musty smell that zoos and circuses have. This place smelled only of cold air made acidic by a few tins of paint.

'Here,' said Jacqueline, probing into a corner behind a stack of broken bedsteads. They looked like hospital bedsteads, of the sort that had sturdy cleanable frames for hygienic treatment wards.

Jacqueline was saying, 'They chose this building for the

giraffes because it was the only one tall enough. The coaches had to go elsewhere. I think that contraption in the corner there is an automatic watering trough. And those pipes running along the wall up there – they're like hothouse pipes, aren't they? They were installed to keep the giraffes warm in winter. Did I tell you that it was Graham Hanley Ashbrook's ambition to breed small giraffes?'

'Of course. In your book.' My reply was clipped. I didn't know why I was resisting her need to be believed. Normally I considered myself to be a relatively unassuming sort of person, easily inspired. Today, I was ready to defend myself, or defend my uncle's integrity, or Robert or someone, until I shook myself out of the distracting memory of that bus ride, and worked a little harder at being nice.

I became the person I was meant to be. I asked in a better tone, 'Did Mr Ashbrook manage it?'

Jacqueline beamed. She was the sort of woman whose happier emotions dominated her face. She had extraordinary cheekbones and her eyebrows were arched and set very high, and they rose whenever she engaged with her obsession.

Then she dampened it all by admitting ruefully, 'I think Graham Hanley Ashbrook was dreaming of the day when he could let loose a domestic herd of giraffes to roam upon the lawn outside his library window with their heads about the height of the rosebushes. But in truth it takes many genera-tions to breed a miniature version of a species.'

Her gaze swept about the coach house. I knew she was imagining better proof than a few nameless pipes on the wall. Then she remarked briskly, 'Breeders of miniature animals aren't seeking dwarfism, you understand? Graham picked his stud giraffes carefully from the Kenyan stock. They were small for their kind, but it takes a lot of selective breeding to create a truly miniature one, and then it has to have other small animals to breed with to make it genetically secure.'

'And are they slow to mature?'

She nodded. 'Normal sized giraffes don't breed until they are about six years old.'

'So how many giraffes did he have?'

I could see that she approved of the question. She told me, 'At its peak, Graham's herd had four males and eleven females but he'd died before half of them had calved even once here. Walter John Ashbrook carried on with the herd until his own death in 1895. He must have had at least some success because that year his son sold two males to a zoo where they promptly died. We know the family still had three females in 1914 because a private park in Bedfordshire wrote to ask about them.'

'Perhaps they had an inkling of what would happen to the herd if Graham's great-grandson met his end leading a charge from the trenches?' I supplied gently.

'Which he promptly did. We don't know whether this park took them or not.' She paused while she turned to me.

'And,' she added with relish, 'we don't know how tall they were.'

I could hear the whisper of the wind upon the roof tiles. For the first time I could feel a sense of the legacy her beloved Ashbrook might have left. Not just this tale of giant animals gradually shrinking. But all those generations of Ashbrooks who had come after him to leave their own traces behind in this house. They were all here, even if only in the alterations to a few windows here and there on the façade of the house.

Jacqueline's passion was infectious. Deliberately so, I thought. She knew what effect her little tour was having and she knew what she was doing when she examined her watch. 'I'll give you a quick walk through the house, shall I? Then we'll hurry back while it's dry to look at those edits.'

She led me out of the coach house and across the yard to a small door that opened into what appeared to have originally been the kitchen cold store. There were stone shelves and the walls were rather green.

She was saying, 'You can see why I had to write about Graham Hanley Ashbrook's work, can't you? His story is bound to be "discovered" when this house is finally restored to some of its former glory, and it's just begging for me to do it first. The son Walter John Ashbrook always meant to write it himself but between you and me, he wasn't a terribly communicative fellow. This hall and the stairwell are the oldest parts of the house. As you can see, the young patients of the wartime hospital weren't vandals but still they couldn't help but leave their mark. It'll come though, I'm sure.'

Now I truly was awestruck. In the sense that for Jacqueline there was no pause in her commitment to the Ashbrook legacy. She didn't see the death of this space in quite the same final way I did. To me it looked awfully like this house's soul had been cut out.

Inside was bare. Like a whitewashed prison rather than a place dedicated to health. This wintery day was never going to show this place at its best, but I couldn't imagine the poor invalided children ever being warm here. Every painting, every wall panel and detail had been removed, brutally in some places, presumably for their own protection.

I asked, 'Where *did* you find this history and the photographs? They certainly can't have been conveniently left lying about for you to discover when you arrived?'

'The local historical society. The village took custody of the family's personal archive shortly after the last Ashbrook died in the Great War. The papers are very fragmentary because I gather all the really important documents from Graham's research were given to a London college years before. But the archive does include a portrait of Graham Hanley Ashbrook as a young man. He had wonderful curling hair.'

She didn't take me upstairs. The rise to the first floor was damaged and the few doors I could see up there hung open onto rooms that were empty of everything except the occasional workman's ladder. She was adding, 'My husband says—'

'Your husband?'

'Well, yes. Andrew did the latest read through of the book. He found all those last minute errors.'

She cast me a slanting look as if she had just unwittingly given away a secret. But not, it must be said, the secret I was thinking of. She had no idea we'd suspected her of being a victim of a wartime tragedy.

She swept across the foot of the stairs and in through a set of narrow folding doors. This room was as empty as all the rest but it had a splendid view across a lawn to the faint line of a ha-ha.

'This was the library,' she said with emphasis, because I think she was a little bit in love with this Graham Hanley Ashbrook, and this would have been his domain. There were no rosebushes outside the window for his giraffes to graze now. Jacqueline was adding, 'Andrew's gone back to help his father in our Blaze Hotel today, but the renovations here are our project. His father's leaving this one to Andrew completely.'

Standing in this room that carried no real hint of warmth or old charm for me, I suddenly knew where the secret lay. 'Oh,' I said on a warmer note of dawning understanding, 'This place is going to be a hotel.'

This was the detail she had omitted to share before. It made her unflinching commitment to the expense of her book make better sense.

You see, I knew the Blaze Hotel. It was near Bristol and it belonged to a chain of hotels that marketed themselves solely upon their panache for occupying a formerly derelict mansion and donning its history like an elegant robe.

Blaze Hotel was terribly near Blaise Castle and traded shamelessly upon all possible connections with that place. Or at least it had done until it had been required during the war to temporarily house engineering officers from the Royal Navy training base.

My husband had been billeted there during his eight weeks of training at HMS Bristol. It had kept the valuable new recruits safely out of range of the terrible blitz that had pounded the city – the same blitz, in fact, that my sister and

I had endured for all that time on a daily basis as we had scurried to our respective places of work.

Knowing the tomfoolery of my husband's fellow seafaring engineers, and the number of men who must have been housed there during the years that followed, I doubted very much that the Blaze Hotel had been returned to its owners in a better state than this place.

Jacqueline was watching my expression. She must have deduced that I was foreseeing the day when her book would be sold from the reception counter with all the little guides to the sights and scenes in the area. But I wasn't misled into thinking that I had also discovered she was a woman who had her eye fixed firmly on the profit. This was just the new excuse.

In truth, Robert hadn't been far from the mark when he had told me that he believed she was pursuing this project as a means of forging a fresh start and a new bond with a child who had been upset by the move to this country house.

Only the child wasn't her own. She was saying, 'You know, he really *did* have giraffes here. Look at this picture.'

She drew out a notebook from one of the coat's enormous pockets. It was bound with a piece of string. She had evidently been saving this moment. She shared it like it was a fragile secret.

The small square print was of a girl of about eleven staring coldly at the camera in that way people always seemed to do in early photographs. Quite crucially, the giraffe was holding its head low so that the girl was able to rest her hand upon its cheek. It wasn't dead like some great sacrifice to a trophy hunter. It wasn't miniature either. It was very tall and very much alive because it hadn't learned to stand like a statue for a long exposure, so it was a little blurred. Jacqueline drew my attention to the small square of white behind the giraffe's left ear. She was convinced that it was the tip of one of the pipes which carried heat into the coach house.

'Who—?' My voice failed so that I had to try again. 'Who is that girl?'

'Harriet Clare.'

Since Jacqueline enjoyed using people's full names, I ought to have realised long before that Clare was the girl's surname. I had a feeling Jacqueline spoke that way as a kind of epitaph to the departed.

I was shaken. I had no explanation for the experience except to blame it on the strangeness of being brought back to a contemplation of the flow of departed lives in this house after the relief of learning that Jacqueline's husband had survived.

Jacqueline was telling me seriously, 'Harriet Clare is the tragic case in this story. She's Walter's niece. Her mother was his sister. His own wife had died five years before. When Harriet's mother died in 1870, the little girl was sent to live with her uncle here. That photograph was taken the following year.'

After all that pressure to immerse myself in her obsession, it was hard to discover that the entire story had been a preparation for steering me into engaging with this. I felt as if I'd been tricked, and the reason why I was finding it so distressing was because it was dawning on me that, while I might never

Lorna Gray

have been capable of deducing Jacqueline's marital status from the evidence available, I had a feeling she could easily have guessed at mine.

Married women didn't tend to have a declared profession, in the main, unless they were poor. Not even my aunt would have gone running about after a job like this in the days when she had still been working with my uncle. But I was here and I had suspected all along that I was being recruited to her cause. Now I was afraid the hook she was using was the loss of my husband.

Jacqueline was adding, 'We know from the few letters Walter's own children wrote that their father wasn't a terribly warm man. And she was much younger than her cousins. It must have been very strange to come here and live amongst these people who were all so terribly grown up. She must have been lonely. You can almost see it in those eyes of hers, can't you? And, awfully, all references to Harriet Clare cease about two years later. It was the year some of the village children died from diphtheria. I always think it a terrible shame that her Great Uncle Graham Hanley Ashbrook hadn't still been alive.'

She meant because the man had done so much work on infectious fevers.

She was waiting for my answer. I think she really did care about the demise of the girl. I thought she believed she had found a good reason to expect me to care too. She was also really hoping to hear me marvel at the coincidence that made this girl, through the possibilities contained within that

80

fragment of pipework in her photograph, the key to proving this entire mad story about the giraffes.

I moistened my lips.

'That,' I remarked slightly hoarsely, 'puts an entirely grim feel on the wartime use of this place as a children's hospital. A bit behindhand, weren't they?'

It was then that it hit me that it was insane to be worrying about why Jacqueline might have led me like this. Or why indeed I might be finding this strange house so sad.

Because what did it matter that I couldn't sense any of the legacy that each new generation Ashbrooks had sought to build in this place for those who followed? It barely even mattered that I could only see that were no Ashbrooks left at all.

My response to this empty, old shell made no difference to anything because I meant nothing to those people. I only mattered to Jacqueline. And we were, as far as Jacqueline was concerned, fully ready to publish her tale of the giraffes. We were already committed to her cause.

I was able to observe then, 'You don't mention Harriet Clare in the book.'

'Except her name. The version I'm laying out for public consumption is, as you know, Graham Hanley Ashbrook's life and contribution dressed up in a palatable form for the children. But, privately, I feel passionately that this is Harriet's forgotten story. That's why I want her name beside mine on the cover. To redress the balance, poor girl.'

And it was then that I understood something more about Jacqueline and her relationship with this house. In a way, she really had succeeded in recruiting me and my emotions.

Because if one small branch of an old genealogy had been extinguished – as must have happened to families all through time – I could finally see that the only legacy that really mattered here was the one that was growing at this moment, when a woman like Jacqueline decided to think of them and learn their stories.

A person's grasp on permanence didn't only dwell the physical traces constructed by them in the course of their lives. It grew gently, selflessly, in the thoughts given freely by of those of us who were still living, who cared to remember them and speak their names now that they were gone.

In this great, neglected house, it was easy to believe that this gift of care was the only real legacy any of us might have.

I didn't have the heart then to tell Jacqueline that it wasn't entirely the done thing to attribute a book to someone without their permission. Even if they were dead, I'm sure it counted as passing-off or plagiarism or something along those lines that wasn't quite lawful.

I didn't really tell her anything of what I was feeling. In that way people have of putting things aside, I managed to enthuse my way through the next few hours of mulling over the edits so that all Jacqueline got from me was positive encouragement.

She was elated.

I was thoroughly unsure of what I was feeling. If, in fact, I was feeling anything at all by the time I caught the bus.

Chapter 7

It wasn't the silence of a town that was shutting up for the night that met me as I alighted at Bourton-on-the-Water in another blustery shower. It was Robert's voice mentioning my name: Mrs P.

At least, I recognised the voice for his when I turned and peered at him through the dark. It was a very odd sort of moment to encounter a colleague in the wrong town when I had just been quietly contemplating the peaceful prospect of an hour between buses and the chance of a cup of tea.

He was clad in a long grey raincoat and a hat that was about as serviceable in this weather as mine. He was stepping out of the shelter of a doorway into the light of the shop window that illuminated the bus stop. About five people splashed past and then we were standing there beside the bus with our heads on a slight tilt because we were each having to hold onto our hats and I was raising my voice above the noise of the gusting wind to say, 'Is this a meeting by chance or by design, Mr Underhill?'

'By design,' he said. I saw what passed for a smile come and go. He added, 'With a carefully choreographed plan that has already gone slightly awry. Mr Lock and I were out with a hired van for a delivery and we had the bright idea that he should leave me here to meet you while he finished the job before coming back to pick us up. Only, he's just telephoned to say he's had to return the vehicle to the garage before they close, so we'd better catch the bus. Shall we take shelter in a tearoom?'

The information wasn't given with charm. It was delivered flatly, with that unease of his that these days seemed to run to asking me unplanned questions about my training, my tastes or my happiness before retreating once again into something more businesslike. This evening, though, the focus of his tension was more immediate. This was like that time when I had met him on my aunt's stairs. He didn't need to ask me questions, because for him everything had settled to a better kind of calm just as soon as I had stepped down from the bus.

I thought he was feeling the surprise he had given me and realising that I wasn't too displeased to see him; which implied to me that he was acting here under instruction.

All the same, I went with him across the great lake that was the high street.

Bourton was very like Moreton in that the opposing faces of the buildings which lined this main thoroughfare were divided by a wide space dotted with trees. The difference here was that there was also a shallow river running down the middle – deliberately that is, and not just because of the increasingly heavy rain.

We crossed at the little humpbacked bridge and dived into a hotel that seemed to be open. And it was as the first glare of electric light slanted across the brim of Robert Underhill's hat and onto the angle of his cheek that I saw again the fading edges of restlessness in his manner, and felt its strain.

I asked with rather too much concern, 'Is everything all right, Mr Underhill?'

We were shown into a neat little corner booth with seats like pews – high backed benches made comfortable by deep cushions. It enclosed us in dim gas light with darkness outside and it was blessedly near the fire, because two hours and two buses had done little to ease my chill after all that walking about the countryside with Jacqueline.

The waitress hovered. 'Soup with pie to follow?' she asked.

'Soup,' I agreed, and so did Robert. There was no question today of shunning the two courses permitted in these days of strict regulations.

The man opposite smiled at the waitress and then smiled at me. Divested of his sodden coat and hat, he was thoroughly presentable in his navy suit and today he definitely matched Amy's idea of a good-looking man worn by hard experiences to a slightly angular maturity. He had hair that was a mid brown shade and a nice sort of height that he carried like someone who had played a lot of cricket as a youth. He was leaning in with his elbows resting on the tabletop.

'So,' he asked pleasantly, 'did you manage to resolve the editing issues today?'

It was an echo of the friendliness that had joined me at my desk yesterday when we had discussed our options for meeting Jacqueline's impending publication deadline.

'No,' I replied. 'Amongst other things, Jacqueline needs time to examine the markings of the giraffe in her photograph for the purpose of identifying its species, so I've got to go back tomorrow to collect the final edit. And on that note, I really wish you hadn't said what you had yesterday about my coping with the idea of encountering a fellow widow. She isn't one, and you rather put the thought of my husband's loss in my mind. At least, I think that's what was wrong today. And besides all that, I really don't see why it's fair that you should get to know all sorts of things about me while I don't know anything about you. Don't you ever speak about yourself?'

If he was looking every inch the man who belonged in this dignified dining room, I on the other hand was looking very much like a woman who had spent the day stamping about a derelict mansion. My windswept state was a fitting accompaniment for my sudden loss of patience.

Then he asked in an oddly braced sort of voice, 'Well, what is it you want to know?'

He was sitting a little straighter, not leaning in any more.

I leaned in myself. 'First of all,' I said shortly, 'I should like to know whether you and the other people at the office call me Mrs P or Mrs Pea.'

He looked nonplussed.

I added by way of a prompt, 'As in – are you using the initial letter "P", or is it the green vegetable?'

Then I allowed an eyebrow to rise.

For once his reaction to my idea of humour was a shy hint of a laugh rather than a prompt urge to bolt. Or perhaps he never really ran away because otherwise this man before me now was too much of a transformation.

He seemed relaxed but contrite as he confessed, 'It's the initial letter. Did you think we were mocking you?'

'I didn't know what you were doing. But I don't see why I can't be called by my name.'

'Mrs Peuse?'

'Lucy.'

I'd surprised him again. And I had surprised myself too, because this was cowardice masquerading as friendliness when really I didn't dare to launch into all the other questions I had. I also had to notice that he didn't return the gesture by inviting me to call him Robert.

After a moment while my mind filled with the memory of that small contretemps we'd had about how equally we were ranked in the office, he merely asked steadily, 'And if that was your first question, what was your second?'

I was determined to be at least a little bit brave. I asked him, '*Are* you all right? You looked as though you'd seen a ghost when you met me from the bus.'

'I'm fine,' he assured me and then the soup arrived. It was some time later that he suddenly grimaced, turning his head as if to shake away some inner constraint. Then he followed it by abruptly fixing me with a gaze that made my hand falter with the soup spoon midway on its journey to my mouth.

His eyes were an intimidatingly intense shade of brown.

He began by saying briskly, 'You've heard that Nuneham's is closing down?'

I hadn't, of course.

My heart was suddenly running unreasonably fast. Because this was frankness after a day of disorientation from being required to be a listening ear or a new convert or whatever it was the doctor and Jacqueline or anyone else had wanted from me. This was the decision he had made just now. To talk to me when he might just be silent.

I asked, 'Nuneham's is closing?'

'Do you understand what that means?'

I nodded. 'It means that another old business has fallen prey to the war. There'll be an unseemly rush from all the survivors to claim the redundant stock of paper and ink before any of the other neighbouring businesses can reach it first. And it'll all be done on the quiet, because it's hardly legal in these straitened times to repurpose supplies that have been dispensed as rationed goods.'

'You're very well informed.' I didn't think he had expected me to be quite so forthright.

I might have also added that I knew that the Nuneham's Book Press was based near Abingdon, just beyond Oxford, and the trainline from Moreton ran there.

I said rather uncertainly, 'Are you trying to tell me that your late return home last Friday marked the end of an attempt to haggle over Nuneham's remaining supplies?'

'Yes. And since your uncle doesn't keep a vehicle of any sorts, I spent yesterday organising a hired van. Today, Mr Lock and I travelled to Nuneham's to stake our claim on the prize we wanted.'

I disguised the force of my surprise by dwelling only on the smallness of the secret, after all that mystery. I remarked lightly, 'Poor Doctor Bates, he will be disappointed.'

'Doctor Bates? Why?'

'He's mentioned Nuneham's once or twice to me in the manner of a rival interest for Miss Prichard's book, and, since we're being honest, I'll tell you that he told me today to pass on the reference to you.'

I saw Robert's eyebrows lift to express mild surprise. He asked, 'When did you meet the doctor for him to be able to tell you that?'

'Well, this morning, on the bus. He travelled with me as far as Stow.'

'Did he?'

'We had quite a chat. I have a feeling he's hoping to use the threat of a rival publishing firm as leverage to encourage you to be generous when deciding Miss Prichard's terms.'

If I was probing for his reaction to Doctor Bates' hints, I certainly won a response of sorts. But not the one I was expecting. I had expected him to treat all mentions of Doctor Bates' name with the same seriousness that the doctor seemed to place upon the name Robert Underhill.

But this man's response was distaste; simple uncomplicated distaste in the form of an unexpectedly direct question. 'Odd that he didn't use his car, don't you think?'

'What I think is odd is that neither you nor my uncle told me this before. When you made me withdraw my question yesterday about my uncle's part in your various excursions, I thought ... Well, I don't know what I thought, but it was nothing quite like this.'

'Thank you,' he said after a moment, 'for not making me break my promise to your uncle.'

I met his gaze steadily. 'So what's suddenly changed? Did you succeed?'

'Take a look at the racks in the printworks and answer that one for yourself.'

It was a strange moment for me because there was something disconcerting about learning that this conversation wasn't so very different from the recent encounters with Doctor Bates and Jacqueline. Here at last was an urge to assume an air of being wise to the ways of the world and be calm – and, in this instance, to refrain from passing judgement about the mild criminality of this act.

Only I wasn't wise and I wasn't even sure if that was what he wanted from me. The single judgement I had was that I understood that my uncle's allowance of paper had been determined at the outbreak of war. It had been calculated by the volume of titles he and my aunt had published that first year. Luckily for Kershaw and Kathay, they'd published a decent handful, but even so the allowance of paper was never enough. So it had fallen to this man to do something to salvage the mess and I wondered how willing he had been.

I said with sudden sympathy, 'You must have found it difficult.'

In truth, I was thinking about this man's self-evident strain in recent weeks and wondering if this had been the source of the worry for my aunt and uncle. Because this task must have been very difficult, otherwise my uncle would have done it.

I suppose they'd decided that my uncle had grown too old to be chasing about the countryside after reams of paper. The doubt lingered, though, that they might have delegated the responsibility to someone else. My aunt was utterly out of the running for obvious reasons, but still they might have thought of asking me to bear the burden instead.

The doubt was echoed in the next moment when, instead of smoothly passing onto an easier subject, the man opposite me added as if there was still more for me to understand, 'Your uncle will be as glad as I am that it's finished with. I've spent quite a few weeks now visiting another ailing business to pick through their stock, but the last lot subjected me to a bit of a run-around. It transpired that they were holding out for a ransom we couldn't pay. Luckily, Nuneham's were prepared to be more reasonable.'

I saw him set his bowl to one side. I felt like I was staring. I probably was. He loosely clasped his hands together on the tabletop and seemed to be waiting for me to ask something.

Only then he told me briskly instead, 'Anyway, even today things didn't go entirely smoothly. Mr Lock and I had a run-in with the bullyboys from one of the Oxford printworks. They were there on a similar mission and I'm afraid they saw the place as their territory.'

'There was a bit of a squaring off?'

'Yes, and an awful lot to do afterwards. And I'm not, I afraid, a man with the patience for a rough scene.'

He wasn't speaking about the questionable legality of buying up redundant stock any more. It sounded like he was describing a blaze of temper; a raising of fists. Some men, I knew, wore their easy fury like a badge of honour, polished up and presented every once in a while to impress.

Suddenly, I was sitting back in my seat and turning my head aside. 'You had to make a stand? How unfortunate.'

I returned my attention to him. It was a false sympathy. I had to wonder now how much Uncle George's concern had been because he had been helpless to say that the paper wasn't needed if it meant tiptoeing around a man's rare but harsh tendency for anger. Perhaps this was why Robert had told me about it now. Perhaps he was one of the men Doctor Bates had described, who had been welcomed home from the war only to prove that they were wracked with rage for all the terrible things they had seen.

Only Robert didn't quite conform to that bleak view. He allowed the waitress to exchange his bowl for his dinner dish and then corrected my mistake with such wry amusement that it was like meeting the man anew.

I watched his mouth as he told me, 'I didn't hit anyone. Heavens, I'm not trying to confess a guilty secret like that. I'm answering your question about whether it was difficult. It was. I'm not fit to cope with the strain of putting my head down and getting on with the real work after a sudden confrontation. Scenes like today shake me. I'm sorry.'

He said it like he knew I must think him weak.

My brows furrowed. I asked quickly, 'You're feeling shaken? You're injured?'

He wasn't moving like he was injured.

I added, 'Perhaps you have a cold on its way. Amy was worried she'd given you the one she had, and Doctor Bates said that sometimes a temperature can muddle things a bit in your mind – in anybody's mind, I mean.'

I bit my lip to suppress the guilty memory of that rotten spell of gossiping in the shop. I certainly deserved the slight sharpness of Robert's reply.

He retorted shortly, 'Doctor Bates again?'

There was something in the way he said the name that struck me. I heard myself saying, 'He isn't your doctor, is he? You barely know him at all.'

Robert contradicted me quite gently. 'Actually, I know the man well enough to be aware that he graduated from the same medical college that taught me, and that he uses it as the excuse to take a slightly tactless interest in the whys and wherefores behind my move away from medicine into publishing – which was why I interrogated you quite so unnecessarily about Miss Prichard's motive for paying you a visit, I'm sorry. I wondered if I needed to worry that he was prying.'

Then he set down his knife to say bluntly, 'But whatever the man's been telling you, he certainly needn't trouble himself with my health. I don't think I'm coming down with anything.'

There was a pause that was accompanied by another turn of his head; as if he knew he hadn't yet quite reached the truth. Then in the next breath he was telling me, 'Today's encounter with the men from the Oxford printworks was really just a few tough words while they tested to see what they could get away with. But I've had enough of mediating between men with an overblown idea of their rights. I learned that during the years I spent being pushed to the fore as a doctor in a camp of POWs.'

This, suddenly, was something I never would have expected him to tell me.

I said carefully, 'You enlisted as a medic, I know.'

He gave a small nod. 'I did.'

Then he added, 'There wasn't, however, a qualified doctor amongst us, so I was roughly promoted to the rank of resident medical officer. It was my job to warily negotiate better care from the guards, always with one eye on their faces in case that slight look of irritation meant I was letting us in for another run of punishment, consisting of sheer mind-numbing boredom and insanely reduced rations.'

I watched as his mouth formed a rueful curve. 'Needless to say, it was always a weak negotiating platform when I was a prisoner too. And, as it was, half the time I wasn't patching up sores and injuries anyway. I was stepping blind into the sort of incidents where tempers might flare up from nothing in a moment and a man could get himself shot in a nasty little altercation with a guard. That particular time, the man on the ground was a friend and I was crouching over him with every word working to fend off that decisive second bullet.'

There was a momentary hesitation before he said simply, 'The guards remembered to be humane, for what it's worth.'

And then, having confessed something vivid like that, he added on a far more ordinary note, 'These days, I consider myself to be significantly more at liberty to speak my mind. And I expect I bear up to the work that follows well enough. But afterwards, as has happened today after the little spat over the paper, I suppose I start to feel the need to remind myself that I'm not confined any more. And, to be quite frank,' the familiar urge to go away on an extremely long journey has only really gone since talking to you.'

For a moment, a very odd feeling rang in the wake of that.

I sat frozen, staring again with my mouth numbed to stillness. Because he was sitting very still himself and it was shocking to finally comprehend the mixture of pressures that were working upon this man. I couldn't imagine how it must have felt to be made responsible for his fellows, all the while knowing the inevitability of failure because his half-trained skills could only go so far, and he was just another prisoner anyway.

I wondered how long this man had taken to regain some idea of what freedom meant upon his return home after the war. And how much he thought he had found it in his work for my uncle's business. I wondered if Amy really was wrong to say that he might be about to leave us, because I suspected that above all things, he was trying to prove to himself that the only responsibilities he had to bear these days were small and within his reach.

I didn't dare to ask him whether the trouble he had met at Nuneham's fell safely within that plan. But still I ought to have spoken. I ought to have found some reply.

In the next blink, the certainty that had fixed his attention so firmly upon me was fading and that old urge to retreat was back in evidence again and I didn't like it. I didn't like it at all.

I had to lean in and find my voice after all to say quietly, 'I'm sorry. I didn't mean to push excuses and explanations upon you as though it were necessary for there to be some temporary influence upon how you've been feeling.'

'No. Of course not.' Then, quite as if it didn't matter that the odd business of the paper had forced him to tell me something utterly private, he united his fork with the knife upon the plate, set the lot aside and asked lightly, 'So what did Doctor Bates really say about me today?'

That trace of shame had gone in him. In fact, my expression made him smile.

'All right,' I conceded while the waitress sidled across with the bill. We slid out of our seats and began shrugging our way into our dampened coats.

I saw my companion sigh at the state of his hat and then I told him, 'Doctor Bates was asking about the fee we would charge to publish Miss Prichard's manuscript.'

'Oh?'

'Yes,' I said, buttoning up my coat. 'He wanted to know what proportion of her payment would go towards my salary. So I gave the doctor a long and entirely uninformative lecture on how fabulously knowledgeable Miss Prichard is. Her old doctor was her peer, not her patron, and I have every faith that her name deserves to become equally established as a figure of respect. And in a way, it means that I'm with Doctor Bates on the question of whether we're a good enough publisher for her. Only, she's so utterly unassuming that I don't quite believe any of the academic publishers would take her seriously. I think she's wonderfully steadfast in her own quiet way.'

And then my flush cooled abruptly because it was at that moment that I remembered the brief encouragement this man had given me when he had passed me the pages and asked me to read them. He had said she was a woman after my own heart.

'Mr Underhill,' I began as a kind of caution. I was conscious now of the other compliment I had received today on the subject of Miss Prichard's work – the one from Doctor Bates. It felt truly offensive to endlessly reduce that woman's endeavours to the level of a fresh form of flattery for me. Particularly when I wasn't in her league in the first place, because I wasn't even quiet.

Robert ignored me anyway. He was dragging open the door to the dark outside. At least the rain had stopped.

Then he remarked gently, 'That was a long lecture you delivered to me just now as well, wasn't it? Presumably because you're trying to hide what he said to you. Only it's too late because you know I can guess what's troubling him. The world of medicine is a small one, and I think it's fair to imagine that he's been able to establish that our old university professor kept a space for me so that I could resume my studies when I came home.'

'You went back to your medical college? I didn't know that.'

'I did. But, as it turned out, I only picked up the old thread of my university life for about three months and then I abruptly left. All of which means that our good Doctor Bates has now got to face the fact that, for no sensible reason, I've pitched up here in a small and struggling publishing company, and I'm suddenly responsible for safeguarding his ageing landlady's dreams. In that light, I think he's right to be concerned. But not,' the man beside me added, 'to the point of harassing you about it too.'

It was said quite coolly. I wasn't entirely sure this wasn't my cue to level my own questions about his inexperience. In a way, it would have been a fair exchange since I could remember perfectly well how this man had recently challenged me about my own skills and ambitions within the scope of my uncle's business.

The bus drew in as we crossed the river and once we were settled in our seats, I remarked rather defensively, 'You know you're good at your job, Mr Underhill.'

My compliment amused him. At least I thought that was the feeling that briefly touched his mouth. He turned his attention to the route ahead where it gleamed in the narrow beam of the bus's headlights. I heard him retort mildly, 'I spent a little over five years in a prison camp, Lucy. My idea of my self-worth is a touch confused.'

We stepped down from the bus in Moreton in a jostling crowd of about twenty people. It was very black in the stiff breeze of the wide market place. The garage where Robert had hired the van was dark and shut up for the night, and the dim face on the clock tower – called the Curfew Tower – showed that it was seven o'clock.

'Lucy?' His voice recalled me as I began to move to cross the road.

I turned my head. 'Mr Underhill?'

He was intending to walk me to my door, it seemed. He joined me and told me, 'I didn't realise I needed to tell you that you can use my name too.'

He didn't mean it too but his utterly gentle concession sent a shiver of recollection through me that came from a very different place from our recent discussion of his past.

To avoid showing this man my sudden chill, I glanced quickly left and right for traffic while tightening my grip upon my coat for the sake of warmth, and said quickly, 'Oh? Well, do you prefer Rob or Robert? My aunt calls you Rob, I know.'

'Either. Whichever you like.'

A simple remark about making me free with his name shouldn't have unsettled me. But it was a nudge back into my memory of today, and it was in that same uneasy frame of mind that I found myself stilling on the approach to the shop door with my head bent while I rummaged in my handbag for my key.

The distant light from a solitary street lamp was casting long shadows. We might as well have stepped back a few years into the blackout.

And it was from that darkness that his voice came with a sudden touch of bemusement beside me. 'What is it? Are you waiting for something? Or are you listening and mapping the sounds of that house again, ready for the night ahead?'

It gave me a second lurch of the heart to realise he was remarking on the intimate bit of chatter he had overheard passing between me and my aunt. For my part, I was finding it even more unnerving to be meeting friendly sympathy in this man. It was as if he could see into my mind and read the echoes there. Then the illusion abruptly passed. This question about the root of my unease wasn't a lucky guess.

This was a product of my unhappy habit of ducking my head and forgetting to smile whenever I tried to hide.

I found my key. 'It's nothing. I'm not afraid up there, you know. I don't need you to fuss about that.'

'Of course you don't,' he agreed. 'And I am sorry, by the way, that I upset you yesterday with my overbearing comments about meeting Jacqueline. I thought I was only showing concern, where I believe your family in the main tends to presume you'll manage everything perfectly well on your own. But I can see that under the circumstances my interference wasn't quite as kind as all that.'

His sudden apology left behind an odd twist of something deep inside that moved halfway between the memory of our first misunderstanding over his view of my role in my uncle's office, and realising once again that all along he had wanted to give me this feeling of being cared for.

I found I had abruptly begun to say, 'I have to tell you something that will sound a little strange. But in a way it has come out of my visit today and you're just the unlucky person who has to bear the brunt of it. My husband was called Archie and I loved him very much.'

Robert became very still.

I found I was rushing into explaining myself. I added, 'I'm sorry. This is Jacqueline's fault. It's an extension of a guilty realisation that first dawned on me in the midst of talking to her today about her Ashbrooks.'

'Why? What did she say?' It took him a moment to find his voice.

'She flung me blind into acknowledging the enduring

legacy we can give to the dead simply by remembering them. And at that moment,' I admitted, 'it struck me that it has been a terribly long time since I have fallen out of the habit of calling my husband by his name.'

I was suddenly a step closer to the door of the shop. I turned my back to the mixture of glass and wood to tell him foolishly, 'So, I'm ashamed to say I've just corrected the error with you. And now every nerve is on edge because you're right; half my mind is indeed listening intently to the silence behind the gusts of wind. My grandmother has been desperate to call out to my husband through the medium of her séances, but I've never let her do it; and this is why. I suppose it has become a kind of superstition with me that I might undo my efforts to let Archie go if I give his name the real form of sound.'

But, needless to say, nothing was happening here with each new utterance of his name. A person's name was not a siren call. It was as Jacqueline used it – like a marker on a gravestone; a means of ensuring that the departed soul survived in memory.

Only, unlike her, I didn't feel compelled to say his name in full.

I was, in fact, achingly conscious of the mistake I was making in saying anything at all. I was suddenly terribly aware that the real living man before me must be thinking of the timing of this sudden impulse to speak of Archie after the liberty he had given me with his own name.

Robert must be suspecting that I was only speaking like this at all because I'd taken his small gesture as a clumsy bit of courtship to a woman whose marriage had been terminated, but my heart was not free.

The tug between the two rival waves of shame was excruciating. It was like standing alone in an abyss.

Then Robert's voice came very quietly out of the dark beside me. 'Your trip to that house has really spooked you, hasn't it?'

And his quick understanding dragged my gaze sharply to the shadow that was his face. He was noticing that absence of a smile again.

I found I had put up my hand to grip my collar once more. The clouds were really breaking to a clear night sky and my breath was misting in the crisp air as I told him matter-of-factly, 'There has been an awful lot of talk today about legacies and dead Ashbrooks, and Jacqueline is determined to keep those people alive in her book and in her mind. I suppose that somewhere in the midst of hearing her theory about the dead girl, I realised all of a sudden that I have a responsibility too.'

'Which is?'

'Of all people, as his widow – as *Archie's* widow – I have to be brave enough to speak of him, haven't I?'

Only I wasn't brave really. Not even now having done it and realising that in truth I had never been afraid that a séance would conjure an answer from the silence. I had been afraid to admit that I had always known it wouldn't.

For Archie was gone, and speaking his name meant acknowledging the wholesale absence of a reply in a moment that was passed in a blink of an eye.

'What dead girl?' was all Robert asked after a time. I suppose this was a peculiar conversation for him too.

'Harriet Clare. She isn't Jacqueline's child. About seventy years ago Harriet Clare was a ward of that house, but she died.'

'Good grief.'

'Indeed,' I agreed. Then I said quite calmly, 'But at least you can feel vindicated for cautioning me about going. Because actually, it wasn't remotely nice to discover that the jolly exchange I'd expected to have with a mother and daughter about their plan to release their book in time for Christmas was in fact only a confrontation with what amounted to a macabre list of dead people.'

'I'm so sorry.'

A single shake of my head set aside the apology. Then I added more decisively. 'Jacqueline meant well enough I think. And how could she have known that my mind's defences had already been weakened to her sense of drama by a difficult night's sleep? Her story about a young orphan girl felt, I don't know, personal I suppose. Particularly coming as it did at this time of year when the long nights are full of family and memories and old traditions in the run up to Christmas.'

This was the moment I stopped pretending that this man was acting as the divide between me and my family.

I admitted that this wasn't just about Jacqueline's story, or even the memory of Archie. It was about me. I drew a steadying breath and told him, 'I don't know fully how to describe what happened today. It was as if the silence of that dead house was scratching holes in the stiff veil between me and

103

the departed, or was making it move a little closer, or something. I already feel sometimes as though I'm living on the periphery of life, as if the war has cut me off from the people I care about. For a while, it was stronger today. It felt as though I might find myself straining to listen to the wrong voices if someone didn't step up quickly and make an awfully big noise. Just as you did appearing out of the rain by that bus stop. And as my aunt and uncle do at regular intervals, thank heavens. Did my aunt tell you that my mother and grandmother and all the rest of that side of the family are spiritualists?'

If he noticed this change of tack, he didn't interrupt it. He inclined his head in acknowledgement. 'I gathered as much when you mentioned séances just now. And Mrs Kathay said something about it. Mainly that your grandmother threatens her with a tarot reading every once in a while – and, before you ask, those were your aunt's exact words. Are you trying to tell me that you're a little bit fey yourself?'

The question was posed lightly and it made me smile unexpectedly. 'Doesn't everybody believe that they have secret talents that they haven't yet had a chance to discover?' Then I added on a more serious note, 'I can read tea leaves.'

I caught a hint of answering warmth in the dark. I felt bolder all of a sudden. I had been angry with this man all day for pushing me into thinking about things I had long since decided were best left well alone. And here I was discussing them for what felt like the first time in years. And now he was asking in that reliably businesslike tone of his, 'When you go back tomorrow, do you want me to come along with you?'

I tilted my head at him. 'Why?' I asked. 'Are you afraid I'll reveal some of this nonsense to Jacqueline and make her threaten us with the name of a rival book press too?'

'You know that I think you're good at your job.'

His quick retort was a surprise. I had no idea this man was capable of easy charm. He made me laugh.

'Actually,' I couldn't help remarking, 'I haven't the faintest idea what you think of me. You never tell me anything unless I ask you a direct question. And I certainly wouldn't ask you that, because the answer might explain why you always retreat into your office.'

I shouldn't have said that. It was what I always did to him – I relaxed and then I startled him by being too honest. For a moment he looked completely taken aback.

He repeated blankly, 'I retreat into my office?'

He really had no idea that he ran away from me. I decided there and then not to repeat the point. Only he must have at least known that he wasn't following the usual pattern of swiftly turning this conversation to something less personal, because I heard him say a shade wryly, 'Well, since I'm here, I might as well tell you that I don't believe your aunt and uncle described you terribly accurately.'

I saw him note the way my eyebrows rose. Then he said, 'They led me to expect a sad and feeble young woman on the retreat. But you? You're formidable. In fact, I find it insane to hear you say that you need other people to show you how to cling to life. Because you didn't bolt for home when things got a little frayed about the edges in Bristol as you said, did you? If you'd done that, you'd have come home months ago when you were first released from your war service. That happened in the spring, I know.'

He left a probing silence as a question. I had always thought that his type of steadiness concealed a deeply thinking mind. I never expected him to turn that mind towards me quite so decisively as this.

I filled the pause unwillingly. 'I came back because I thought my aunt needed a helping hand.'

'And instead you found her managing perfectly well despite the rheumatism, and a lodger already installed in your old family home. I'm sorry.'

It was said dryly, without meaning to offend, but perhaps it betrayed again just a shade of that raw measure he seemed to place on his own self-worth. Then, while I digested that, he added on a note that was so ordinary and practical that it almost came close to relief, 'What time is the bus tomorrow?'

'Twenty-five minutes past seven,' I told him, without being entirely sure what I was admitting.

He watched me unlock the shop door. My hand found the light switch on the wall. In the sudden blaze of yellow, I heard him mention my name again and turned to see him squinting on the threshold.

In that same warmer voice that was like his own, and yet new to me, he asked, 'Lucy? What would you do if your uncle's business folded as Nuneham's did? Do you have reserves?'

It was asked so naturally, it felt as if he were merely extending the question about the time for tomorrow's bus. And yet I was suddenly acutely aware of the two yards or more of wintry air that lay between us now because he hadn't followed me inside. He quite patently did not consider the office his territory by night.

I lingered between shelves of books and told him, 'My parents-in-law are still living, so all Archie and I had was what we could earn. And he left me a signet ring, but I put that into trust for his nephew. It seemed the right thing.' I don't know why I told him that. I ought to have just said I was poor.

'And?'

This truly was turning into a very odd farewell. My reply was instinctive because I had already thought about the future. It was just very unusual to be giving it the solid form of a declared ambition.

I told him, 'If Kershaw and Kathay folded, I'd begin my own book press by buying a few favours with the little I have. Then I'd absolutely beg Miss Prichard to let me publish her.'

I didn't expect my answer to make him laugh, but it did.

All the same, it wasn't ridicule that came and went in the night. 'Fair enough,' he said. 'Well, if you do, will you do me a favour?'

'Which is ...?'

I had a sense that this conversation wasn't quite going as he had meant it to. I saw him frame his words carefully in the form of one last remark before he left me.

He asked with such humility that it rocked me, 'Would you take me with you?'

He meant as a fellow editor. He meant as my assistant. Now it was my turn to laugh.

I didn't reply but it was very certain that the slow manner of my shutting of the door was an answer all the same. There was the warmth of companionableness in the act and the prospect of further talk tomorrow, instead of exclusion.

Chapter 8

If my urge to tell Robert Underhill my husband's name had
grown from a heartfelt wish to break away at last from my
terror of the séance and the proof it carried of my absolute
loneliness, imagine my pulse when I woke sometime after two
o'clock to feel Archie's presence in my room.

The dream had been a pursuit of those ridiculous heating
pipes in the Ashbrook coach house. They mattered because
hot water and steam were Archie's field of expertise. He had
been training for a career as a railway engineer – of the scientific sort who moulded their talents at university. He had
graduated and been immediately snapped up by the Royal
Navy for rigorous instruction in Bristol. We'd met at a dance
there two wild weeks later – and the whole rush had suited
him because he had been one of those nice capable men for
whom amiableness was a marker of his wonderfully energetic
grip on life.

By contrast, when I woke these five years later, I was flustered and my attic room was an unmoving box filled with
cold air.

The light switch on the wall above my mattress was found

with a fumbling hand and went on with a brief blue shock of an electrical spark. The chairs, the bookcase and the door were all as they had been, standing upright or shut depending on the need. The small fire in the hearth was out but still giving off that pungent smell of coal. The only real difference was that my small, brown handbag had fallen from the table to the floor.

I slid out of bed in the glaring light of the rose at the centre of the ceiling. The leather bag seemed an alien object, somehow. The contents were in danger of tumbling out because the flap had been left open and now it had landed face-down.

I righted the handbag and returned it to its place on the tabletop. Then I heard the board pop on the stairs.

It wasn't the step that tended to groan in the night. The sound was the crack of old wood finding release after bearing weight.

By rights, I ought to have barricaded myself in and stayed put to talk sense into myself until morning. I'd had dreams like this before, of course, where ghosts and memories muddled my reason.

As it was, I was already dragging open the door in my nightgown – a stiff floor length affair because it was winter and the world beyond the heavy blankets of my bed was utterly freezing. I passed in one barefooted stride across the silent space of the landing.

Closed doors stood inoffensively to my left and to my back. They barred the kitchen and the storeroom. The staircase below was a steep narrow descent into utter blackness.

I arrived at the bottom in a blind slither and dragged heavily upon the grip I threw out to the banister rail. My shoulder met the door that rested upon the bottom step. It swung. I was out into the space beside the box of the main stairs. I could hear my footfalls and the rustle of my nightdress. There was light here because a distant streetlamp was able to penetrate the dark through the open door of my uncle's office. My desk showed ghost-like in the far corner. A second glow from that streetlamp spread from Robert's office. His door was open too, only that was wrong because all these doors were usually shut.

A short rush across bare floorboards towards that vacant doorway was all I managed. My pulse was rapid, but not pounding enough to smother the sudden whisper of movement behind.

I span. My heart lurched. The door to the main stairs was open. It was swinging shut. I lunged and got my right hand onto the door's rim just as it neared the end of its final arc. There was a gap still between the door and the frame. There was glass in the door itself. But no face shone white out there beyond, and that was worse. There was nobody there at all. Not even the ghostly form of a departing figure.

And in that single wild moment of seeing that no one was leaving, I felt the cringing sensation at the back of my skull as my senses began to wonder if the door had been opened to let someone in. I forgot that I was still gripping the rim of the door. And then I remembered. Because the door slammed like it had been caught in a sudden gust of wind and it carried my hand with it to meet the frame.

I remember even now the sound I made.

It was a product of that awful cringing anticipation of knowing that my hand was trapped and imagining what I would see when the door eased a little. And what it would mean for my hand if it didn't ease at all.

Then the prison of that wooden trap opened for long enough that instinct was able to snatch my hand away.

There was a line across the bones. I was clutching at the limb and barely even clear when the suck of cold air jerked a second time and slammed the door onto its catch.

I tottered. I remember finding enough room within the fierce inrush of pain to know that if a person were truly here, he cannot have been deaf to the sound he'd dragged from me. But the door closed and stayed closed.

And I reeled and shook my hand as if to drive the pain away and gibbered because it just wouldn't stop. It wasn't broken because the fingers still worked, and yet the pain wouldn't stop. And then I was suddenly intensely afraid of more pain, or to be accurate, the first real violence, because there was no thought in my head of ghosts now, but still nothing was moving out there. No telltale shadow was fading away behind the glass into the dark below. No foot-steps were beating a reassuring retreat. I couldn't even be sure that the glass window wasn't about to darken with his shape before the door opened once more to let this madness back in.

I called it 'him' because it was the only way I could frame the strength of this night. In the seconds that followed I was kicking the guest chair across the floor to jam under the door handle. And cringing even as I dropped into the seat to add my weight to the barrier, and sobbing a little now as I nursed my injured hand.

It was a while before I felt the decidedly unpleasant draught of cold air that wafted through the gap under the door. And it was later still that I discovered that the breeze had come from the opening of the shop door. The force that had dragged upon my hand really was made of flesh and blood, and his exit had been secret to the last. I didn't, needless to say, have the presence of mind to run to the window to spy upon his departing form.

I only had the mind to give up the chase, to stay bound to that securing chair where the telephone was within my sight and to twist back against the office door with my leg braced; while my skin crawled from the bitter cold of the painted wood through my nightdress until the shock eased.

It was in the last few hours before dawn that I stopped cradling that injured limb and went upstairs and dressed.

I had to do it gingerly with my left hand only. The waistband of my skirt was hard to fasten like that. Then I bound up the increasingly swollen right hand with a bandage. It wasn't broken. I was certain it wasn't broken, but it still benefitted from the relief of being bound. I think it was terrified of being touched.

I hadn't even probed the bruise. The skin was too frightened to bear the idea of any more contact after the brutal line of that doorframe. And I was treating it as if it had an opinion of its own because, to be honest, it did. The bandage gave it comfort and a shield to hide behind, and then I could function again as me.

When six o'clock came and the first car drifted past in a wash of headlights, I slipped downstairs into the shop. It was still and calm and the only thing out of place was my set of keys lying on the mat before the door. The door was locked as though it had never been opened. There was a letterbox in the door to explain the arrangement, and there was no ambush waiting within the utterly black ranks of bookshelves. He hadn't laid a lure for me. He truly had gone.

I returned the keys to their home in my handbag. It was quite something to realise that my ghoul must have claimed them from my room while I slept. It meant he must have been here before I had locked him in with me last night. He must have been trapped inside even before I'd had that complicated conversation about names and farewells outside the darkened office with Robert.

He had been near me all the time that I had been shuffling about the rooms upstairs and listening to the news on the wireless. He had heard me go to bed and finally he had decided to find the means of making his exit.

I didn't know what he had been doing in Robert's office, because the papers on the desk were always disordered. But there was certainly a sign that he had let himself into the print room to examine our new store of paper.

I stood there staring at it, wondering just how much of a row Robert had truly had with those fellows from the Oxford printworks.

Chapter 9

Formidable. I believe the term had been meant as a compliment – a young woman who might be considered admirably capable, possessing an unexpected steadiness in her course. This morning, I bore the term in the manner of an intensely focussed wrath.

Half past seven came and went and I certainly didn't go to meet the bus. The hard reality of our night-time invasion, and the necessity of telling my uncle about it, rather put paid to any little outings of mine.

Or perhaps that was just my excuse for staying safely within the small territory of my desk.

A little over an hour later and my uncle drifted in. I was intercepted in my pursuit of him into his office by the boy from the print room. Mr Lock's young assistant Larry had been the lucky recipient of my uncle's unwanted sweet from the advent calendar, and now the boy thought he might try his luck with a drawer today.

There were two days to choose from, today's and yesterday's and, happily for him, one yielded a treat. The other he shyly returned to me. It was a brittle seed-head from some dead and dried summer weed, and not the treasure I had secreted there.

By the time I made it to the threshold of my uncle's office, I had lost him to the lure of the telephone. The Willerson archive was a problem that would never sleep, and today brought no respite for him. But at least he could privately console himself with the knowledge that he had the paper on which to print it now.

Robert didn't come in at all.

I went down to the shop, but found it empty of both visitors and Amy. I was a little early for my usual tea round so I suspect that I only went downstairs because I wanted to prove to myself that it was growing easier to face that gloomy space.

There was a distant murmur of voices from the passage beneath the stairs to the print room, but I didn't bother to join them. Then, as I turned to stamp my way back up to the sanctuary of my desk, a well-dressed customer broke my fragile bravery with a rattle of the door and an inrush of cold air.

I wasn't remotely ready to be faced with the sound of an opening door. He was broad and dressed in a smart raincoat. And that was the moment when I acknowledged that this whole morning was being occupied with the fear that at any minute someone would step in, and I would match them to some small detail from last night, and I'd be forced to identify the culprit.

But nothing but ordinary memory stirred in my mind. The incomer was Doctor Bates and he was politely removing his hat.

'Good morning Mrs P. How are you?'

I had turned on the second step. It took me a moment to speak my reply. Finally, I said, 'This isn't your usual hour for visiting us, Doctor? I thought you had your morning surgery around this time. So if you've come to share tea with Miss Briar, I have to tell you that I haven't had the chance to make it yet.'

Then I shook my head because I was being rude. But it didn't matter anyway because Doctor Bates was walking directly towards me and telling me clearly, 'I have a string of calls to pay this morning to various old people with the 'flu, so I thought I'd stop in while I was passing. I've only got a few minutes to spare, and as it is ...'

Notably, since he'd broken his commitment to his patients' confidentiality by giving me the details of what was wrong with them, Doctor Bates didn't breach the rest of the rule by adding their names.

Instead, I saw him remark severely as he reached the counter, 'As it is, I can tell that I ought to have visited you first. What on earth have you done to your hand?'

He made me stiffen. He was staring at the space near my right hip. My other hand was gripping the banister rail where it had remained while I had turned to greet him so that it still passed across my body, both as a security and a disguise. But the bandage was shining there in the gloom beside me. I hadn't concealed it as well as I had thought with the twist of my body. Now, quite unwillingly, I released the rail and was reminded very sharply of the injured limb.

The sudden ache was disorientating because this narrowing

of my thoughts onto that bright bandage actually proved to be the most unpleasant part of these past hours, even beyond the bruise. It wasn't natural to dwell in this hard land of distrust where my mind had clearly learned to anticipate fresh pain.

And then I realised that the doctor had stepped briskly around the edge of the counter – and I've never felt anything like it.

The doctor was reaching out a hand. 'Will you let me see?'

The bruise twinged sharply. It still loathed the idea of contact. I said hastily, 'It isn't broken.'

'That's for me to say. May I see?'

His stern reprimand scolded me into obedience. Numbly, I let him take my arm at the elbow to draw me off that last step into the space beside him behind the counter.

I felt the lightness of his touch as he tethered me there while he carefully set down his bag upon the glass. Absurdly, it occurred to me to realise that I had never made contact with this man before. Not even during our bus ride yesterday, where I had the vague idea he'd finished by asking me if I might like to meet him alone at some point.

Then he turned back to me and unravelled the bandage.

The last time I had seen the bruise, there had been a pronounced groove tracing the course of that wooden door jamb. Now a bulge was consuming the entire back of my hand with a small band of dull colour at the heart of it.

Doctor Bates didn't touch the bruise but he did probe all the bones in my fingers. His touch was steady but utterly light. I watched him as he discovered the score line across my palm. His eyelashes screened his thoughts from me. But his concentration as he did his work matched the fierce rhythm of my heartbeat.

He made my pulse jump when he declared crisply, 'It isn't broken.'

Then he let me retreat into the relief of binding it up again. And the release came like a flood – uncomfortably.

I had never meant to show anyone this small part of last night, not even my uncle. I knew that whatever I told my uncle would have to be told to Robert as well. And speaking about this meant admitting to him – to all of us – precisely what we had been brought to by that business with the paper.

And now the doctor was asking me calmly, 'Will it worry you if I ask how this happened?'

His grey eyes were being lit by the slanting electric glow cast by the nearest wall lamp, and his backdrop was the unrelenting dark of the old stained wooden bookcases receding in ranks through the shop.

I wasn't expecting to hear myself say in reply, 'I don't mind the question at all. Because Robert has a key.'

I meant that Robert would have had no need to go skulking about my room in the dead of night for the purpose of stealing mine.

And suddenly, I was free. I'd had no idea that the use of my key had formed the heart of one of the more obscure terrors that had haunted me since the early hours. Now I was able admit that my distress ran far beyond the idea that at some point someone would step in and I would recognise them as the person who had crouched behind that closing door. I was terribly afraid that I would be forced to learn that the person who had dragged that awful cry from me was someone who knew me – and still they had left me there.

But no one could tell me now that it had been Robert. And in the next moment Doctor Bates was dragging my attention back to his face. He was looking severe. Beneath his well-bred uniform of the town doctor, there was utter bewilderment.

'I'm sorry,' I said with the slightly giddy exhilaration of relief, 'I suppose you have no idea what I'm talking about.'

Then he swept aside my clumsy apology by repeating the name, '*Robert*?'

Incredibly, there was a breath of a threat in his tone.

He remarked, 'You've progressed very quickly since yesterday from formal titles into the familiarity of first names with your uncle's newest editor.'

'I—' I began uselessly. I drew back. I hadn't braced to find more reasons to worry, but the feeling was here all the same.

I'd have called his reaction jealousy, except that the last time the doctor had used that tone to speak Robert's name – as we'd shared that morning bus ride – he'd been weaving in strong hints about his landlady's offer from a rival publisher.

So it was with a very uncomfortable degree of courage that I stemmed my urge to feel flustered and innocent, and instead asked him, 'What precisely do you know about Mr Underhill and Nuneham's?'

Now I was remembering that the secret of the paper was dangerous.

Not to put too fine a point on it, there were elements of its purchase which might be classed as criminal.

Doctor Bates was looking like a man who was wishing he had merely tutted over my hand before hurrying away to resume his round of morning visits. He had noted my retreat from using Robert's first name, though.

'Mr Underhill,' he said, 'took a hired van from the garage by the Curfew Tower yesterday, and later it came back from Abingdon fully laden.'

He knew all about the paper.

Carefully, as if measuring every word, Doctor Bates told me, 'I was at the garage a few days ago getting them to put fuel in my car ready for the week's rounds when Robert Underhill stepped in to speak to the owner. He mentioned Abingdon and the need to take a van for a trip to a fellow book press. A few telephone calls later and I had the name Nuneham's and the details of their fate.'

I saw him bite his lip. Then he added, 'You should know that I meant to catch him in the act of leaving yesterday morning. I might even have planned to follow him in my car. I didn't fully know what he was up to just then. But then I saw you step out of the shop and then you boarded the bus to Stow.'

My throat was dry. It took a moment for me to be able to say, 'You followed me instead. Why?'

The doctor's expression suddenly crumpled to a grimace. 'Because I acted on an impulse. I thought you might be able to give me some information that would help. But it was a mistake and by the time I'd made my way back to town,

Underhill had long gone. In fact, it's Rob by name and rob by nature, wouldn't you say?'

'I beg your pardon?'

'I'll say it plainly, Mrs P. I think you must have been Underhill's decoy.'

Suddenly I was flushing. 'His *decoy?* I most definitely was not.'

Doctor Bates' chin lifted. Condescendingly. 'I'm sorry, Mrs P, but you were. My blame is entirely reserved for Mr Underhill because I think he's been manipulating you. I think it safe to say that once I got chatting to you on the bus yesterday, I realised quite quickly that there was absolutely no point in asking you about his business. Because at the time, the name Nuneham's meant even less to you than it did to me, didn't it?'

I couldn't refute that, because it was true.

Then the doctor's expression was shifting into something oddly like sympathy and he was asking, 'When *did* you learn about his trip to Nuneham's?'

'Yesterday afternoon, but—'

'So how did he manage to get you onto that bus?'

I was vigorous shaking my head. 'I wasn't manipulated into doing anything, Doctor Bates. I was paying a perfectly innocent visit to one of our authors.'

'But who asked you to go?'

I didn't reply. But my sudden loss of speech wasn't solely due to the pressure of knowing full well how this man would react if he learned that the giraffe book had come to me from Robert.

Instead, I was turning over a different part of what Doctor Bates had said about the van's return trip from Abingdon. I was trying to calculate precisely how it should have befallen that Robert had decided to wait in Bourton to intercept me on my way home.

Because the route back from Nuneham's to Moreton didn't pass through Bourton. And yet Robert had passed it off as a mild happenchance that Mr Lock had set him down there for the purpose of waiting for me in the rain.

The doctor didn't leave me any room in which to unpick this thought. With such swiftness that it hurt my mind, he dragged my attention back to his own concerns.

He confided, 'I've been studying that man's steps for weeks. You know I have. I'd imagined I was establishing just precisely what sort of place he'd taken in this business, because I'm decent enough to recognise that the man's education and opportunities in life ought to have set him above his quiet style of work here. Don't *you* find it odd?'

I didn't particularly care to answer that. I found that I had stepped backwards to reclaim the first step on the foot of the stairs. It wasn't nervousness that drove me to retreat there this time. In a way, I ought to have thanked the doctor for curing me of my terror of this dark staircase. I really was ready to face Robert now. In fact, there were many things which would have to be said upstairs, only I wouldn't get the chance – because Robert was not there.

The doctor clearly wasn't going to let me go anyway. He swept on with increasing energy to say, 'I thought at first that

Underhill's little trips away were a sign that he was trying to patch things up with his old college in the hope of finishing his studies. I thought I might need to warn you that your uncle was about to be left high and dry. However, a quick telephone call to my old lecturer was enough to shine quite a different light on that theory.'

I was supposed to be troubled by this. But instead I supplied with all the coolness of my new mood, 'And during that telephone call, Doctor Bates, was your old tutor able to tell you that Robert passed up the chance of finishing his training, and left his college for the second time only a few months before he came to us?'

I saw the doctor frown. 'You know that?'

'I do,' I confirmed.

'But aren't you curious about *how* he left? Because the details I gleaned put me onto the idea of truly worrying about the man's fitness to be in a position of trust here. And then to crown it all, I was on hand when Underhill abruptly needed to hire that van.'

He was studying me beneath lowered brows. I think he must have noticed the hardening of my resolve, and the endless drift of my attention to the office upstairs. And then he observed, 'Do you know that I saw you yesterday evening when you and Underhill arrived back at the door of this building together?'

Suddenly, I had focused solely upon his face. So much so that I think the abrupt turn of my attention startled him. I saw him blink and then I said quite sharply, 'Is that a return to that slur of being a decoy?'

'Of course it isn't,' he assured me hastily. 'I don't fully know what I meant. I suppose I was simply observing that you seemed to give the man a cool farewell.'

Doctor Bates was running a hand through thick hair. He gave me a nervous little flicker of a smile as he lingered there by the counter.

And all of a sudden, I had the strange experience of suspecting that the doctor was in fact reviving the nature of his own parting from the morning bus, where he'd hinted at a certain kind of interest.

My doubt gave me that unfamiliar feeling again; that sudden consciousness of every inch of my presence here. This time it was his own glance that made me very aware of the style of my clothes, my defiance and the unintended elegance of my reach towards the banister with my left hand. I thought he was seeing something vividly alive in me, and setting me against the sweep of that dim and colourless staircase.

In a way it was profoundly empowering. I suppose anyone who generally dwells in that bruising no-man's land after a sad end to a relationship ought to have at least one brief moment of being reminded of her strength.

On the other hand, I was hardly standing like this for the sake of feeling attractive. And when he spoke, it turned out that he had only meant that he was aware of the repeated drift of my gaze to the stairs behind me, and it was allowing him to believe that we were both united in distrusting Robert.

'What really irritates me about Underhill,' he was saying, 'is that this sort of thing runs precisely along the lines of what

Amy – Miss Briar, I mean – was probing when she was worrying about the man's unnatural lack of interest in pursuing excitement now that he's free after his incarceration.' He added with intense distaste, '*This* is where Underhill's been hiding it.'

The doctor was a very different stamp of man when his mind showed its energy like this.

'Please, Doctor. I don't know that he enjoyed his trip to Nuneham's, or any of the publishers.'

The doctor didn't hear my protest. He was already saying, 'You do see, don't you, that the contradiction between how the man speaks and how he acts is the clue?'

'No, I don't.'

He swept on, 'Underhill gives the impression of being quiet and unassuming but he must possess some metal to have worked his way into the heart of your uncle's business. And my old lecturer explained how he and that band of fellow student doctors went off to war. Underhill led the way, and they all trotted after. So let's not pretend here and now that he doesn't know perfectly well how to lead people into all sorts of peculiar places.'

I must have abandoned any thought of upstairs. I was conscious of my position on the step in a very different way and I felt every whisper of movement as I stepped cautiously down to the ground again. 'What are you talking about?'

His eyes had dropped to my new level. He said, 'I'm suggesting to you that someone is steering this business of tearing about the countryside after failing publishing firms, and to me it just doesn't quite bear the hallmarks of your uncle's usual indecisive style.'

I stared. The doctor meant this to be a stark warning, only I didn't quite know where he thought the danger lay.

After a moment, I observed carefully, 'You seem very angry about this, Doctor.'

I must have released the feeling in him. Doctor Bates was suddenly telling me quite tersely, 'In my opinion, Mr Underhill is a man who has developed a very unreliable idea of how to undertake normal business. He learned through years of striking horrific bargains with the prison guards over a few prohibited medicines for the suffering inmates, and all without, I might add, having any of the necessary qualifications.'

We were both standing in this little pool of light cast from the nearest wall lamp, and it was having a similar effect on him as it had on me. It was emphasising his features so that he was almost too vivid against the plain backdrop of the shop as he continued, 'Underhill is perfectly capable of striking underhand deals. But not so keen on facing the consequences that come afterwards, wouldn't you say?'

He asked, 'Have you noticed how Underhill tends to retreat just as soon as things get a little tense?'

He didn't even leave me the room to draw breath for an answer before he added, 'Apparently, he found the strain of going back to his medical college too much after the guilt of what happened to those boys who'd followed him to war.'

'Is that what your tutor said?'

'Near enough.' He swept on. 'Then Underhill came here instead, and now the pattern is repeating itself all over again with your aunt and uncle ... And with you – because you've only just found out what he's got your uncle involved in, haven't you, and now you and I have to decide whether to tell the necessary people before he runs away again.'

'You mean to report us?' I asked while my mind stumbled. 'Not you. Him.'

In a way, this bruise ran deeper than the nightmare of the trespass into a darkened office because this was being said in daytime and it was clear that every mention of Robert's name was personal.

I heard myself saying carefully, 'Just to be clear, Doctor, you do understand that you're talking about the acquisition of a little surplus paper for the sake of printing a few books, don't you? You aren't imagining that you've uncovered something truly horrific?'

Doctor Bates flinched. I suppose it was a little unexpected to hear me voice for the first time the truth of his discovery about that paper.

He tried to contain the feeling by telling me to be free with his name – Terry.

Then he must have grown calmer, because suddenly he was telling me on quite a plaintive note, 'Do you know that my study of that man only began as a small matter of curiosity?'

He reached out a hand to fiddle with the clasp to his medical bag. With his eyes on it, he told me, 'I like order. I like to make things better. That is my job after all – I'm good at it. Then I mentioned Underhill's name in passing to my old lecturer for the sake of understanding the path the man took between that place and here.'

'And got in return an awful lot of nonsense and gossip?' I supplied.

He nodded. 'Afterwards, the question of what the man was up to ran on into a bigger and bigger complication, until, somehow, I've finished by standing here, cursed with the job of acting as judge and justice.'

He stared bleakly at nothing while he drew an unsteady breath. Then he told me helplessly, 'It's got to the point that I'm actually growing a little afraid of my own power as a witness. I have no idea what I'll be made to do next.'

There was a sense that Robert was to blame for that too.

It hurt me when I had to say firmly, 'It *is* only one small van-load of paper. If you'd seen our stock room, you'd know it isn't exactly on the scale that people go to prison for.'

Doctor Bates jerked his head at that.

Then he set both his hands to the task of fastening his bag because the clasp was stiff. 'You're saying that Underhill was acting for your uncle's business?'

'I am.'

I watched him nod over his bag as he accepted my decision. I was confirming that I was part of my uncle's business too.

Then he asked almost idly, 'So what *would* happen if you were to be exposed?'

I told him quickly, 'If our purchase of the paper were to be exposed, I imagine the company would have its allowance of paper revoked and my uncle would have to pay a hefty fine.'

I caught his glance and shrugged. 'Ultimately,' I said, 'this is Uncle George's business, and my aunt's.'

'Your uncle's,' he repeated flatly.

I felt again his strange determination to force me to consider the possibility that Robert had been driving this rather than my uncle. And wondered how it was that neither of the editors had thought fit to let me know much about this, and yet here I was, fighting to negotiate a safe path for us all through this idiotic debate of right and wrong.

As it happened, there was only wrong here anyway, and it led me to tell the doctor, 'We bought enough paper for one job, perhaps the Willerson archive. I'm sure that's what my uncle had in mind when he decided to take the risk – and Robert really did say that he was acting for my uncle, I'm sure he did.'

The doctor's head lifted at that. He made me very conscious of every small movement as I added sympathetically, 'You see, we think the Willerson book is likely to sell, just so long as we can print a large enough number to meet the first rush of demand.'

I drew breath to add something else, something about the issues facing small publishing houses these days. Then I let it out again. Because it was only one short step from there into speaking about our other titles, and I wasn't about to start sliding in references to Miss Prichard's manuscript as if I intended to offer up his landlady's name as a bribe.

My uncle couldn't afford it and, besides, I wasn't yet that desperate.

That last realisation came harshly, in the midst of knowing that I'd never been so calculating in my life before. I knew the doctor was watching me when I finally asked, 'Well then, Doctor, what do you want to do?'

For a moment, Doctor Bates didn't have a reply. Other than to reaffirm that I ought to use his name.

I told him, 'You aren't at fault here, you know. You really aren't. And we needn't spend all morning debating the likely consequences for my uncle. You probably ought to be getting on with your morning round of visits to your patients as it is.'

I was cheating there. I kept reasserting that the danger here was to my uncle.

Then something about the doctor's expression jarred in my mind. It was the complacency of his nod after I'd referred to his list of morning visits.

He made me consider again the timing of his arrival here, and the way he had immediately noticed the bandage on my wrist, even when it had been concealed behind me.

I thought he was here because he had known before he had even stepped in this morning that he needed, for the sake of his peace of mind, to check the bones of my hand for a break.

He was here because I was one of his patients too.

So, with that in mind, it occurred to me that he'd been entirely honest when he'd said just now that he was afraid of what he might be led to do by his interest in Robert.

I had to wonder how he had felt last night, crouching silently in that space behind the doorframe in the dark of the stairwell, when he had eased the door by those few crucial inches to let my hand go.

Chapter 10

Doctor Bates wasn't aware of the shift in my concentration. He still believed we were speaking about Robert.

That confident mouth was answering my question by telling me rather doggedly, 'I don't want to *do* anything about this. I want Underhill himself to decide what's right. It's in his nature to move on after all.'

'He'll move on?' I repeated flatly.

The doctor didn't notice the way my posture changed. 'Of course. He left his former scene of disgrace just as soon as the shame grew too much. So I want him to give way to the same urge now. I imagine he'll realise what he's done, he'll quietly take himself off, and that'll be all the rest of us will need to think about it. He'll leave.'

The doctor's certainty flooded my skin. I wasn't sure I would have spoken if he hadn't jarred me into it.

I barely recognised my voice when I asked, 'How did you get yourself shut in last night at the office? Was it when Mr Lock left after they unloaded the hired van?'

I might have imagined I'd struck Doctor Bates in the throat from the sound he made.

I suppose that after everything, we were all finding our darker limits here. This counterattack was at last the proof of how fiercely my own mind could behave in the face of a perceived threat.

I felt its stain. As I say, I hadn't truly decided to confront this man at all.

Then the faint tremor beneath my skin stopped. His mouth was moving without forming sound. His shock grew from the sheer nakedness of perceiving that I knew.

When he still didn't speak, I remarked quietly, 'You must have had an uncomfortable few hours until two o'clock came and you felt brave enough to creep upstairs to take my key. I suppose this is why you've been so determined to teach me that Robert has a history of leading people astray. If he's a corrupting influence, it allows you to hate the man for bringing you to this.'

I stood there while the man who had trapped my hand in a door swallowed and worked to find his voice. He stammered, 'N—no. I didn't even mean to talk about Mr Underhill just now, until you shocked me into it by calling him Robert. I thought I might need to show you who he really was – and quickly, because we're alike, you and I, aren't we? We're both victims here.'

'*Victims?*'

'Of course. I've been led to this brutal place purely because I was curious about that man's criminal act, and now he's thrust you into the path of harm. I'm sorry.'

Now that Doctor Bates had found his voice, he couldn't be stopped. He rushed on to tell me plaintively, 'I saw the print room man come back with the van at five o'clock. I was watching for about an hour before they came.'

'They?' I prompted. 'And don't say Mr Underhill.'

'Mr Lock and the boy who helps him. I followed them in through the big carriage doors. Your uncle had already gone home so no one saw me slip from the workshop into the back door of this shop, or from here upstairs to your office.'

He hesitated before adding, 'I had to wait up there until they'd finished clearing the van.'

'Were you down in the print room when I came in?'

He winced. Shame made him add very reluctantly, 'I was having a second look for a spare key. I'd already exhausted your desk, so I was in Underhill's office when you climbed the stairs to your bed.'

It chilled me to realise he had been so close. The doctor was watching me carefully as he told me, 'That was how I knew you and Underhill had come home together on the same bus. I watched you from his window. I was afraid you'd noticed my mistake when I mentioned that.'

I hadn't noticed. It went some way to explaining the sweep of the man's emotions at the time, which, naively, I'd taken as a kind of compliment.

I saw his mouth dip when I didn't give a retort. He was more relaxed than he had been when he had to tell me, 'You locked the front door when you went up to bed so I took your key from your handbag – it was either that or wait until morning and politely tell you all about it by knocking on your door as you poured your morning cup of tea. I was only trying to do what was right.'

'I can see that.' It was said dryly.

Somehow he'd cured my temper. He had been, after all, a very accidental burglar. And he really had thought he might come here this morning, the well-intentioned gentleman, to assure himself that I was unharmed before slipping away with his integrity intact, to brood endlessly upon the criminality of my uncle's new editor.

I asked, 'Were you ever intending to publicly expose our new store of paper? Would you have reported Robert if I hadn't stumbled into discussing him with you this morning?'

'I don't know,' he admitted. 'Probably not.'

He drew a breath. 'I certainly didn't expect to end up feeling like the wretched villain of this piece. And,' he added, 'I didn't mean to hurt *you*.'

Doctor Bates was telling the full truth at last.

His mouth had formed a rueful line. And I could really see the real difficulty ahead for me and this man, because there was a trap here, and this one was a snare for my peace of mind.

It grew from knowing that everything hinged now upon how I proceeded from this moment. I was the real judge of these deeds. Now that the doctor had shed his disguise, no one else could decide how far his suspicions should justify the way he had first followed me to the bus, then spied on this place and finally stalked about my house after dark. And no one except me could decide how much responsibility Robert should bear for this, or even how much he should know.

If this was my chance to bury this, I should capitalise upon the doctor's guilt now.

I lifted my head and met his eye plainly. It was another of those moments when I was very conscious of every small movement of my body. I repeated frankly, 'What do you want to do?'

He was stunned into speechlessness.

I added, 'This isn't one of those moments of threat and counter threat, you know, it really isn't. I don't want Mr Underhill or my uncle to be dragged into a deeper mess, but I don't intend to bully you into silence either.'

I saw him wet his lips before he asked numbly, 'You're giving me the advantage?'

I gave a nod which eased to a slight smile as I turned my head aside. I told the gloomy space of the shop, 'Take this as one of those serious gestures which are not exactly considered good tactics, but are meant as a mark of truce.'

There was no scheme here, no ploy. I wasn't expecting the doctor to react to the undemanding nature of my offer in the way that he did.

I turned back to him in time to catch the faintest of twists upon that mouth, like the uncoiling of strong emotion. His gaze on me was suddenly wide and unwavering. He looked utterly thrown by the discovery that I would not blame him.

Then he took a small step towards me.

He told me hastily, 'I've never felt anything as confusing as this. We've both been thrust into something utterly revealing, haven't we? I know you feel it too, because you've been left as unbalanced as I have by everything you've had to face here. You never asked to be put in this position, any more than I did. And yet all the while you're standing there wearing that

137

same ethereal look you always have, and you're mesmerising.'

Unexpectedly, I saw bewilderment blaze upon his face.

I believe I may have recoiled slightly as he swept on, 'This is just like that moment when you travelled on the bus with me, when I think I might have asked you to dinner. I never seriously expected anything to come of it. But these past days have been a whirlwind with you as the only clear point. Finally, I think I understand why. You care for me, don't you? And what man would say no?'

I froze when I felt the brush of his fingers as they ran across my cheek and into my hair. He had stepped again and now he leaned in. He meant, impossibly, to find a kiss.

I will state here and now that I did not for a moment believe his reach for me was an insidious bribe. This wasn't the act of a sinister male taking his idea of redemption from a woman in the form of a certain fee.

This must have been as he had said – the instinctive conclusion to the intimacy that had already been forged between us by our proximity to someone else's mistake.

Only, even as I felt the whisper of his touch against my cheek, I was already pulling back. Because I hadn't meant this. I hadn't even foreseen it.

He must have misread my sympathy. He must have been swept into this, when I hadn't imagined that I might need to be more guarded. I was finding it disorientating enough these days to be suddenly reconsidering my idea of who I was as a woman after all the years of quietly thinking of little beyond my work. I hadn't realised that he had even noticed my newfound determination, or the self-consciousness which for me was coursing like a fever through this entire wretched morning.

Now the misunderstanding tugged drunkenly on almost every nerve. Because the doctor thought I had been battling for his sake. But he wasn't the man who had been foremost in my thoughts during that dead-of-night rousing, and I wasn't even sure my husband had been that man either.

A distant voice was heard in the passage beneath the stairs that led from the printworks. We were suddenly yards apart because Amy Briar was calling out her parting words to Mr Lock.

I couldn't face her as well. Not when Doctor Bates was her friend and, until this moment, Amy had always been the person he had visited here. I was the coward who slid away to my desk.

I was sitting there when Robert walked in at about eleven o'clock.

Chapter 11

On Robert's face, there was the sort of irritation a man wears when he feels he's spent hours chasing about after some vital piece of missing information, such as why I had left him to catch a bus this morning on his own. It was mingling with concern, and there was also a remnant of the steadiness of our farewell last night, where his remark about being my assistant had seemed to be a signpost for beginning to be my friend.

He said by way of a greeting, 'Did you oversleep? I've just been to Stow and back. I nearly pressed on without you, but then I remembered your uncle's workload, so it seemed sensible to turn back at the first available town. Inevitably, I managed to pick the time of day when there was a long wait between buses for the return trip.'

I watched him fold his damp coat over the back of my guest chair and set down his hat upon the top. It was a peculiarly vivid experience to see him so thoroughly at home in this space around my desk after what had just passed between me and the other man.

I wasn't sure I could even speak without betraying the new

secret of my parting from Doctor Bates. I didn't want this memory. It meant straying into that difficult place of imagining that for a moment I'd reciprocated in the surprise of that near-kiss.

I hadn't. I absolutely hadn't. But, all the while, I was sitting here in my chair while Robert waited for me to give some cheery excuse that made everything all right, and as I did so I knew that it had been for his sake that Doctor Bates had gone roaming about this office last night. And now the doctor had entangled himself even further with me this morning, and for some ridiculous reason the only detail I was certain about was that I was feeling personally responsible for the lot.

I managed to find my voice after all. 'I thought you would go to the meeting with Jacqueline on your own.'

'No.' Robert's hair was dark and ruffled where his hat had been. This was the moment when he noticed the bandage about my hand. The injured limb was resting in my lap with my chair drawn in close in an attempt to hide it. He was beginning to stare when my other hand lightly moved to drape itself artfully along the edge of the desk.

I seemed to release him to remember what he had been about to say. He said, 'It's your project now; you might as well finish it. What happened to your wrist?'

He knew I couldn't reasonably ignore a direct question. 'It's fine,' I told him quickly. 'Doctor Bates has already looked at it.'

I thought for a disconcerting moment I had slipped into using the doctor's first name, Terry. But I hadn't. I added, 'Anyway, it's my hand, not my wrist. I caught it between the door and the doorframe on the stairs last night. And it isn't broken. It's just bruised.'

Robert had already moved around the corner of my desk and now he was easing himself into a crouch in the space there.

I turned in my seat towards him. I believe I tried to say something crisp and orderly but he didn't even hesitate. He was saying, 'Will you show me that you can make a fist?'

The space behind my desk was very small when he crouched before me like this. His voice was different. It was suddenly more focussed, like a medical man getting to work.

I stirred uneasily. He was the second man to ignore my protest about my hand today. At the same time, his manner prompted me to remember everything I knew about his experiences at that awful camp. I didn't want this injury to be the one that made him revisit them. My fierce effort to avoid this latest pitfall came out as a defensive, 'Don't you ever listen to a single thing I say?'

Clearly, he didn't. First he got me to prove that I could still grip with the hand. Then he made me perform various movements with it. He didn't take hold of it even once, or attempt to unwind the bandage. It was a very different method from the examination Doctor Bates had given me. I wouldn't like to say which was the more medically correct, but this one preyed less upon the poor hand's aversion to being touched. It didn't make me feel as if he was affecting its increasing tendency to swell either.

And, very clearly, despite the running theory that life in a prison camp had given Robert a profound aversion to doctoring, he was able to use those skills readily enough now.

Now I was truly restless. The doctor's accusations were prying into every thought of mine – the hints about the path that had brought Robert here and the pressure that might drive him away. All that remained was to risk everything by explaining how much had been exposed.

I drew back as I told him, 'Doctor Bates knows all about your stock of paper.'

A wiser person might have finished the confession there, but an impatient urge to speak the angry truth rushed in with the ache of finding this man caring about that hated bandage like this.

I made his attention lift from my hand when I added, 'In fact, the doctor thinks you asked me to lead him aside as a distraction while you got away with the hired van. And that little insult has led me to realise something very strange about you.'

'It has?'

From his mild manner of asking, I might have believed he had nothing to hide at all.

'Yes,' I said firmly. 'When you questioned me over dinner yesterday about Doctor Bates' references to Nuneham's, you must have at least suspected that his hints meant he'd uncovered your plan. Only, instead of worrying about that, all you wanted to know was what else he might have told me. So then I began to wonder what other secrets you might be guarding. Doctor Bates is convinced that you're using my uncle to hide a habit of black market trading.'

'And is that what you think?'

'Not in the slightest,' I replied flatly. 'But it has finally occurred to me that yesterday, when you met me in Bourton, it wasn't a matter of convenience or kindness. You were tasked with keeping me away from the office.'

There was a pause while Robert adjusted to the agitation in my tone.

He had his right forearm laid along the rim of my desk by way of support while he crouched before me. He considered the drape of his hand over the edge for a moment, then he replied, 'I didn't keep you away from the office.'

'Yes, you did. You—'

'You caught the same bus home from Bourton that you had always intended to catch.' His insistence made my brows lower. He remarked, 'I even told you about the paper.'

'Yes,' I agreed. 'Yes, you did tell me about the paper. And once you had successfully coaxed me into making light of the shady deals you've been making in my uncle's name, you made an awful lot of references to the state of this company's finances. So what I want to know is whose idea was it to leave you in Bourton to meet me? And what have you really been up to, if telling me about the trip to Nuneham's was the easy part?'

I didn't say it out loud, but I very nearly added that I particularly wanted to know why it was acceptable that my uncle should be involved, Mr Lock and the print room boy, and even Doctor Bates. But not me.

The colour in my cheeks was the pain of exclusion again. Not of myself but of him. I had been struggling all morning on the cusp of some unpleasant conflict. I had battled my own fear, and I'd tiptoed around the effort of defending this man while the doctor weighed up the risks of doing his civic duty.

In the process, I had been left trying to answer the disturbing question of how on earth I had spent the past minutes feeling terribly responsible for misleading Doctor Bates, when I ought to have been asking how it had happened that a trained medical professional should have visited a woman for the purpose of inspecting the injury he had caused, only to find himself contemplating romance.

I was increasingly angry with the doctor. And frustrated with him for deciding I was keen.

Now I was disturbing myself all over again with the effort of trying to guess what Robert might be reading in my distress at this moment – because if nothing else, the misunderstanding with Doctor Bates had taught me that what I thought I was saying and how my actions were interpreted appeared to be two very different things.

The simple solution was to withdraw, to busy myself with my work, to pretend that I didn't care to hear anything this man had to say at all.

Robert's manner wasn't exactly warm any more, anyway. He was watching me from the nearness of that crouched position by my chair. His forearm was still claiming the support of the rim of my desk.

Then, while I reached for a sheet of paper to feed into the typewriter, there was the brief turn of his head away from me towards my uncle's closed door. The act was followed by the short nod of a decision being made.

It was the smallest acknowledgement of the hurt beneath my temper. Then he rose to his feet.

I watched in silence while he walked to my uncle's door. I heard the light rap and his muted request for permission to enter. My mouth went dry.

If this was capitulation, it left behind a very peculiar feeling.

Chapter 12

A minute later, the office door opened again. Robert was there. He tipped his head at the room behind him. 'Would you come in for a moment?'

I expected him to step out as I entered but he didn't. Or, at least, he did step out but only to claim the guest chair from my desk before bringing it in to set it beside the seat I was taking. I thought he intended to supervise this talk.

My uncle was watching across the wide spread of his desk while Robert shut the door and took his seat. The older man's chair was set before a window so that the natural light brightened the pages of notes in his hand. My uncle looked as he always did. Tall and willowy, but comfortable about the edges.

Beneath the familiar wooliness, though, there was that undertone of preoccupation that had concerned me before. Even now it didn't fully take any specific form. At once his expression matched the general worry of a kindly relative; in the next a remoteness that must have stemmed from being the man in charge.

Uncle George certainly sounded unnaturally crisp when he leaned in to lay his work down upon the crowded tabletop

149

and told me, 'Lucy, dear child, I hoped to keep you blissfully ignorant of this, but Rob disagrees. He's said it before, and now he's said it considerably more loudly that he never approved of this particular aspect of our plan. He's said that I'm acting as though wishing that all will be well is the same as it actually being so; and that it's irresponsibly naïve of me to go on burying my head in the sand about the wider consequences of misleading you.'

My uncle left a pause long enough to give this the weight of a direct quotation and to receive a grimace from his second-in-command. Then my uncle's attention returned to me. 'So here you are. We needed the paper because I've spent the reserves keeping the business afloat.'

'I don't understand.' I couldn't help the sideways glance to my neighbour, but he was no help.

My uncle was saying, 'My reserves are what your Aunt Mabel would call our pension. Only we haven't got much left after the expense of the war. You know how hard it has been for small book presses like ours to weather the years of shortages. It's what claimed Nuneham's, and all the rest.'

I don't know why but it startled me to hear my uncle mention the source of that paper so easily. I expected Robert to react too, but he simply sat in his chair with one leg crossed loosely over the other and his fingers laced around the knee. He looked, in fact, like a man who had been stepping in and out of meetings in this room for years, not the paltry eight or so months it had truly been.

Uncle George's own fingers were mindlessly tidying the papers on his desk. He stilled his hands and sat back to say grimly, 'About four years ago, while you were busily turning out notices from your office in Bristol, we began producing very short print runs and took to making up the shortfall in our income by spending our reserves. It was a common enough practice for those of us who were feeling the effects of the paper shortage. For your aunt and for me, it was the choice we had to make between closing down there and then – with the knowledge that we mightn't have enough money for our dotage – or pressing on in the hope that conditions would improve enough to remedy some of the disaster.'

I hadn't often seen my uncle look so grave. In a way, Robert had been perfectly accurate when he'd dubbed the older man naïve, because this kindly presence from my childhood had always existed within a wonderfully innocent world of books and writing. He was the man who had made up silly stories and left them on scraps of paper about the house to make a little girl laugh.

At this moment, however, I was feeling every one of my adult years, because my uncle's narrow face was drawn as he explained, 'The work *has* improved slowly. We've got new titles on our list; we've won the enormous challenge of publishing the Willerson archive. But the shortages of the war haven't eased to match. We lack resources. Mabel and I are close to sinking. And I don't mean we're just a touch poor. I mean if we don't fulfil these next few jobs, we'll have nothing left. We'll have to sell up. And we'll lose the bulk of the sale of these buildings to the cost of settling our breaches of contract.'

'You'll have nothing left?'

My uncle knew it was a query for specifics. He tipped his head uneasily. 'Mere pennies. Mr Lock and the print room boy will be out of work too. And Amy downstairs. All our responsibilities are hanging on by a thread. And it's a terrible secret because it won't matter how hard we work if even the smallest rumour gets out.'

He added, 'When that happens, we'll find our authors ringing to cancel our current projects quicker than we can answer the telephone. *That's* what really did for Nuneham's. The rumours. Which is why Rob here has been working to save us ever since he came. He's the only one who could act without drawing attention to himself. I could hardly go dashing about the country chasing contacts – I'd be bumping into friends and neighbours at every turn. So it fell to Rob. He's barely had a moment's rest.'

That last part was said more briskly with a sideways glance at his fellow editor. And it carried the warmth of affection.

Whereas I was thinking that his note of excuse carried that trace of innocence again. And this time, the naivety didn't quite ring true. Because Uncle George was always travelling to meetings if the query couldn't be answered over the telephone. He had met the Willerson family at least five times since my return home, and the contradiction was reinforced when I caught the faint stirring beside me as Robert changed position in his chair. Something had surprised him too in my uncle's speech. There was an alertness in the younger man like puzzlement, only suppressed to nothing very quickly because he knew I had noticed.

It was an odd time to remember the doctor's harsh suspicion

that Robert might have been more than my uncle's lackey. That Robert might, in fact, have been driving this.

I didn't believe for a moment in the doctor's darker insinuations. But I was absolutely certain that Robert had expected my uncle to give a different excuse for leaving the work to his second editor.

Focusing very hard upon my uncle's face, I asked, 'Who else knows about the situation here? Presumably, Mr Lock and his assistant do, if they were involved with the hired van. Does Amy know about the risk to her job?'

'No, of course not. She's too gentle for me to risk upsetting her for no good reason. I know she acts as if she's been managing our shop for years, but she spent her war wearing an air of frantic jolliness and daubing patches over holes in damaged training planes. She knows everyone – she even knew our man Gilbert Willerson before he died. If we worried her, she might let it out in conversation over her shop counter. The rest of us – myself, Rob and the men from the printworks – meet the public on very different terms.'

I wanted to bridle at that – it sounded like a criticism of Amy's ability to bear bad news; and, by omission, mine too.

But Robert's voice was making a quiet addition beside me. 'It's a basic fact that we needed the paper stock to print the books. We can produce all the Jacqueline Dunns and the Miss Prichards and so on within the scope of our usual allowance, but the Willerson project is likely to sell. If we're going to meet demand we've got to print a good volume of books from the first moment. If it really takes off, we'll need to licence the title to one of the big producers. But in order to achieve that, it's vital that we first get it out and earning recognition.'

'I know that.' I had, in fact, said as much to Doctor Bates.

Perhaps Robert had guessed, not unreasonably given the way my left hand had tightened its grip upon my chair, that I was noticing once again the division that seemed to be perpetually being raised between the men and the women.

Perhaps he meant to bridge the gap by bringing this back to plain facts.

I told him as an aside, 'You really needn't explain yet again why it was necessary to purchase that paper. To be frank, it has been discussed so much by now and by so many different people that I feel we've established that you and my uncle wanted to combat the paper shortage.'

'I wasn't trying to justify myself,' he replied quietly.

'So perhaps you're trying to distract me again?' Somehow, I was almost making light of it. 'Or are you directing my mind towards something I'm overlooking? You've led my thoughts before, after all, with that well placed query about my plans for the future. I suppose you couldn't say more that time, without breaking your oath of silence to my uncle.'

He acknowledged the remark with a faint tilt of his head. His manner suited mine. There was a precision beneath the steadiness, and in the process he reminded me that I still hadn't been given more than a partial answer to one of the many points I couldn't quite comprehend – the point where I specifically couldn't have been told.

'What are you two talking about?' My uncle's voice drifted across the desk. The older man was bewildered.

I turned my head. My voice was bolder than I meant it to be when I asked, 'Why didn't you get me to contact Nuneham's, or whichever of the other failing printworks you had Mr Underhill try first?'

'I offered to help. I didn't mind.' This was said more crisply, by Robert.

I thought he was reacting to my unplanned stumble into the formal use of his name.

Or perhaps he was trying to show that his disapproval of my uncle's decisions only went so far. That must have been my mistake based on my wish to assure myself that Robert was on my side. But I ought to have guessed that the younger man considered himself fully committed to his role. He had, after all, said as much while I'd been worrying about his tension during that companionable little meal between buses.

My manner was less reasonable than it had been when I told my uncle insistently, 'All the same, it wasn't right to let him take such a personal risk like this. When I might have done it.'

'Lucy, don't. Please.' The agonised correction from my uncle checked my heart. He said desperately, 'Please don't make your offer like that. Like this business with Nuneham's is something that would taint him.'

I hadn't realised how close I had come to apportioning blame. Then my uncle's distress changed everything. I think until this moment, I had still been feeling the tug of the doctor's nastier suspicions about Robert's influence upon these decisions. Now, though, I could remember that I really hadn't been alone in noticing the very real toll this had taken on Robert. My uncle cared terribly too, but still he had leaned upon his second-in-command.

The raw adjustment to my temper made me straighten a little. Somehow I had my bandaged hand hidden from my uncle by keeping it behind me, between my back and the chair as though bracing for action. And yet even this small secret felt like a risk because, really, by hiding my injury, I was doing it too – I was making a decision to exclude these people. And I was calling it protection.

I was gripping the rim of my seat with my other hand when I tripped into saying with rather too much feeling, 'I meant that kindly. I meant that I might have helped. You needn't have felt remotely guilty about asking me, would you? After all, I've taken enough care from you over the years. Surely it might have been fair to let me pay something back.'

Beyond his desk, my uncle only smiled in a watery sort of way. 'We couldn't ask you, Lucy.'

'Why on earth not?'

I looked from man to man and caught the last seconds of another silent exchange between them. And then the sympathy of my previous thoughts evaporated.

The sense of collusion between them made my mouth tighten with a sharp pang. Here, despite every swing in my emotions, was proof that everything was being said, more or less, to an agreed script. And Robert was driving it.

With that man's silent insistence, my uncle added reluctantly, 'Your aunt and I think you've had enough to worry about in recent times. We decided we shouldn't add to your burdens.'

Archie. He meant Archie.

After all this worry about motives and the personal cost to these people, I found I had been blind. Everyone had been involved except me, and for one very specific reason.

I felt my voice grow small and disbelieving. 'You couldn't ask for my help because I was widowed five years ago?'

Somehow, I hadn't prepared for this. It felt like a trap. It had to be. And it had to be Robert's because he had orchestrated this meeting, and yet I felt his sideways glance that took in my bewilderment as I shook away Uncle George's explanation with a brief turn of my head. It made no sense because these people knew me. They knew I was fine.

Whereas I had never seen my uncle like this. There was no mask here. No fresh concealment. He was alive; he was the same man I had always known when he adjusted his position in his chair, and yet he was utterly aged.

It burned my spirit when my uncle asked gently, 'Lucy, what would you have done if I had asked you to go to Nuneham's?'

'I'd have tried to find another way.'

His expression made it clear that this wasn't enough of an answer, so I added, 'I'd probably have saved the money you spent on the paper and attempted instead to buy the assistance of one of the other struggling printworks. It would have cost us fractionally more to produce each book by sending the work outside these walls, and we might have had to explain why we weren't fulfilling the contract ourselves. But surely people can appreciate the toll the war has taken?

And at least you wouldn't have had to worry about all this secrecy.'

And while I heard the seriousness of my reply and began to feel the smallness of defeat, my uncle nodded and sat back in his chair as if I had just confirmed something for him. Presumably that my stubbornness was why they hadn't told me.

I asked rather too sharply, 'Who really decided that you would do this? And when?'

My uncle looked bewildered again. 'Your aunt and I decided in the midst of last winter. We realised that the business was going to fail at about the same time when it became clear your aunt was going to have to retire. I took steps to halt the decay very early this year. Rob was drawn in some time later through the course of general conversation over dinner.'

The routine of their quiet family dinners made my heart ache. For a moment I thought the feeling was resentment again. Then I realised it was protectiveness.

Because Robert had taken a seat at that warm kitchen table in their cosy little house, and had agreed to do this for them even when it had turned him into the man who had met me from the bus in Bourton: the uneasy male who had told me as much of my uncle's business as he could within the scope of his promise, before hinting at all the rest.

The doctor's theories about Robert's influence in this business were wrong. This was where the shadow of Robert's wartime incarceration lay. It lay, as Robert had said, in the difficulty of feeling he had the responsibility to act where he was needed. I only had to look at the age that had etched itself upon the old man's face today to understand why my uncle had felt unequal to the task of managing this alone.

Now I thought I understood that Robert wasn't any more pleased with my uncle's idea of a solution than I was. But he'd possessed the grit to do it for them all the same.

My uncle had moved on. He was giving room to his real preoccupation – that dread of wasting all this by letting his business collapse – and saying crisply, 'Rob, did you say that Doctor Bates' information about the trip to Nuneham's was limited to the paper?'

'Lucy said as much just now, yes.'

As Robert glanced at me, the fingers of my bandaged hand spread sensitively against the chair behind my back. I could feel every grain in the wood.

My uncle added, 'Someone will have to talk to the man.'

Meaning, presumably, that Robert would have to talk to him.

I woke abruptly from my trance. After everything I had just said, my uncle still meant to turn to Robert rather than me.

I straightened in my seat and said quickly, 'Honestly, I don't think it's necessary. When Doctor Bates and I spoke just now, he didn't give the impression that he was going to do anything.'

I said that with some certainty. I couldn't bear to imagine what damage would be done if Doctor Bates were to be confronted about what had happened last night and today.

I could guess how my uncle might feel if he discovered that the risk with the paper had lately extended to include physical harm to me, and that alone would be bad enough. But I very definitely did not want Robert to be thrust into the responsibility of dealing with all those layers of blame.

I knew that Robert had noticed the change in my sense of urgency. I could feel the intensity of his attention upon the side of my face when I told my uncle again, 'You really don't need to worry about Doctor Bates. I've already talked to him. He hasn't any reason to say anything.'

Uncle George didn't believe me. He was insisting with sudden weariness, 'We have to be sure. If you truly object to Rob doing it, I'll go. But perhaps, Lucy, if you're already on terms with the man, you might pay him this little visit? Would you do that?'

My mouth moved to frame speech; meaning to say, I don't know what. I was shuddering at the idea of going in person. But I hated the way my objections had been interpreted by my uncle; where he had linked my name to Doctor Bates in a manner that might give Robert a very specific gloss to the knowledge I had of the man's intentions.

Now, presumably, I was going to pay this visit, purely because it was fractionally safer than admitting the truth of the injury, the suspicions, the mistaken intimacy, everything.

But I was interrupted before I could even really make a sound.

'No,' said Robert quite tersely from his seat near my side. 'I'll talk to him.'

He didn't leave room for debate. He didn't look at me either. He kept his eyes fixed upon my uncle's careworn face.

In fact, I thought the set to Robert's jaw was even tougher

than the way he had made me let him test the health of my hand. This decisiveness was a shelving of personal concerns; it was a glimpse of the hard resolve that must have carried him through all those unhappy visits to other failing publishers.

This was a man bracing to meet a difficult scene and, shamefully, I didn't argue because I was too relieved that this particular decision was being taken out of my hands.

Robert made my sense of shame even grimmer when he caught me as I climbed the stairs to the kitchen. We'd been sent out of my uncle's office after a few more quick instructions had been passed between business owner and second-in-command. Despite everything that had been said, there really was fresh exclusion here.

And even if I could pretend to understand why my uncle might still value the support of his friend and colleague more than any help I could give, I thought that I, in my turn, must surely have earned the right by now to claim the attic kitchen as my own while I made the morning round of tea.

But Robert was lingering there in the open doorway at the foot of the stairs while I turned to face him several steps higher up. He was in the light cast by the lamps on the first floor. I was in shade where the light failed halfway to the top. I had imagined he was following me to prolong the discussion.

But, in fact, I got the impression he was at a loss himself as to why he was standing there.

He covered it by allowing the door to close slightly until

it was propped open by his shoulder, then he asked me, 'Are you bearing up all right?'

'Of course I am,' I said. 'I ought to be asking you the same thing.'

I could feel the drama of my place in the dark of these narrow stairs. I felt its power too. I had turned to face him with my hand outstretched to grip the rail. In my mind was the shadow of those terms he and Doctor Bates had used to define me – formidable and ethereal. For a moment – a very fearsomely triumphant moment – my jaw lifted to match the pulse in my veins, and I was tempted to test this man.

Then I reverted to myself with a rush. The harsh angles of my body and the stairs softened as I sagged back against the solid wall.

I confessed, 'I still don't fully understand why I wasn't to be told.'

'I know. Mr Kathay surprised me too when he sidestepped that point. I thought he had decided to explain. But the clue was in the way you answered your uncle's question about the shortfall of resources. You described how you would set about forging links with our neighbouring publishing companies.'

'I'm irresponsibly naïve, you mean?'

I turned my head and found that a dry idea of amusement had touched the presence at the foot of the stairs. He shook his head. 'Too predictable. They knew perfectly well that you'd never have taken the job if you'd found out they couldn't afford your wages.'

'*Really?*'

That jerked me out into the middle of my step once more.

Then the soft release of something like affection came out on a slow breath.

His voice drifted up the stairs to meet me. 'As it is, long before you telephoned your aunt to say that you were thinking of moving back here, they gave me to understand that you, Lucy, are the one aspect of their life they absolutely never meant to risk.'

The smallest of hesitations, then, 'They've waited a long time to have you back.'

Later, when I took the opportunity at lunchtime of slipping away to my aunt's house, I discovered just how long that wait had been.

My uncle's reference to Archie hadn't been an accident. It hadn't been designed to bewilder my questions about his ongoing determination to lean on Robert. I learned from Aunt Mabel that ever since I had moved away to Bristol, she had lived with a terror of being too far away to help.

She had never met Archie; there hadn't been time in the brief few weeks that had remained of his training to make the long run by train out of the city to here. But she and my uncle had seen the photograph of our wedding and experienced all the grief of guessing what war might mean for me. And they'd endured the distance of hearing that final news and the years that had passed since, which had never, until these past few months, drawn me back to them for longer than a routine visit.

Now, though, as I stood on my step at the midpoint of this gloomy stairwell, I hadn't yet had that conversation. I was still standing here and thinking that all the time that Robert had been squandering his good name for the sake of helping them with their financial disaster, he must have also been working quite seriously for me.

It was a peculiar feeling, knowing that this man had quietly, steadily, been a fundamental part of this conspiracy to smooth my pathway home.

'Robert,' I felt compelled to say as he turned to go.

He paused with the door open in his hand.

I said simply, 'Thank you.'

Chapter 13

Thursday was a day for sharp gusts and sunshine between low grey skies. It gave a cold beauty to the final stage of our journey to that overdue meeting with Jacqueline Dunn – and I say it was ours because Robert had shed another day from his busy programme and was beside me.

I could really have come alone because the trepidation of a second meeting with Jacqueline felt entirely distant after the emotional marathon of yesterday. But he was here and there was shyness but no acrimony as we walked along the drive between Jacqueline's gatehouse and the main house.

She had left a note pinned to her door telling us that she was wrestling with workmen and to come and find her. Robert was asking me about that move I had made from my farming home to Moreton to live with my aunt and uncle. Previously, I had felt that he was asking personal questions of me as a means of distracting himself from some deep internal tension. This wasn't like that.

He was probing the connection between my aunt and uncle and my parents.

I told him, 'Uncle George is the blood relative. He's my

mother's vastly older half-brother. My grandfather's first wife died and when he remarried, her son – Uncle George – was sent away to be apprenticed to The Kershaw Book Press.'

'Not the Kershaw *and Kathay* Book Press?'

'Not at that stage, no. So you can hazard a fair guess that the apprenticeship worked out pretty well for him. Mr Kershaw was Aunt Mabel's father. Uncle George married her, and the company became Kershaw and Kathay. It's all so wonderfully dynastic.'

I didn't add that I had been quietly wondering lately if the name were set to move on again into Kathay and Peuse. Because that would mean admitting that I suspected that there was a far greater chance it would become Kathay and Underhill instead.

I said inconsequentially, 'The view from here is spectacular, isn't it?'

The drive was on the high ground and rolling clouds and bleak farmland competed with each other to form the most unforgiving horizon. I was holding the collar of my coat closed at my neck in that way a person does to keep the draughts out – futilely, I might add. I hadn't bothered with the wind-shy hat this time so my hair was running in curling wisps past my face.

I risked a glance at him. He had the collar of his raincoat turned up. The coat was well made and it gave me a hint of the life he must have fitted at his medical college. I knew his absence from the office yesterday afternoon had been for the sake of talking to Doctor Bates, but there was no new shadow in this man's face to tell me what had been said. I didn't dare ask. If we spoke about that again now, it would feel raw, exposing, like forgetting the value of what he had done for me yesterday in the course of that small exchange on the stairs.

'Do you know,' I was saying instead, 'I'm not surprised that my uncle's business is struggling. Look at us both; taking a day to visit one author about a book she's already had us edit twice.'

I made him laugh. Overhead, the pollarded limes which lined the high point of the drive were rattling their thin fingers.

Beneath their reach, Robert remarked seriously, 'Brace yourself. Now you know the truth and you've promised to help Mr Kathay chart his path through this mess, he'll have you working all hours.'

'Well in that case, he'll be getting very good value out of me, because I've already decided to work for the smallest remuneration I can afford, for the time being.'

I saw his disapproval. 'They'd never let you.'

'They won't have a choice,' I said a shade tartly before easing the tone to something more wry. 'They don't know what power they've given me by making me the woman who types up the letters and answers the telephone. I deal with the bank as well and write out all the payslips at the end of each month. So please don't tell them.'

His promise came in the form of a single shake of his head.

'That's the little church near the bus stop, isn't it?' I was looking at the curling line of the distant river where it passed into a smear of trees.

A small farmstead was crumbling in the wintery light nearby, but there were no other signs of life. Even so, I could remember seeing a notice that had been pasted up by the bus stop there, advertising a carol service. I couldn't imagine how this desolate landscape had enough people in it to even make up a congregation.

His thoughts must have been running along similar lines because he asked, 'Do you go home for Christmas? To your parents, I mean?'

'No, I'll go in the new year. What about you?'

'No. That visit I paid to my family last week will do for a while. My relationship with my own parents has never been as smooth as yours.'

It was the brief silence that followed that made me remember where comments like that usually led. I pre-empted it by telling him freely, 'I'm not estranged from my parents, you know. They're still Mum and Dad. It's just that their house tends to be very full at this time of year. When I was a small child, it always seemed to me that there were so many of us that we barely bothered to see anyone else – and I was only the middle child of an eventual seven. It's no wonder, when you think about it, that my life with my aunt and uncle seemed so much simpler. I suppose this'll be your first Christmas with us? Kershaw and Kathay really does collect people, doesn't it? First my uncle, then me, and now you?'

It was then that I realised that I was rambling and he hadn't been asking about my background anyway since the evidence was there that he already knew. To make matters worse, I suspected that I was the one who was prying here, and I was in danger of breaching that personal line I had drawn about asking and being asked about things that had grown from the war.

He made the feeling stronger when he said, 'Is that a very circumspect way of asking me how I met your aunt and uncle?'

His head had turned towards me. He didn't mind. The faint teasing note made my heart give a sudden tilt as I gripped the collar of my coat and gave the smallest of consenting nods.

He told me, 'Your uncle met me at the end of a drizzly day in March after he'd stepped down from the train in Moreton. He'd been in Warwick all day, talking to other publishers.'

'Is this the time when he'd begun to take steps to resolve the company's problems himself?'

'Yes, and it wasn't going terribly well. Night had fallen by then. I'd arrived about half an hour before. I didn't have enough money in my pocket for a hotel and I'd stalled where the last gas lamp from the platform fades into the terrace of filthy brick railwaymen's cottages. I presume you know the spot?'

I did. The place was dirty with soot and the debris from the nearby factory workshops, and fearsomely bleak at that time of day.

'I was standing there, just wondering if I had the energy to think my way through this latest pitfall. I let my bag slip from my shoulder to the ground just as this tired old fellow passed me. I heard him murmur, "You too?" Then he offered me a meal. You have to understand,' added Robert in a tone that certainly didn't match the vision I had of the kind of weariness that defeated a person at the darker end of a rain-soaked day, 'that I'd walked out of my medical school about three months before. And when I say I walked out, I mean I started walking and kept walking. Or moving by bus or train, or a lift in a stranger's car. I picked up the odd rough job in return for bed and board here and there along the way, and that path led me to Moreton.'

'You were a vagrant?'

He made one of those tips of the head that conveyed both agreement and yet an adjustment to the term to make it fit. Slowly, he settled on saying, 'Close to becoming one.'

He said, 'I certainly chose an awfully hard time of year to take to moving about the country. A "Gentleman of the Road" is what they call us, isn't it? Referring to those war-damaged old soldiers who can't quite settle to normal life. Only I wasn't fully down to my last penny, and I wasn't hopelessly unemployable. I was rejecting the life I was being moulded to. And I was barely a soldier at all when you think about it. Is this the house that's destined to become a new hotel?'

His eyes had abruptly fixed upon the tattered façade before us. It looked both really grand and painfully tired of its former life today too, and I presumed that this was his way of neatly closing the subject. I was willing enough to let him do it.

But in the last few yards before we approached the steps, he added the next part with sudden steadiness as if it wasn't so much that he thought I wished him to explain any more, but that he felt it necessary. 'I never wanted to reclaim my place as a medical student as if the war had never happened, but I would have borne it. Just. Do you know what really drove me to finally abandon my studies once and for all?'

I shook my head.

'It was the endlessness of going home after all those years away and realising that I was set to forever hear myself being called Doctor. When I like being merely Rob, or Robert.'

There was the smallest emphasis in the way he added that last variation of his name. As if the addition belonged here, with me. After the easier back and forth of the moment before, it chilled me a little. It made me think of the sting I had given him yesterday when I had briefly reverted to calling him Mr Underhill.

And because of that, I found myself saying a shade too briskly, 'So are you telling me that you've stayed and helped Uncle George out of gratitude? Because of the way he and my aunt gave you back your name? I don't believe you.'

I saw his jaw lift in a manner that somehow met my challenge and countered it. 'I didn't say that, Lucy, did I?'

He had drawn to a halt on the strip of gravel before the steps and so I stopped with him. This ridgetop walk wasn't desolate any more. It was rattling with the secret whispering of those dormant trees. Their black fingers crowded, and I was almost wishing that I could break this intimacy because it was perfect, and yet at the same time it was making me feel strangely uncertain.

I watched as his head turned away to run his gaze up to the open door of the house. Then his eyes dropped back to mine and there wasn't any difficulty in them to mirror mine. He seemed entirely unaffected by the current running beneath all this honesty when he confided, 'It's idiotic to admit I threw away an entire career for a name, isn't it? Particularly when I've studied enough medicine to know that a sense of rootlessness is a pretty common experience for newly demobbed souls. And I knew that with time the feeling might pass; or at least reduce itself to a dormant undertone. So, by all logical means I could have stayed and qualified and established my practice. And eventually I probably would have even found some idea of normality within my old family home.'

With an effort, I swept the hair back from my face with my free hand and found a lighter tone. 'Do you know, I realise I've never asked where you're from?'

'I was studying in Birmingham, but my childhood home was Coventry.'

'Good heavens. Were your parents bombed?'

'Not at all. Perhaps the easiest way to convey the life I've left is to ask you to imagine a respectable house filled with dark wallpapers, glass cabinets and clocks that tick.'

'I see,' I said. 'Oh dear.'

'Yes,' he said, smiling. 'Whereas I gather you were significantly closer to the dust and rubble during your years of service in Bristol?'

I didn't rise to the reference to yet more tales my aunt and uncle had been telling about me. The rooms my sister and I had shared were hit once. Instead, I countered it with an unguarded retort to rival his own idea of a teasing note. 'I suppose all those clocks and things explain why you're so at home in my uncle's office – with the endless yards of dark

172

wood, and the thoughtful silences which practically grow in the corners?'

I shouldn't have said that. I was already beginning to frame a retraction because my sort of instinctive humour had the capacity to ruin things. And, besides, there was a private concern of my own in there to do with my relationship with the place, and I didn't want him to see it.

But I found that I had made him laugh. 'You think I sought the familiar? Not a bit of it. If you knew my childhood, you'd know the idea of working at the office of a small, unambitious printworks counts as very careless indeed.'

He caught my eye. I saw him cast a brief sigh into the cold wind, like a release from the past in one breath of air. He told me on quite a different note of confidence, 'My parents wanted me to treat my return to my studies as the cure for all their years of unhappy worry. But I'm nearly thirty years old now and it turns out there is a world of difference between the idea of responsibility held by this man before you today, and that of the reckless youth who hurt them terribly by dashing off with his friends to do something very patriotic but entirely foolhardy.'

He added, 'I'll make amends and go back for visits as I did last week – my sister's just had a baby, by the way, so we were all very polite to one another. But I didn't expect them to approve of my part in your uncle's absorbing, challenging work. And I certainly didn't forget how easy it was to leave them and come back to your Uncle George, or your Aunt Mabel. Or you.'

His declaration of his commitment to return to us after his trip away absolutely stunned me.

Whereas he seemed oblivious, as if he had barely noticed the strength of those last few words while the nearby house snared his thoughts. There had been movement in there.

Then the man beside me turned his attention back to me with a suddenness that made my heart miss a beat.

I heard him say quickly, 'By the way, before there's any confusion in that house, I'm not here to take over responsibility for the book. I'm here to make amends for laying you bare to Jacqueline's manipulations, and also to carry anything she gives us. Your bruised hand is terribly sore, isn't it?'

'Not really.' Now my heart was beating in a different way.

'Lucy,' he said severely. 'You've been trying to keep your hand raised by gripping the collar of your coat, so I know you wish you had it in a sling to ease the ache a little. Do you want us to attempt to fashion one out of your scarf?'

'Fashion what? A sling?' Suddenly, my attention was upon the injured limb; instinctively releasing its grip upon my coat like a guilty secret. 'No. It's fine really. It's more habit than anything. The swelling's reduced already, as you can see.' To prove the point, I showed him the neatly turned bandage and then thrust it into a coat pocket.

He didn't mean it to but his observation cooled every heating feeling. It hardened me all of a sudden, and not because he was wrong to suspect that the throbbing of the bruise still ran as an undertone to every thought. This was an unexpected tumble back into the sense that it wasn't so much that he didn't speak about himself, but that getting to know him made everything more complicated.

I had barely absorbed the description he had just given of his retreat from his sense of obligation to his parents. Now he was bewildering me because I could perfectly recall the undeniable strain he had shown in the course of his recent management of my uncle's affairs, and yet it had never even occurred to me to ask him if he could cope with the trip to this place.

His decision to ask me about my own fitness now, all of a sudden, as a footnote to all that intimacy, struck me like an act of sabotage.

It was as if all along he had been working towards laying me open to this when he said insistently, 'If you're sure? Just, please, don't wear yourself out.'

My nerves were on edge. I was bristling.

He had done this to me once before, when I had planned my last visit to this place. This time the injury was worse, because now I had the memory of all our recent minutes of companionableness, and I had the sudden chance to realise that, before him, the last man to cut this close to my idea of confidence had been my husband.

'Robert,' I said. 'I'm fine.'

From my tone and posture I might as well have reverted to calling him Mr Underhill. And then it was too late to explain the sudden defensiveness because I was too cold to find words that would be more like my usual manner; and then Jacqueline was coming out of the house.

Chapter 14

Jacqueline's first act was to prove that it was all my own fault that I'd been unsettled by the way she had sought to increase my commitment to her book. Because she certainly hadn't tried to use Archie's memory for that purpose. She greeted Robert as though she believed he was my Mr Peuse.

It was possible, of course, that she had simply forgotten that detail about me. The business of my previous visit was all old news today – even her scheme to use her photographs of the young ward of the house, Harriet Clare, to prove the existence of the giraffes had faded. This time, she was passionately determined to show us the present-day repairs to her stairs.

'Come in, Lucy,' she said excitedly. 'The workmen have begun the process of smoothing the damaged plaster on the walls, and the staircase has been made safe so I can finally take you up to the first floor.'

She was terribly stylish again. She was also a little flushed and wafting graceful hands to show us the vast entrance hall and to take in the sweep of the stairs and the marble, and the heavily ornate newel post.

I stopped the rapid flow of her enthusiasm when I said

firmly, 'Jacqueline, this is Robert Underhill. He's the editor you dealt with when you first got in touch with Kershaw and Kathay Book Press.'

She turned to stare at him at the moment of setting a foot upon the first step. She looked, in fact, a little bewildered, because as well as forgetting most of the details from my last visit, she had apparently also forgotten who she had greeted at the front door just now. It was flattering in its way because I thought it was my presence that counted.

'Oh,' she said, aghast at the oversight. 'I wasn't really thinking about the book, but of course you're the editor. And you're very welcome.'

She didn't notice the way my formal introduction had briefly made Robert's mouth compress into a line. Whereas I heard the way he added his own amendment as Jacqueline shook his hand. 'Thank you,' he said. 'And I'm glad to finally meet you too. But I will just make it clear that Lucy is in charge of the edits to your book now.'

It was an odd experience, being aware that it mattered to me that he should say that, but still feeling the way my mind had been irritated outside. It showed in the brief sideways glance he and I shared as we followed Jacqueline onto the stairs.

And that was where my irritation abruptly ceased. Because although I had been thoroughly unsettled by Robert, it wasn't the memory of his caution to take care that hit me as I climbed to the midpoint of the sweeping staircase.

These stairs were set to be the equal of the grand staircase that had climbed through the heart of the other Dunn hotel

I had visited – the Blaze Hotel near Bristol. Here, a tall and arched Regency window lit the turn before the final rise to the first floor.

The last time I had seen a similar fall of light, I had been running upstairs with my hand firmly enclosed in my husband's.

It had been a late summer's evening then, and the hotel had been full of noise because the men were celebrating their last night before travelling to Portland. They would pass from there to their various stations on board their new ships. We wives and lovers had come for the dancing and the bustle and the idea of pretending that such a send-off was heaven.

Today, in this great derelict house, the step onto the landing of the first floor marked the end of that memory. I had only Robert and Jacqueline for company, and, instead of the jangle of a gramophone, the floor was empty and echoing, and lined by open doors.

They were elegant panels of painted wood. Jacqueline's voice ran up and down the row as she stepped towards the room at the brighter end of the house. 'I'm pleased to say that I've uncovered the plans of the house within my collection of documents.'

I observed, 'And, clearly, they're proving useful?'

She grinned as we joined her. 'They are. They state clearly that this bedroom here is the one that belonged to Graham Hanley Ashbrook. And the view is absolutely perfect, isn't it?'

Against my expectations, this wasn't the beginning of discussion about the giraffes.

Instead she said wistfully, 'This is the same view over the

179

ha-ha that he had in his library. I think it gives a wonderful insight into the spirit of the man.'

I could see why the giraffes might have lost their allure. The parkland was dipping away uninterrupted into distant hedge lines and, even on a day like this one, it was spectacular. There was a tangible sense here of the life and tastes of an old Victorian gentleman who had sought retirement after his great African quest for dangerous diseases.

Behind me, Jacqueline conceded, 'The bedroom itself is less perfect. The recent war has left the walls stiffly white-washed and the floorboards bare.'

In fact, the bare floor meant that every footstep, every breath sounded brash.

'But,' she added, turning in an arc, 'the fireplace is still present with its alabaster surround. And, if I ignore the chips in the ribbed plasterwork on the ceiling, I really do get a sense of the man he was. The son, Walter John Ashbrook, claimed the bedroom at the eastern end of this floor. Shall we go up to the second floor?'

She said that last part rapidly, and then she whisked us back to the stairs.

Jacqueline was already at the head of the stairs when Robert and I hurried up to join her.

She had barely even glanced at Walter's bright, silent room with a view over that avenue of limes. For me, the son's choice was prettier than his father's and there was something odd, I realised, in the way Jacqueline had used his name.

I was used to her manner of giving respect to the dead by

180

using the name in full, but the emphasis this time was different somehow. And it was unlike her to steer us past any remnant of the Asbrook existence without giving it a friendly greeting.

Now she was merging with the flood of light that was dancing its way along the gallery, even on this cold, wintery day. She said in the manner of the best tour-guides, 'This floor is where Graham's grandchildren slept and learned their lessons.'

The second floor was less grand, stretching in a corridor along the length of the house to be lit by high windows that overlooked the stable yard. It was cold enough to make our breath mist, but still there was a kind of cheeriness here, in the form of a faint whistling.

The muted tune was coming from a workman who was attempting to restore some usefulness to the much narrower staircase that rose in a damply neglected corner to the servant's floor in the attic. He was whistling a popular song from the music halls. For a moment, this might have been another return to the bright cheerfulness of the Blaze Hotel, if only he had been fighting to be heard above forty or so boisterous young men wearing the Royal Navy uniform who were diving in and out of every doorway after drinks.

'Did I tell you, Lucy, that I managed to unpick where each of the family members must have slept?' Jacqueline was beckoning at me from a narrow doorway at the end of the row.

'In here?' I asked as I passed her. Robert was already inside.

I turned to meet her smile as she followed me in through the door. I remarked on a sudden note of understanding,

'Whose room was this? You've been waiting to tell us this all along, haven't you?'

Then I answered the question for myself. 'This was *Harriet's?*'

She beamed, triumphant. But for a moment, the merest portion of a second, I thought there was a brittle note behind the expression in those shining eyes.

Then she swept it away by sending an expressive hand in a thoughtful curve towards the doorway before conceding, 'It's actually disappointingly ordinary in here, isn't it?'

'Well, yes,' I said. The room was utterly empty. The walls were plain and uncomplicated, and whitewashed like all the rest. This space was, in fact, completely devoid of, well, anything significant at all.

It was almost funny. The disappointment was my own fault. Or perhaps Robert's. I suppose I had been braced, after all his cautious words outside, to enter into a further dark encounter with my past. Those fleeting memories of running up the stairs at the Blaze Hotel with my husband had felt like a forerunner to something bigger. And I had known, even without Robert's warning, that it was only a matter of time before Jacqueline gave me a second brush with the sad story of the girl with the thick dark hair and the dress from a genteel era.

So I suppose I might have been imagining in a small way that I would learn that I shared my grandmother's somewhat fearsome sensitivity to the world of ghosts. Because, really, if any room should awaken those skills in me, I had thought it would be Harriet's.

But nothing manifested itself between these plain walls. This narrow little bedroom carried no sense of her life, or her passing. This was a room that had lately housed a number of hospital children, and Harriet's residence was swept up by the seamless continuity within these unadorned walls, so that one bored child's presence was indistinguishable from the rest.

She didn't even come in with the sudden bolt of discovering that Robert was watching me.

He gave himself away by abruptly fixing his attention upon the damaged fireplace as soon as I turned my head. I waited until he looked again. This time he didn't pretend to hide his question – the one that went with his earlier concern for my welfare – and he received, after a moment, its answer.

We were both amused, actually, because there was nothing wrong here at all.

It was with a better feeling that I turned to join Jacqueline in the doorway. She was gazing out of the windows that lined the narrow corridor.

'Do you see those doves?' asked Jacqueline. Her tone made it clear she wasn't thinking about ghostly memories of any sort. She was thinking about something tied to facts and physical details and she was drawing my attention to the view we had over the coach house.

A screen of trees beyond gave the illusion that these buildings stood alone in a damp landscape, but doves flew in the distance where the woodland tapered southwards.

Jacqueline pointed towards them. 'That,' she said, 'is Bramblemead, where Graham Hanley Ashbrook's estate manager lived. It's a farm. You can see it from the drive.'

Suddenly, it was clear to me that some stronger feeling really was driving this tour after all. Beyond her, the workman's whistle seemed to have stuck upon the same few memorable lines like a gramophone record that kept skipping: 'Every little girl would like to be; The fairy on the Christmas tree.'

Whereas it was with an entirely different spirit that Jacqueline told me, 'The estate manager is in that old photograph I have of that collection of gentlemen all standing on the front steps. Sampson Murray is the fellow on the second step down, do you remember him?'

'I remember beards and top hats,' I admitted, 'and very little else.'

She caught my eye. 'I bet, therefore, that you didn't notice that he was a black man?'

She was hugging herself as she told me insistently, 'Absolutely, he was. When Graham Hanley Ashbrook sold the Kenyan estate, he brought Murray back with him. I don't know on what terms it was done, but as far as I can tell, Murray made his mark just as soon as he'd settled in here.'

The floor creaked as Robert joined us. She told us both, 'He was running that farm over there, running every part of the estate, even to the point of walking in and out of this house with the same degree of intimacy with the son Walter. And,' she added a shade sourly, 'I have that photograph to prove it.'

'Whatever do you mean?' For a moment I had been cheerfully waiting for Jacqueline to tell me that Sampson Murray had been employed as keeper of the family giraffes. I had even been readying my smile.

But somehow she was making me revisit the memory of my wartime home in Bristol, where houses with rooms to rent had been heavily papered with signs declaring, 'No Irish, no coloured'.

I was thinking that her hotels mustn't need any signage of that sort since wealth was a pretty robust barrier. I was afraid she was about to say something foul about Mr Murray's place in this house now.

She wasn't of course. She was saying, 'Don't you think it infuriating that such a man should have moved here at the height of the Victorian Empire – even within living memory of the era of all those Acts for the Abolition of Slavery – and yet barely a story about him remains? He must have been the first black man to live in these rural parts; I thought he would have left behind a spectacular record. But it turns out that seventy or eighty years is a long time for the memory of a man, regardless of skin colour, when the people who knew him are long-since dead too. Murray travelled across continents but left me nothing except a few surviving references to his name. His descendants own the farm these days.'

She added glumly, 'There appears to have been a clause in the Will after the last Ashbrook died, which allowed Murray's son to buy the place.'

'And that's a problem for you?' I was utterly confused now.

'Only because,' she replied, 'I can't make contact with him.'

At last, I thought I was beginning to understand her frustration.

After a moment while her gaze still ranged over those distant trees, she added, 'I think I met the son in question roaming about in that woodland when I first moved here – he was aged at least eighty-five and just as unassuming as his father. But I didn't know then what I know now about the Ashbrooks, so I didn't think to tackle him.'

'Well,' I suggested, 'can't anyone in the village introduce you?'

She cast me a sideways glance. 'I refer you to my earlier statement about the lack of local stories.'

She sighed. 'I don't mean to say that the people in this neighbourhood are strangely silent about the present day black man in their midst. I think they're trying to help. But all I can get from them is the reoccurring encouragement to find Murray's son at Bramblemead. So you should know that I've been to Bramblemead – and the farmhouse there is a ruinous cowshed.'

She was glowering at those distant doves once more when she added, 'There is a great-grandson – the young folk in the village do know him, at least. But he's still out on manoeuvres in the Far East, so who knows what he'll be able to tell me when he gets back.'

I didn't quite understand after all. I said, puzzled, 'Tell you what? Do you want to ask him to confirm your theory about the giraffes?'

'No,' she said so crossly that she made me jump. 'I want

to speak to Murray's extremely elderly son about the girl who died when he was a boy. I want to ask him about Harriet.'

Jacqueline had already swept away along the corridor and I followed with Robert just behind. The movements of her hands weren't at all graceful now.

She was saying fiercely, 'Do you know what diphtheria does – *did* – back then? My children are vaccinated so it's becoming less common, but all they had in Harriet's time was hopelessness and the cries of plaintive parents begging to understand how a sore throat could kill. Six of the village children contracted it within a matter of days in 1873. Four of them died.'

Suddenly, she wasn't telling me this. She was stopping at the top of the stairs and reaching past me to draw Robert forwards. She was gripping his sleeve and saying accusingly, '*You* know what it is, don't you? And can you guess what Graham Hanley Ashbrook's son and heir did while Harriet Clare was suffocating? He went away. Walter's account ledgers say that he went off on some business trip to London and didn't come back until all traces of the infection were gone. It's the only part of these people that I can't reconcile myself to. It's so ... so *cold*. How could he do it to her? How could he leave a poor parentless girl of thirteen to the care of servants, until her presence had faded from every record in this house?'

Her voice caught on a shrill note as she told Robert fiercely, 'I'm a parent and it's inconceivable. I *wish* I'd never looked in the wretched archives.'

I had my hand out upon the rail that shielded us from the drop over the stairwell. My grip was so firm it hurt. I released it. Oddly, it was seeing the reaction on Robert's face that made me begin to understand the impact of mine. I saw the shape of his mouth barely change from its usual steady interest but I knew he was surprised. I was certain he was sensing the tug of his years of doctoring, just as I had felt her claim upon my widowhood. It was the effect Jacqueline created with her passion. And now I thought that she had to be completely unaware she was doing it. She didn't know Robert. She couldn't know how this appeal would affect him.

Jacqueline was hurrying Robert down the staircase into the light falling from that impressive arched window. It overlooked the stable yard and she was describing the legacy Graham Hanley Ashbrook had passed to his son. She was explaining the continuity of many generations who had cared for this house. However, the script didn't follow quite the same pattern as before. Instead of using this window as a means of directing his mind to the myth embodied by that coach house, the legacy she was speaking about was the ownership that had passed through generations, and the memorial that Walter's children had installed in his name.

By the time I had reached the landing of the first floor, she and Robert had already moved onwards to the turn. Jacqueline was quoting softly, 'A man dies not while his world, his monument remains.'

It was the inscription I was supposed to be including in her book.

She was adding, 'There's a note that says that the memorial

was installed by his daughter. It lists all his children's names. By convention, it ought to have been put up after Walter's death by his son, but some years had passed by the time the monument was installed. It's possible that the son and heir had died by then as well; I need to check the dates. But Janet Ashbrook – the daughter – may well have been the last of them.'

They were so far ahead of me now that I was free to linger for a moment on the second step down from the first floor. I heard her tell Robert, 'At the time of Harriet's death, the daughter was living almost entirely in London. I'd understood that Miss Ashbrook was already married but the occasional reference to "Miss Ashbrook" in various letters implies that she came here more frequently in the years after Harriet's death until abruptly a single melancholy line recorded that she was married and she wouldn't be staying in this house again. If she was banished,' she added grimly, 'it doesn't paint a very cheerful picture of Walter's idea of fatherhood, does it?'

I didn't really hear what Jacqueline said next. She had passed down into the entrance hall below me and I was pausing with my hand on the banister rail.

Then some change in the pattern of my thoughts intensified and grew clearer. I followed the impulse back along the landing towards the open door of Walter's bedroom.

Somewhere in that wide expanse downstairs, Jacqueline was saying, 'Perhaps the daughter felt differently about her exile, because she certainly cared enough to have the memorial to her father installed in the parish church.'

I heard Robert's voice; a question. Then her reply, 'No, not the little church you passed on your way here, but the more distant one in the nearest village. You can just see it from one of the east windows.'

I hadn't noticed before that the workmen had gone out. It was time they had their lunch. I had the floor to myself and a glimpse of views over the stable yard and the parkland. And now, as I stepped through the door into that overlooked bedroom that belonged to Walter, I had that view to the east along the lime avenue.

These details were all monuments to the Ashbrook men. And through Jacqueline's lecture about the memorial in the village church, she was undoing every idea she had given me of the role we have in building our own legacy for the dead by remembering them.

What did it matter that I had learned the Ashbrook names, when their house cared nothing for the memory of all the other people who had passed beneath its gaze? The inscription on the family memorial implied that a man built his own monument, so what did that say about the legacy of those who had no wealth, no property? My husband didn't even have a grave. Archie had been buried at sea in the tomb of his sinking ship, and, like that estate manager and Harriet, we were all forgotten people here.

Only it wasn't quite true. I knew it wasn't true. Because, regardless of the Ashbrook taste for permanence in the form of stone and bricks and mortar, for me things might have been becoming a little more free, a little closer to my happier nature since I had rediscovered my power to speak of my husband.

I had less fear of calling to him now. I knew my strength,

and the relationship that had underpinned it all. It was the same strength that in this quiet, thoughtful moment had led me to visit Walter John Ashbrook's bedroom.

I think I must have done it with a defiant idea of assuring myself that rooms weren't everything to the memory of a man.

It was a perfect invitation for the shock of silence that met me.

It was the silence of emptiness. Of daylight and of the drifting consciousness of someone else's thoughts. The sense of it came as an assault. Far more physical than the one that had trapped my hand in the doorframe. Because he was here. I couldn't see him, but he forced a disbelieving question from me.

'Archie?'

Silence answered.

Because no one was here in this bright, whitewashed room but a fierce absence of life.

It crowded round like deafness while instinct sent my heart-beat hammering across the floorboards. It consumed my husband's friendliness. I should never have tried to put a name to it. I'd called it to me.

This space became a hostile void. Unkind, unhealing; the weight of it crashed in from the corners. It swept like a flood through this house, pursuing the whisper of my footsteps as I turned and hurried for the stairs.

It came with me as I ran downwards. It blinded me and travelled a few yards ahead. I had a giddying sense of being half enclosed and half breaking free into fresher air. I was made dizzy by the way my eyes knew that I was racing onwards, and yet my mind behaved as if I were being snatched backwards into a return to that memory of racing up the staircase in the Blaze Hotel with my husband.

I was descending still. It was impossible that there should be any doubt about it, but I only knew this because I had a hand – my left, not the one my husband had gripped – out on the broad banister rail. It was stone and it ran like ice beneath my palm in a swoop towards the ground floor. It was blacker down here; duller out of the glare from that high window. The silence swept up from the space of the entrance hall like a barrier. It flung me back like grief. It stopped me with a thump upon the last step.

Then, at last, my senses met something I could put real words to.

The stout crown of the newel post caught me in the crook of my elbow. This too was stone. Glorious Victorian reconstituted stone dressed up to look like grey marble. The newel post snatched at me as my leading foot slipped over the lip of the last step. I saved myself by sort of crumpling over the heel of my trailing leg. I sat down hard upon the stairs with a suddenness that punched the air out of me.

I wasn't sitting there for long. A fresh shadow swooped in along the foot of the stairs and this one was familiar and it took hold of me to haul me to my feet. I went gladly into the curve of Robert's arm. I turned there against him, fingers knotting into a tangled grip upon the fabric of his coat. The staircase behind was desolately empty. I barely spared a thought for the curious presence of his companion hurrying out of the library just beyond.

I felt the strength of Robert's hold on me. I clung to him for shelter from the maddening effect of this house, and begged him on a grim whisper to explain, 'How did you know to warn me?'

Chapter 15

Robert hadn't been warning me about anything. I realised in the next moment that his concern about my fitness to make this trip had been nothing more than friendly care for my hand.

I felt his confusion by the way that his grip slackened so that he might study my face while he tried to answer my question. He asked, 'What did I warn you about? Did you hurt yourself just now?'

'No, not at all,' I said with remarkable steadiness, and stepped back to claim the support of the banister rail once more. This time it held me and the space around us had returned to its ordinary shabby self.

Sorry,' I said hastily. 'I must have tripped on the stairs in the process of hurrying after you.'

I used the edge of that bandaged hand to sweep the hair from my face. I did it because I was overheating all of a sudden and I was worrying him terribly, and, besides, there was something horribly corrupt about clinging to a man, when I had lately been thinking wild thoughts about the memory of another.

*

Jacqueline didn't really know me well enough to guess at any of that. She thought I was tired and said that we had better go and find lunch if we were to have time to dissect her final edits before Robert and I had to meet the bus.

I believe I chattered my way through the soup and the innumerable questions about giraffes – she hadn't forgotten them after all – and then I was free and hurrying along the lane that passed before the gatehouse through more of that interminable wind.

Every action of mine had a peculiar energy to it. I had been walking for about fifteen minutes before Robert broke into my thoughts to ask, 'Is this the way to the bus?'

He was with me. His question was given in that way a person has when he knows speech will be unwelcome but feels compelled to breach the cheery charade anyway. He had noticed that I wasn't leading him back across the fields towards that little church by the river. He had certainly noticed the decisiveness with which I was marching along.

I confessed far too blandly, 'I want to take a quick look at the family memorial in the village church. Do you mind? The bus stops there too.'

That was the last thing I said for some time. It hadn't really occurred to me that I hadn't been speaking before. Now I had the surprise of suddenly wishing that I had left him with Jacqueline, or sent him back along that footpath over the fields to the main road; or anywhere, just so that I wouldn't have to acknowledge that I wasn't quite calm.

It took us another twenty minutes to reach the village. The church stood at the heart of an uneven assortment of grand houses and rotten little cottages that ran in a straggling line along the lane. It was built of a strange white stone that shone against the heavy browns of the surrounding wintered landscape. There was no tower. Like the riverside church, this place seemed to have been limited either by wealth or the instability of what was effectively an island in a vast water meadow.

Inside, the whitewashed nave was so deeply silent that for a moment I was afraid again – I thought I was stepping back into that obscure oppression of the senses. The hush was certainly strong enough to absorb the heavy creak as I pushed the stout wooden door closed behind me. But this time Robert was with me and the silence was the sort that belonged to ancient walls built to withstand the winter outside.

I drew a steadying breath and finally found my courage. I said quietly, 'Is that the memorial? On the end wall of this aisle?'

It was a vast marble plaque with ornate scrollwork, and Walter's motto – that defiant declaration that he could never die while his monument remained – had been picked out with black pigment against the veined stone.

My bandaged hand was gripping my collar again, but this time it was definitely for the sake of warmth. This place was cold, like an ice house.

I remarked with a whisper, 'Do you think Walter's inscription is a bit tactless for a church memorial?'

'How so?'

'Don't people buried in church generally subscribe to the belief that eternity dwells in the strength of their faith, rather than tangible things like earth and stone? "He who believeth in me shall never die", and so on?'

That was all I said. Because Robert was checking how much time we had left before the bus went past and I was noticing that Walter John Ashbrook's parents were recorded here too. Their mortal remains lay under the great slab at the base, where someone had set a vase of dried flowers. They were lavender and a teasel, and the fragile seedheads of what looked like forget-me-not.

Walter's wife was mentioned, and so were his children; three sons and a reference to Janet, the daughter, who had been interred in the fullness of time with her husband elsewhere. The youngest of them had installed this tribute with the note, 'Given by his daughter with love'.

The sequence ran on in a different script to include a painfully emotional tribute to the last of the Ashbrooks who had been lost in the Great War. But there was no memorial here to my real target.

Harriet Clare was as neglected in this place as she had been at the house.

She wasn't in the graveyard either. A hasty search identified a shattering cluster of children robbed before their time in 1873, the year of the diphtheria outbreak. Their names swept after me as I moved out into the lane again, a mutter on the wind.

I barely even noticed when I passed the bus stop sign at the turn where the lane joined the main Cirencester road. I know Robert saw it.

In a profoundly unpleasant and claustrophobic way, I was certain now that I really wished he had stayed there and let me go on alone. He was like a guard, an increasingly doubtful guard, and I don't know at what point I had stopped feeling grateful for the way he had picked me up at the foot of the stairs, but I didn't like this feeling that I was doing anything wrong.

I thought he was suppressing the urge to start asking me searching questions. I marched on just so that he didn't get the chance to catch my eye.

We reached the little church by the river as the cloud crashed in at about waist height. It filled the air with a fine icy rain that stung, and it was as we ducked beneath the brief shelter of an ancient cedar that it finally occurred to me to wonder if Robert's disapproval was coming from the responsibility of accompanying me like this.

I remembered at long last that this was not a man who had the nerve for mediating between peace and a rough scene.

I asked him quite seriously, 'Are you managing all right? You aren't feeling restless? You don't want to leave?'

'Well, it is a touch chilly to be striding about windswept churchyards.'

He cannot have understood the reference. In fact, the brief flare of my concern was swept away by his simple and uncompromising honesty. After all, he must have known that a person only ever asks after another's health at a time like this when they wish to either be told that all is well, or told categorically that it very much isn't. In this instance, this benign airing of his discomfort made it plainly my fault, while leaving it entirely to my temper to decide that he was actually saying that he would stay with me while I did this.

And now the bus was due and that infuriated me too.

The riverside church was sinking. It was dark and damp inside, and far too poor to bear a memorial of any sort beyond a few ancient slabs before the altar.

My race moved into the graveyard. The first short rows yielded nothing except the final resting place of that brave traveller Sampson Murray. He had died a few years before Walter John Ashbrook, but lay alone here amongst all these names I did not know.

I was diving along the next row – all uselessly modern – when the bus clattered into view.

It came with a curse for me. I wasn't ready to leave this place and every movement seemed to be taking longer and longer. The feeling of panic grew stronger when Robert left me and crossed the fifteen yards or so to the kerb to put out his hand as a signal for it to stop.

'Lucy!' The hard call of my name carried across the grey stones and snatched at my attention. I had been struggling back to Murray's badly weathered inscription when I blindly turned my head.

Robert was tramping back through the dirty ground to the limit of the graveyard. The bus had slowed to a halt beyond him.

Now I saw his face clearly for the first time. His urgency was a shock for me. Robert was a serious and characterful man with cheeks cast to harsh angles by the bitter air until

200

he looked pale and cold. The flaps of his coat were guttering wetly. It was a shock for me to see that the energy that had been flowing through my veins was being reflected in the stark purpose of this man. He really didn't want to stay here.

'Lucy. The bus!' His hand swept out towards the road where the conductor was itching to close the doors.

Even while I began to obey his call, from somewhere I mustered the intelligence to say impatiently, 'You're acting as though wishing to visit this part of the Ashbrook story in person is a thoroughly unnatural thing to do, and it isn't kind. I shouldn't have to justify myself.'

'No?' he retorted. 'In that case I shouldn't have had to notice that something has been upsetting you ever since we left that house.'

Then he added more persuasively, 'We can come back.'

The lack of answers amongst these graves matched my numb mind, and my frozen limbs. The only heat in me came from the urge to keep on searching. But his determination to get me away was a burning plea of his own. It snatched at me. He sharpened my focus and intensified it. For a moment, a deeply alien moment, the tug of his wishes almost tore my mind.

He almost unleashed an aspect of my nature that would have made him get on that hateful bus alone. It was so close. I very nearly snapped out the unforgiveable. I felt it curling in my mouth. Only, I knew nastiness would just force him to bear his responsibility and burden me with his presence until one of us was worn down to an apology. There was no way

Robert was going to abandon me in my distress, so I knew that ultimately the apology would come from me.

Dignity made me get on the bus, but I couldn't look at him.

I didn't glance at him when the conductor took my ticket, nor when I stepped along the narrow channel between the rows to take the first available seat by the nearside window. I certainly didn't acknowledge him when I felt the springs give as he claimed the seat beside me.

And I wasn't looking at him now.

He didn't want to speak to me either. The temper ran both ways. And suddenly I was turning my head to the misted glass while the verge ran away outside, and my eyes were burning because I had the burden of knowing his retreat into silence stemmed from the shock of my mood, and this was my fault too.

I didn't want this feeling. The scenery was growing infuriatingly blurred. This was reaction, I suppose. It was slowing dawning on me that I had spent the past hour obeying a blind compulsion to go chasing after gravestones.

It felt like I was drawing my first breath after waking from the influence of that awful moment upstairs in the house, where I had been compelled to call out my husband's name. And yet I didn't even know why it should be so disturbing, except that since then the only emotion I seemed to have experienced was rage.

And now the bus was jarring unpleasantly over a pothole. This was reality. This was the flood of every normal emotion returning after the wild hunt, when the world reduced itself to the scale of a bus ride with an ordinary, rattling crowd of people. There was a woman two seats behind who was telling her neighbour all about her Christmas present to her husband. It was going to be a maroon jumper from a second-hand shop because the clothing coupons were needed for socks.

It was suddenly hard to draw a steady breath. I rummaged impatiently in my bag for an absent handkerchief and then I gave up. I focussed very hard on blinking, and did not look at Robert.

It seemed an extension of that simple determination when, between one stinging second and the next, I felt Robert move beside me. His hand passed over his lap to draw my attention. It wasn't a mark of further blame. It was simply a gesture of solidarity.

That loosened the controls as nothing else would. It hurt. I placed my hand in his and gripped him. I kept my head turned to the glass and took the gift of calm from him while the strain kept bursting upon me in waves. It would ebb and I would think I had managed to win this battle and then it would crash in again and make my eyes burn.

It was about ten minutes later that I realised I had made another fool of myself. Robert hadn't been offering me his hand at all. He had been meaning to pass me a folded and unused handkerchief.

'Oh God,' I said and practically flung his hand away.

Now every part of me was livid after all this time of feeling chilled to the core. I was blazing, really, because nothing had changed. I hadn't woken from anything. And still I didn't have a blasted handkerchief so that in the end I had to ask for his after all.

Then the bus was stopping in Cirencester and we had to climb down and walk across the town to the stop where the northbound bus would depart. We had an hour between buses but I was hardly going to suggest a cup of tea today. My eyes had dried at least, but I gripped my collar to keep out the cold and scurried along as if I might leave him behind. In fact, I truly expected him to leave me now, I was behaving so appallingly.

But his question when it came was a restrained note of grim perseverance from about a step behind me. 'Would it help you to talk about it?'

I turned my head. I said bitterly, '*Of course* it wouldn't help to talk. What on earth do you think you're playing at, anyway? You said I was formidable and why would you say something like that, when you know perfectly well that I'm not? You keep building me up and then asking me questions that prove I'm pathetic. It's as if you actually *want* to make things worse. When I'm fine as I am, thank you.'

His reply came a little later. 'You say that word a lot.'

'Which word?'

'You're "*fine*".'

'Whereas you say absolutely nothing.'

This was a repeat of an old lie.

After an inward battle with the truth, I stopped in the windswept street where we were to catch the next bus. I turned to him and finally conceded, 'Very well, you say all sorts of things; it's just that I don't always understand you. For example, everyone keeps saying that you're going to leave us, but here you are. Perhaps you *should* go, Robert. At this moment, and there's an end to it.'

It was a truly nasty thing to say, for both of us. And revealing too.

For him, it was enough to make him turn aside slightly, with hands thrust into the deep pockets of his raincoat. In this dingy light, he was looking, I don't know – remote, I suppose. For me, my remark was a deeper echo of my brutal wish to be left alone in the churchyard, only I had been too wise to speak it there.

Now, all of a sudden, I had chosen this moment to regain my voice; and all I had done with it was speak to him in a way that came close to repeating the act of taking his hand on the bus – it was another terrible mistake.

It stung, just knowing what he might read in that statement, and I couldn't have honestly said whether I was bracing to cringe away from a cold reply, or one of care.

As it was, he didn't leave, and he didn't speak. He did nothing very much, in fact, except turn his mind to the few cars which were running past on the dregs of their rationed petrol between the horse-drawn delivery wagons.

Robert's steadfast refusal to argue with me was somehow steadying. He gave me room to hope just a little that the break of my temper into speech might be my release after all; when I had at least attempted to answer his question. He had asked me to explain what was upsetting me and, in this very poor way, I suppose I must have begun.

It certainly allowed me to try again when someone needed

to squeeze past behind. Joining him in his contemplation of the thin traffic, I finally confided bleakly, 'People are going to say that the plight of the dead girl is making me confront my memories of losing Archie, aren't they?'

At last, my voice was more like my own.

'Not at all,' he replied while a bus approached – it wasn't ours. 'They'll be more likely to say that she's dredging up memories of your own abandonment after your parents gave you away. Finding her grave would mean unearthing proof that Harriet – and by extension, you – were wanted after all, wouldn't it?'

I stiffened.

I supposed I deserved this rather damning reply. It hadn't even occurred to me that there might be an alternative explanation for my agitation – that I was reacting to the more distant bruise from my childhood.

But it didn't quite fit, anyway, because I was certain that Robert knew I would find this second theory considerably easier to dismiss. He knew my aunt and uncle, after all.

He allowed himself to meet my eye. 'Lucy,' he added firmly, 'I'm trying to say that I'm with you all the way. But what do you want to do?'

He hadn't meant the barb at all.

Suddenly, I was able to breathe and notice that dusk had fallen. I thrust my hands deeply into warm pockets and confessed in a completely new voice, 'I haven't the faintest idea what I want to do. Nothing, probably, except beg to never have to go back there?'

And then, because I didn't think he was really asking about

Harriet at all, I told him, 'I had a very strange little turn upstairs in that house.'

My lips were dry. And so was my voice when I added plainly, 'In a way you really have been making things worse when I go there, because you persist in putting thoughts of my loss in my head. I wish you didn't keep feeling that you need to ask me how I am. I don't really think of myself as vulnerable as such, so it shocks me to perceive that you do. And it shocks me even more to think that you may be right to worry. Because there was a moment when I was alone in that end bedroom, when I felt I had to say Archie's name.'

'Did he answer?'

The fearsomely direct question sent a cold touch across my skin.

I shook my head. 'No. No one was there at all. Nothing but silence. Unless ghosts speak with the opposite of sound? And, honestly, I don't want him to communicate with me. It's true.'

I saw Robert's doubt. His features were being lit by the unsympathetic glare of passing headlights.

I told him quickly, 'I don't *want* to feel that Archie is near my side. I don't want to be brought to the point of believing that I have to reach out to the dead for the answers to this life.'

I faltered. I had stumbled into the type of honesty that left ripples in the mind.

It was, I suppose a little bit of proof of why I always said that people shouldn't be pushed into speaking about such dark things as their war experiences. Only now I was realising that I had only ever really meant that I shouldn't be made to talk about my own. This was like the rudeness I had thrust at him before; this was the sort of confession I would never be able to retract.

It certainly was unstoppable now. I blundered into adding earnestly, 'I am sorry, by the way, about how I've been behaving. I mean in general rather than just today. I keep growing so frustrated and I'm afraid that it does, in its way, stem from Archie. You see, you're the first man I've been friends with since him.'

'You're feeling guilty?' Robert's question was brusque. And for good reason, because this was the sort of terminology that was the usual reserve of lovers. He braved it anyway when he asked flatly, 'You feel as if you need to remain faithful to your husband?'

I cast a brief twist of amusement out into the grey dusk, but not because of the difficulty of the subject. I was amused because if I agreed with him, this idea of guilt would be such a conventional way of passing off my recent behaviour that it would probably work where all previous explanations had failed.

The temptation was there to simply accept this excuse. But I found myself saying firmly, 'No.'

My hands were still thrust deep into my pockets and they felt like miles away. 'And this isn't one of those platitudes either where I say that Archie would just want me to be happy. To be honest, if Archie's thinking of me at all these days, he certainly wouldn't be troubling himself about the small matter of my heart. Archie always was focussed on the bigger things.'

It was better to speak emphatically like this. It became a dispassionate discussion between calm adults. I added, 'When I met Archie at a tea dance, it was like falling into marriage at a breakneck speed without even really being asked. It was what nearly everyone was doing. And he was charismatic and brilliant and there was no time for delay when the abyss of the war was crowding in with the blackout.'

Abruptly, I drew an unsteady breath. This was threatening to slide into an agonised description of a beautiful man's final days, and I didn't want that either. I bit down on the pitfall and stepped into another instead.

I said, 'I'm trying to say that somehow my experiences from that time are all muddled in my head like you were the one who hurt me. I think I'm angry with you because he was fiercely committed to me – and I to him – but I barely knew him and then he was gone. And while I'm still reeling and working very hard to pretend my feet are fixed upon solid ground, someone like you *keeps* asking me how I am.'

I admitted, 'I never really knew Archie. I had no time to become friends with him. In the six weeks before he went to sea, I barely even learned the names of his family. Sometimes I think love and friendship get turned the wrong way round. I think I fall in love very easily, but it feels as if it might take me a lifetime to truly get to know a person. And when it comes to you and the questions you ask ...'

I faltered and then gathered myself for the push onwards into revealing the last. I told him clearly, 'It all belongs to friendship. And it's magnetic, when I can't bear to feel this sense of diving headlong. I don't want to live this race again, as if becoming friends is an illusion that has to be overcome quickly in the narrow space before the world charges on.'

I found that my blood felt thick and heavy.

It was very hard to catch my breath. I suppose it came as a shock to me to admit something like that.

Suddenly, I couldn't look at him again. I said on a painfully humble note directed at the kerb sweeping away from my toe, 'I'm sorry, Robert. I thought I should explain why I react so sharply whenever you make me tell you that I'm fine. And, besides, you *did* ask.'

I think I must have still been experiencing the extreme of mood that had dogged my steps since that tumble on the stairs. I found I was focusing very fiercely upon some approaching headlights, feeling the handkerchief knot itself within the grip of my hand in a coat pocket, and wishing that I had never spoken at all.

Then the bus came in. As we moved to board, I thought Robert and I were just going to pretend I hadn't said anything in the past run of minutes. But then he paused with his foot on the step to tell me, 'My sister's name is Chloe and she lives in Leicester.'

And I felt my pulse settle to a completely different rhythm, and it was like freedom.

When we reached Moreton, he walked with me through the dark to the shop door and this time he stepped inside. I thought he was searching for something from his desk, but

I saw the truth when he stepped out of his office empty-handed and it burst upon me with a sudden, unexpected laugh.

I said, 'You've known all day about my late night brush with a fleeing burglar, haven't you? That's why you were so stern this morning about the state of my hand.'

Now he was assuring himself that no one was being shut in with me tonight.

He conceded, 'The doctor and I had a chat that was surprisingly frank.'

I waited by my desk while Robert came out of his office and joined me in the angular light of my desk lamp. He was saying, 'There was some truth in your observation that we might have been better off finding another way in place of buying that paper, wasn't there? When it turns out you've been paying the price for our tomfoolery.'

He said it grimly because the injury to my hand wasn't a secret he liked. And in the process, he left me racing to calculate just how much he had really grasped about my recent run of encounters with Doctor Bates.

I was hardly going to ask him about it. Instead I said, 'If I tell you I'm fine, will you believe me?'

'No.'

Robert's quick return made me laugh again.

Then he said, 'But while we're skirting around the subject of that paper, might I ask a more personal question? Will you tell me about the plans you've inevitably been forming for your uncle's rescue?'

'My ... plans?' I was completely taken aback.

'Yes. We could make time to discuss them now, if you like?'

'Now? You mean here? Or over dinner, or something?' Somehow I was flushing. This was happiness. His confidence in me was gloriously like a continuation of all that had been confided while we were waiting for the second bus, except that my mouth was already galloping into confessing, 'I can't, I'm sorry. I've promised to put on my best frock for an old school friend's little evening party. She's recently married and enjoying showing off her dinner service. Tonight she's feeding her husband's friends so I mustn't let her down. Unless you'd like to come?'

For a moment, willingness seemed the right feeling. Then the reality of what I had just said hit me hard.

There was something excruciatingly complicated within that last question – too much like a contradiction of everything I had lately said about wishing that friendship might take a slower path.

My offer to share my evening was nothing like his simple invitation to discuss my aunt and uncle.

Nothing I did today would stay within normal bounds. Survival made me beat a retreat to the corner where the coat-stand lurked. And yet I hadn't lied just now when I had revealed the value I placed upon the idea of having his company tonight. I really hadn't.

All the same, I was making a business out of unravelling my scarf from about my neck, while every nerve in my body focused intensely upon the short distance I had created between us. The dark span of the office was practically humming with the memory of the wider space he had crossed earlier to take hold of me after my slip upon the stairs. It was like I was inviting him to revisit it.

But he didn't move. He didn't even suggest tomorrow night for dinner instead.

When he spoke, he only said gently, 'It's sweet that you would ask, but it probably isn't the done thing to turn up unannounced to another person's party. By the way, might I borrow this until the morning?'

He showed me the copy of Jacqueline's book he had carried all the while in his coat pocket.

Then he finished by wishing me a good night and framed it around the smallest serious mention of my name.

I didn't know what he meant by that. Except that he left me alone with nothing but the usual creaking floorboards and the bewildering sense that in the midst of stumbling into offering up this new small part of myself, I must have finally taken the mistakes I'd made today one stage too far.

Chapter 16

I t was hard to be at my desk by nine o'clock the next morning.
 The first minutes were an excruciating marathon of greet-
ings where I tried, at the very least, to show that I was free
of that horribly energetic excess of emotion once and for all.
My uncle bustled by and then Robert stepped in with his
collar turned up and his hat pressed down on his head. He
met me as I was fiddling about with papers, braced for stiffness while I found out how deep the alienation ran, in him
and in me.

Robert removed his hat. He returned my greeting easily.
Whatever mistakes had been made yesterday, the newfound
friendship still stood.

He made me brave enough to follow him as far as his office
doorway as he went in to take off his coat. I stood there at
the point where the light from his window met the heat from
the glowing hearth, feeling faintly uncertain but trying hard
to be bold, and asked him, 'Have you been tampering with
my advent calendar?'

Larry, the boy who helped Mr Lock in the print room, had
appeared by my desk at half past eight to ensure he got to

open the next drawer. Besides the expected boiled sweet, Larry and I had discovered a neat little sprig of foliage nestling in the tray, which I vaguely took to be marjoram.

Now Robert only moved me aside into the cramped space between the doorframe and a set of shelves so that he could hang his coat on the back of his door. As he reached for the hook, he asked, 'Tampering? No. Is it a problem for you?'

I shook my head. Dark wood was against my shoulder and behind my back. He was barely more than a foot away from me but focused upon the task at hand.

I told him, 'Miss Prichard's study of historical medical essays asserts that marjoram was used to promote a contented state of mind. With the rosemary and what I think was a very tiny piece of arrowroot, wouldn't you say that whoever is leaving me these odd little presents is, at the very least, taking care to gift me the ingredients for a good health-giving drink?'

His hand was setting his hat upon the hook as well. 'Do you think so? Well, I'm sure you'll get to the bottom of it soon.'

'By the twenty-fourth drawer, presumably.'

My remark was a test that failed. Sarcasm didn't quite have the same effect on him as it used to. This time it simply made him glance at me as he let his hand fall. Friendship really had established itself here. Comfort ran like warm silk between us when he returned to his desk.

He took a moment to tidy some papers. 'By the way,' he said, 'Mr Lock claimed Jacqueline's final edit off me as I came in this morning. I hope you don't mind? And has your uncle had time to mention that he's got the first of his notes of approval for the Willerson archive? No? It sounds as though we're going to have another very busy day.'

He looked up to catch the moment that I gave the smallest turn of my head towards the thin partition that separated his office from my uncle's. This was the first reference Robert had made to yesterday. I could remember his comment on the serious challenge ahead of easing my uncle's worries. I remembered too how Robert had denied my claim that his own commitment to this course was being driven by gratitude.

I didn't get to express my doubt a second time. We could both hear Uncle George moving about just beyond the panelled wall, preparing to bustle out to give us our instructions.

I certainly didn't get the chance to tell Robert that I had used Miss Prichard's manuscript to look up the dried plants and seed-heads we'd noticed during yesterday's visit to the Ashbrook memorial.

I didn't tell him that lavender bored the author since various ancient records had been so thoroughly reported in other histories. I didn't manage to describe, either, the entry for forget-me-not, which wasn't a true herb and could give patients a nasty case of liver damage. Teasels got a better mention because of the worm that dwelt in them and their documented use in medieval times as a remedy for fevers.

I probably didn't want to speak about any of that anyway, because then I would have been forced to admit that although my urge to read distress in every brief silence had very definitely faded with yesterday, the cure wasn't complete. Even now, Harriet's diphtheria-ridden death persisted in running like a subtle thread through almost every waking breath.

It made me take the first opportunity to reach for the telephone for the sake of calling Jacqueline.

I caught her just as she was about to go up to the house to issue new orders to her workmen. She had been putting it off because she was feeling overwhelmed by everything today.

The voice by my ear was saying, 'The list of repairs is barely shrinking, the workmen have uncovered a fault in one of the chimneys and the boys are supposed to finish school next weekend. I haven't managed to get anything ready for them.'

I heard the line crackle as if she were taking a moment to steady herself. Then she confessed, 'I feel as if I've taken on an impossible project and it's never going to come right. So what is it,' she added bravely, 'you need to tell me about the book?'

She was clearly hoping for good news, but bracing to hear bad. She made me feel terribly guilty when I had to say, 'I'm really sorry, but I'm not actually calling about the book at all. I wanted to ask what else you knew about Harriet. I'm so sorry. I shouldn't have done it.'

She showed how unhappy she was by leaving me an awful lot of room in which to ask a few minor questions. But then, all of a sudden, I heard her take a funny little breath before she broke in to say, 'Oh God. I've got to tell you that you needn't apologise for wanting to know more about that girl's origins. It isn't really the repairs to the house that are bothering me. The workmen are fine. I'm really cut up about this nasty little secret to do with Walter's treatment of his niece. It's awful, isn't it? And I did so need this place to be wholesome.'

Now I really heard a tremor in her voice. She admitted, 'Lucy, I think I must be like Graham Hanley Ashbrook. I've retired from a busy life and made the job of writing about those giraffes my distraction, my cure.'

It was the way she phrased that remark that startled me.

It was too precise. Now I asked carefully, 'The giraffes are your cure?'

'I had blood poisoning about three years ago. It started with a small insect bite on my hand.'

'Good heavens.'

It struck me with a sharp little tightening of sympathy that I had spent an awful lot of time at that house worrying about its effect upon me. I really ought to have been paying more attention to its affect upon everyone else.

She was saying, 'That's the least of it. The doctors treated the infection with M&B, as they would if you have the money to cover the expense. And you know how they say that you have to have a high chance of dying from the infection before they'll risk the chance of killing you with the treatment. I can only say that I really hope the new penicillin will be better. Antibacterial drugs are not nice.' She said it dismissively, angrily.

'No wonder,' I observed, 'you've been feeling an affinity with Graham Hanley Ashbrook.'

'Because we're both obsessive about dangerous diseases, you mean?'

I heard the breath of a humourless laugh.

'Do you know,' she added, 'that when I first moved here and discovered his account of his giraffes, it felt like starting afresh. I've been living on tenterhooks for the past few years, waiting to see if my body had managed to pick itself up from the ruins. It even overshadowed the usual worry about whether every fresh midge bite was going to set it all off again.'

'I can imagine it would.'

'So when I discovered Graham's story, it felt as if he had been waiting for me. It seemed meant. And writing this book for his memory was like a friendly wave from a patient who only survived unscathed thanks to the ground laid by many generations of old doctors like him.'

'Oh, Jacqueline.'

She told me, 'We bought the Ashbrook house as a place for my recuperation. And that's what I'm doing while I oversee the restoration. This book was supposed to be my personal contribution to the process.'

She drew a breath before plunging on. 'Only, all of a sudden I've uncovered this wretched bit of family cruelty, and it's infectious. Walter's meanness has worked its way into every corner of my mind. He's making me aware of the uselessness of my expensive little book – because who's going to read it really? And what good is it going to do?'

I had my hand up to my forehead. It was the one that had sported a bandage yesterday. Today the hand was just a little stiff and the bruise was a mildly interesting colour. It made it seem as if I had exaggerated the entire thing.

I dropped my hand and said rapidly, 'But the book's nearly done now, isn't it? It went down to the print room today. And it's wonderful and I love what you've written. Besides, the book mainly focuses upon Graham and his giraffes, doesn't it? Walter is just a footnote to their story.'

'Where the brute deserves to be, you mean? Sweet of you.'

I heard the steel in her voice when she added, 'But let's not mislead ourselves. The wretched man's claim on his father's house is everywhere. It's on that girl and those giraffes, and it's on me now. He's made me think that I don't even want to *see* the finished books.'

She hesitated, then said in a rush, 'I was in half a mind today to call you and tell you to pulp the lot, when you called me and saved me the job. Can you do that? Cancel the order, I mean?'

I said after a moment, 'I can. I could run down to the print room and ask Mr Lock to stop.'

'But I've practically paid for them, haven't I? I wouldn't get a refund?'

I felt my mind stiffen. It's what it always did whenever I found myself abruptly lurching from friendly concern into a debate about the money, even when it was being led by authors who were thoroughly keen. I always ended up feeling as if we were somehow running a fraud.

I told her in a considerably more businesslike manner, 'You've just got the balance to settle, yes. It's technically payable on receipt of the books, but we only do it that way for clarity. If we were anyone else, we'd expect payment in full before commencement of work.'

'Really?' she asked dispassionately, while I tried to avoid thinking too deeply about my uncle's likely panic if the job were to be cancelled. This was why he always insisted upon a sizeable deposit. This was why we ensured the basic cost of materials was covered from the outset. Now, if the job failed, we'd only lose the value of Robert's time and mine.

Then Jacqueline was adding, 'Of course, I've also got to think about the fact that I've been asked to give the address to the Historical Society.'

'You're delivering a speech?'

'Didn't I tell you? That's why the turnaround is so tight. That, and the fact I wanted to give the books as presents. Did you think it was for the hotel launch? When that great rotten pile clearly isn't going to be finished for months?' She laughed. 'No. I'm the guest speaker at the Historical Society Christmas Dinner. It marks the start of their centenary year, so I can tell you it's quite a coup. Harold Winterbourne was their speaker last year. He wrote *Battleship Grey;* have you read it?'

Needless to say, I hadn't.

She was racing on anyway. 'Do you know,' she said with renewed energy, 'I'm feeling a little better about it all. I'm so glad you called. Would you tell me ...? Will you tell me what you would do if you were in my position?'

This was the moment when the fraudster would step up. Jacqueline was ready to be galvanized into fresh action. She was, in fact, practically begging for encouragement. So the fraudster would tell her to commit, to finish the job, to perhaps even invest a little more into it.

It was at times like these that I could begin to believe that I must at least be reasonably nice.

I only said quite truthfully but not at all coldly, 'I really can't tell you what to do, I'm sorry. I'll still happily answer any questions you may have about the book, though.'

'Then, do it.'

'Finish the book?'

'Yes, absolutely. Finish the book. We'll show that rotten Walter John Ashbrook what an insignificant little man he is.'

She rang off.

I returned the telephone receiver to its cradle and almost immediately heard my uncle claim the line for himself in his office. The other office door – Robert's – was still firmly closed. It indicated that he was working hard to conclude the task he ought to have finished yesterday, so I invented the excuse to disturb his peace by making the morning tea round.

I began, naturally enough, by going downstairs first. And it was then that I realised that I should never have allowed myself to be prevented by personal concerns from making this tour earlier.

Because the shop was shut and was still as dimly lit as it had been when Robert and my uncle had passed through at the start of the day. Amy had left an uncharacteristically brief note upon the countertop, and it read:

Dear Lucy,

   My cold is worse so I've decided to take a few days off.
   I've seen Doctor Bates and he says that this is absolutely the right thing to do.

That last line was the part that really lodged in my mind. Her style of writing made me wonder what precisely the doctor had told her. And how much my uncle had been right to fear that the first small rumours of our decline would flow from this shop.

It also made me wonder what had passed between Robert and the doctor during their private meeting, and if it was going to turn out that Robert's discussion with the man hadn't been quite as frank as Robert had thought.

Then I noticed the way that the note was addressed to me. Amy's elegant script had placed my name at the top. And then I had to worry that Doctor Bates had helped her to decide that part too.

Chapter 17

He came to see me on Saturday. Doctor Bates found me as I was helping Mr Lock, who was floundering in the inky fug of his print room. We were battling with the first test sheet for the giraffe book. Mr Lock had been muttering over it since Friday, and I had left the shop closed today so that I could help him to finish laying out the text.

We were bending over the great table that stood at the heart of the room. It was cold in here beneath the long ridges of glass which hung overhead on fine iron girders. A potbellied stove was huffing away in the corner but I was rubbing warmth back into my hands while I observed, 'I can see at least three misspellings of Ashbrook on this page.'

I wasn't levelling an accusation. It was easy to misspell the name when the fingers hurried. Our printing machines ran on the letterpress principle, where each printed page was laid out as raised type and printed directly onto the paper. But instead of assembling hundreds of single letters of loose type by hand, Mr Lock would cast the text a line at a time in soft metal using a 1920s linotype machine.

On the test print for the first set of pages, I could see at least one Ashrbook and several Ashbroks. It was the sort of error that made me realise that when I had been tutting over the misspellings in the proof copy, they must have been Mr Lock's mistakes, not Jacqueline's.

Now Mr Lock was grumbling because today was Saturday – not his normal day for work. Tomorrow was definitely his day of rest and then Monday counted as less than two weeks before Christmas.

He was saying, 'I don't know the book. I can't tell at a glance where the errors are. We're already running tight on time to meet the author's deadline, and now I've got to go through it all, piecemeal, to compare it to the original. Or scrap the lot and start again. You do see, don't you, what the problem is?'

I did see the problem.

Our books were very small – about the size of a respectable pocket book really – so our main press was large enough to print eight pages on one sheet of paper. Efficient though this was, I knew that it took many days to produce the pages, trim them, fold them and get them stitched before he and Larry could bind them into their covers.

On the other hand, I also knew that for once I was in the position of being able to state that I had read the book, so I could find the errors. I would mark up the test print myself and it would be simple enough then to replace the faulty lines with him on Monday.

This was one of the wonderful benefits of laying out the text in lines like this. Single lines could always be altered without having to remake the entire set.

Only I didn't get the chance to say any of that because I saw Mr Lock's eyes flick beyond me. 'Can we help you, Doctor?'

I've never moved so quickly from complacency into sharp attention in my life. Mr Lock and I were standing at the heart of this cluttered old workshop. Our neighbours were the presses and the copper kettles which filled this place with a disgusting smell of fish glue on binding days.

Doctor Bates, on the other hand, was standing at the mouth of the arched passage from the street front, where he had no right to be, and staring at us.

Doctor Bates seemed to think that we were accosting someone else at first. He was dressed in the long coat of a respectable man-about-town, and beneath the customary mass of fair hair, his eyes coursed the old rough stonework of the office building. They ran to the vacant door that gave access to the back of the shop, then drifted back to me. He explained, 'I was hoping to speak to Mrs P.'

He seemed confident, as though I should be pleased, and all of a sudden I was wooden.

'How did you get in?' My voice was brittle.

'Through the coach doors?' It wasn't said with any kind of swagger, just plain honesty. 'The shop door was locked, but they weren't.'

I was thinking that I really needed to have a private word with Mr Lock about leaving the place more secure when he was working here out of hours.

I was also thinking that the doctor didn't seem very aware that he was guilty of trespassing here a second time.

The paper that had inspired his original break-in was there

behind us in the racks that lined the workshop wall. He didn't so much as glance at it. He also wasn't quite acting like a man who was busily recalling his last encounter with me.

Instead, his question was insistent but very mild. 'Might we have a chat?'

I felt Mr Lock's curious glance at my face. I was feeling curious too. Doctor Bates didn't seem to be assessing my delight at being near him again. So then it occurred to me to be afraid that if this visit wasn't for me and it wasn't for that paper, it had to be for the sake of giving me a few more searing judgements about Robert's fitness to work here.

I was afraid the doctor had gathered new material during the visit Robert had paid him. I thought he might be about to cast me once again as his ally. In which case, I very much did not wish Mr Lock to hear what I would have to say in reply.

It was when I came downstairs after fetching my coat, that I really felt I was back in that misunderstanding from my last encounter with the doctor.

He met me at the turn on the stairs as I stepped back down from the office. He surprised me in the same dark corner that carried the memory of that interview by the shop counter.

Behind me was the shadow that must have concealed him in the dead of night when my hand had been caught by the door. And today he came here as if this old stairwell didn't still echo with the memory of how he had subsequently tried to turn every word of blame back to Robert.

He did it amiably, charmingly and quite as if I hadn't, in

fact, specifically asked him just now to wait for me downstairs with Mr Lock in the print room.

I took him to the little teashop by the Curfew Tower. I did it very plainly after explaining my plan about the edits to Mr Lock, and without leaving Doctor Bates any room this time to misunderstand my wishes.

I poured the tea, and then I asked coolly, 'What is this "little chat" about, Doctor?'

'I need to tell you that I am going to marry Amy.'

I have to admit that this wasn't remotely the reply I was expecting.

I set the teapot down and abruptly sat back in my seat. It was my first moment of truly examining my companion's face. He didn't look threatening at all. In the fussy setting of teapots and tablecloths, I saw fair eyelashes lift beneath that boyish tangle of hair and then he gave a small and amiable shrug.

He added, 'I thought you ought to know. First, I mean, before Amy gives notice to Mr Kathay. I arranged it that she would wait for a few days.'

Suddenly I was laughing. I wasn't afraid at all any more of how my manners might be interpreted. Relief was easy. I fiddled with the placing of my teacup and said with an attempt at seriousness, 'Congratulations. Has this been coming on for long?'

'For some time, yes.' The set of his mouth implied that laughter was not perhaps the most polite reaction I could have had.

Then, a different aspect of this struck me. He had implied that he had needed me to know first.

All of a sudden, there was something deeply unnerving in this man's mildness as he sat opposite me in this gentrified tearoom. I watched as the expression on his mouth moulded itself into sympathy.

The doctor remarked with the gravitas of a professional giving dreadful news, 'Perhaps you should take some sugar in your tea.'

'Whatever for?'

'Amy was afraid we might upset you. I said I'd talk to you.'

'Don't be absurd, Doctor Bates.'

Because he knew I wasn't distressed. And I was pretty certain he hadn't come here to tell me that I was in love with him, either. Regardless of what he remembered of our odd slide into intimacy during that highly-strung conference over my bandaged hand, he couldn't have come to confront me about it. Because if he was here, publicly, that meant he wasn't remotely afraid that the ensuing scene might embarrass his future wife.

And yet the doctor was saying quite genuinely, 'She *was* worried. We both are.'

With my eye on the teapot and thinking I really didn't want to play this game any more, I asked, 'Why?'

'Do you know, I worry about you, Mrs P. We don't want you to be alone.' He said it kindly, in a way that made me shiver.

It was the mention of my married name that did it. He was talking about a specific kind of loneliness to do with the loss of my husband.

Bracingly, he remarked as if we were finally getting down to business, 'I was bemused to find that it was Robert Underhill who visited me on Wednesday and not you. It told me precisely what place that man has in your uncle's office. And I should have thought *you'd* have an opinion about what that means.'

'Please, Doctor Bates. I don't want to speak about Robert any more.' He'd swept on as if this still related to that reference to loss, but I couldn't quite see how. I said clearly, 'Don't you think we discussed his apparent failings enough the other day? I don't want to hear anything you have to say about him. And I most definitely do not wish to hear what new dire accusations you can add after his visit to you at your home. So if you'll excuse me, I'll—'

He didn't let me finish my attempt at a neat goodbye. He stopped me in the midst of gathering up my handbag and gloves by saying 'Surely, you must realise by now that Amy is going to leave you alone in that office?'

My brows furrowed. It was Doctor Bates' turn to show amusement because I was still missing the point. He surprised me by saying earnestly, 'You'll be the only woman. And I was entirely wrong, you know, about Robert Underhill. My old lecturer painted a very inaccurate picture of the man, and I don't think he's going to leave you all in the mess of your uncle's failing business at all. I think he means to stay.'

My heart gave one unpleasant jerk in my chest as I gave up my attempt to rise from my seat. I set my handbag down again.

I stared at him as he added, 'In fact, I'd go so far as to admit that Robert Underhill was unexpectedly decent when he came to see me the other day. And I believe Mr Underhill when he says that he counts himself a friend to you, and your aunt and uncle. Which is rather telling, don't you think?'

I might have thought he was hinting about feelings – Robert's and mine – except that I just didn't trust that I could ever fully understand this man, and I didn't think he was ever going to be capable of reading me. I said carefully, 'I don't know what you mean by that.'

The doctor adjusted the arrangement of the tea things to make better room for telling me, 'I think it's time, Mrs P, that we considered your place in your uncle's business. And how that relates to Mr Underhill seniority as your uncle's right-hand man.'

I'd been right to distrust him. He was saying, 'I'm trying to observe that we already know Underhill feels a certain degree of responsibility for you all. I think you need to consider how much that feeling extends to the long-term upkeep of your uncle's business. If Underhill thinks he's got an important duty to fulfil there, do you really think he's going to just quietly hand all that down to the woman who answers the telephone when your uncle George Kathay retires?'

The doctor was adding in a low voice, 'Amy and I are terribly worried about you. You're a widow. You're alone with no one to safeguard your future unless your friends step in.'

Suddenly, I began to understand. I should have guessed when he had given such emphasis to my married name. I said slowly, 'You aren't trying to bully me. You're trying to warn me. You're speaking about the struggle I'll have to keep my place at the helm when my uncle retires. You're telling me that I'm about to lose my livelihood to the better man.'

Doctor Bates was nodding as if I had given him the clear answer that would end this. He had given his warning, he had done his duty and now he could move on. But then his mouth moved and he said, 'Were you never formally adopted? Were you known as Miss Kathay as a child?'

The muscles in my jaw tightened. He was hinting about my inheritance, but there was an awful lot about ownership in that question, or belonging or something. My voice was acid. 'I kept my father's name.'

I set my cup aside with an unsteady but determined hand. I said, 'Let me be perfectly clear, Doctor Bates. I do not have and never have had any claim on my uncle's property in that way.'

I saw his eyebrows rise. I told him, 'They may have brought me up, but I have no expectations on that score. As far as I'm concerned, they're fully within their rights to keep the business, sell it, gift it to Robert; anything, if that is what they want.'

Doctor Bates looked as if I had just betrayed the utter loneliness of being me. He leaned in to confide sadly, 'I can't help thinking that the swiftest solution here would be to take back control now, before it's too late. I know you don't want to face the real error Robert Underhill made by buying that paper, but it needn't injure your uncle, if we're careful.'

'No.'

He took my negative as a question. He assured me, 'Absolutely. I believe I know the man well enough to suggest which few well-placed words from you might do the trick. Let's help him to realise that he really ought to go away, shall we, and restore your peace of mind?'

It was like he was promising to speak to Robert for me, man to man.

He meant it as an act of kindness. An unanswerable, undeniable act of charity. And now I really was close to the distress the doctor was expecting. The feeling belonged to the burning realisation that this man had convinced himself that I needed a friend; someone, anyone to act for me to preserve my income. Since I had no one else to keep me, not even a husband.

This ridiculously stuffy teashop was smothering me. I said unsteadily, 'Why are you doing this?'

This was an extension of that infuriating intimacy that had grown from the injury to my hand, only it wasn't quite the same because the doctor didn't like me. He wasn't even afraid that I liked him. We certainly weren't friends. And that was when it struck me.

I said on a low note of realisation, 'You've come to me because you're trying to patch up your own mistake again. The simple truth is that you can't bear the memory of nearly kissing the wrong person. So instead you've reduced me in your mind to something less than the level of a woman. You've decided that I'm fragile and needy, and you've used that detail to talk yourself – and Amy – into doing this last noble deed to save me.'

He didn't fully understand me. He blustered, 'But you *are* vulnerable. You're a widow.'

I added in a voice made flat by the force of trying very hard to be utterly, uncompromisingly clear in every word, 'Can't you just go off and marry Amy and be happy, and leave me to muddle along by myself?'

I can't describe how painful it was to finally grasp that the term 'widow' wasn't mine to define. Some years ago, when the news had been fresh, I had imagined my relationship with my past marriage would be a private matter; personal and wholesome, like the memories I had of the man who had given me his name.

Here, though, the term was worse than a shackle upon my capacity for independent thought. Today, the fumbling steps of Mrs Lucinda Peuse also seemed to be tainting Robert's choices and the future of my uncle's business.

Before this man could find words to contain me further, I asked rather more pertinently, 'Do you love her?'

I was beginning to feel concerned for Amy. I didn't want to have to learn that this man was my enemy. I didn't want to find myself deciding that the pleasant, uncomplicated woman who ran my uncle's shop needed my help.

She had chosen Doctor Bates after being his friend for a long time, and I didn't want to assume responsibility for her welfare with the same damaging fervour I was experiencing here.

So I did what I could to seize authority with the tools within my grasp. I surprised him with my question. I leaned in and repeated, 'Do you love Amy?'

The doctor stumbled into speaking with the most honesty I had heard from him yet. He nodded and confessed shyly, 'When you popped upstairs after our little chat on Wednesday morning and she stepped in from speaking to Mr Lock, I'm afraid it just stuck me there and then who I had been visiting all this time. You're nice to look at, but she's ... well, whatever she is, I tripped headlong into asking her. I don't want you. I want Amy Briar. And she wants to be my wife.'

He was flushing his way into a complicated smile. If anything, I suddenly had the impression he was near to tears. Doctor Bates wasn't predatory. He was desperate to be free of me.

I began to gather my coat and my handbag. I said quite seriously, 'Well then, Doctor. I wish you and Amy every happiness, and that's that, really, isn't it? There's nothing else to be said. I do not wish you to think of me. I don't want you to interfere in my choices. I don't want you to steer me or otherwise manage my business at all. Good day Doctor Bates. And thank you for the tea.'

This was, I'm afraid, a rapid bit of management of my own. Of myself, I mean. I knew that if I didn't tell the man plainly what I wanted from him – which was nothing at all – I would only end by feeling responsible for whatever he decided to do next.

After that, I went home. I attacked the edits to Mr Lock's test print in a silent and deserted office. I was still pretending that the giraffe book was occupying every thought in my mind when I was called down the stairs about five hours later by a light knock upon the locked door of the shop.

My visitor was Robert and he greeted me cheerfully with, 'I've been sent by your aunt and uncle to fetch you to our council of war.'

Chapter 18

It seemed to me that my life was set to always swing from one extreme to the other these days. My first step that evening into my old childhood home was a blast of merry bustle. I had expected to be met by the first scheme in a plan of campaign. But all I had was the sudden brightness of the hallway, with Robert beside me as we struggled our way out of our coats after the bleak cold of the night outside.

We could hear my aunt and uncle in the front room. My aunt had just finished wrestling with the Christmas tree. This wasn't a real tree, just a wooden contraption that was basically a collapsible many-pronged coat stand, with boughs that were hinged from the main trunk. It always developed a list in the third week.

Today it was upright and bare, and when I moved into the light of the doorway into the front room, I found that Aunt Mabel was glowering upwards at the bands of crepe paper Uncle George was running across the ceiling.

'It isn't straight, George. You'll have to do it again. Hello dear.'

This was another one of those wonderfully familiar patterns

of this household, like the baking of the Christmas cake and the drinking of the sherry. The paper was ancient and patched and irreplaceable because, as I believe had been observed once or twice in recent days, new stock was in very short supply.

Robert passed me to take up one of many cardboard stars from the footstool as Aunt Mabel told him, 'That's supposed to unfold like a fan to make its finished shape. I think it's broken.'

I saw the way my aunt smiled at him when he held up the flimsy bit of cotton which was meant to hold the whole thing together. I was dispatched to the bay window with decorations for the tree.

The decorations were a potted history of generations. Paper and glass more ancient than memory dwelt in this box to be greeted like old friends each year. The small and bespeckled ceramic mushrooms always seemed to me to be an odd choice.

Robert must have thought so too. As he came near me to hang the star upon the picture rail, he asked me, 'Why *have* you got mushrooms?'

I studied the little decoration standing proud on its wire fastening as I held it between finger and thumb.

It turned slightly, as I repeated what my aunt had once told me, 'They were my Great-Aunt Gert's.'

She'd said it as if that answered everything, which in a way I suppose it did.

Family folded round me like a cloak. Peaceful and assuring me that this was why my steps had brought me home. It was peculiar to go from such simple happiness to the discovery that my uncle had come in with a tray and was offering us a glass of something.

It was my aunt's fearsome homemade dandelion wine. Robert was reaching to take his own drink and saluting me with it in a discreet and silent toast. I didn't quite know what he meant. It wasn't about festive things. It was more personal; a mild way of saying 'over to you'.

I sipped my drink and found that a sudden flurry of activity had directed Robert to take the armchair that nestled in the space between the fire and the bay window. My uncle was already sitting on the settee that ran along the hall wall. My aunt took her place beside her husband and then looked at me. She was laughing at me quite affectionately because I looked stranded somehow, as if I had missed a vital cue.

Then Robert was getting up again and offering me his armchair while he went to claim a hard dining chair from the kitchen and I was saying quickly, 'Don't bother, please.'

I sat down abruptly upon the round footstool that had been pushed aside into the space between Robert's armchair and the prongs of the Christmas tree. I found I was flushing a little when Robert finally reclaimed his seat beside me. I hadn't anticipated that instinct would make me take the spot quite so near him or that my uncle would instantly begin teasing Robert into admitting that the offer of the armchair had been hollow anyway. I saw Robert's grin. It was all so homely.

And it was in its way an answer to Doctor Bates' many and varying ideas about the nature of my place in my uncle's world. The doctor had never seen this side of things. The experience shook me into acknowledging what I had known for some time: that Robert belonged amongst these people too.

I didn't intend to be the one who ruined it for him.

Abruptly, certainty defeated the nervousness that was working like a worm upon my capacity for speech.

It shook off the sense that I was feeling a little like a spectator of this bustling scene. It had been a familiar sensation of late. I will admit here and now that sometimes I have this insane feeling that it wasn't Archie who died, but me. That I had succumbed to one of those dreadful near misses in the Blitz on Bristol.

It has felt sometimes that this pathetic craving I have for the old comfort of my childhood home is a stretched out memory ringing endlessly in those last few seconds of thought while life fades. And that my refusal to attend one of my mother's séances in my husband's name had grown from the fear of having to learn it was my name she meant to use; and that it was my soul that needed guiding into what lies beyond.

I have sometimes caught myself listening to the sound of my breathing just to establish one of the usual patterns that went with living.

This was the opposite of one of those moments.

I knew I was very much alive. And very much present. I could feel the way my hand was smoothing my skirts over the neat fold of my legs as I perched very near to the floor. Every muscle was sensitive of the warm glow of my aunt's cosy living room as I sat up and lifted my head. My voice interrupted my uncle as he was explaining that the Willerson archive would be a good step in the right direction if it finally went to print, but it would only keep things afloat.

'You're perfectly right,' I agreed. 'Publishing the Willerson archive won't rebuild what you've lost. But you might make things easier upon yourself if you'll consider leasing the business to me.'

I probably said that a shade too earnestly. My gaze ran from my uncle's face to my aunt's, faltered and ran back again. After a dumbfounded silence, my uncle mustered nothing more than a blank, 'Right.'

I could tell my aunt was going to follow him by explaining reasonably how I'd ever so slightly misunderstood the point of this meeting. My own seriousness made me laugh at myself. Because the doctor had repeatedly attempted to galvanize me into working to unseat Robert's claims on my uncle's business, and this might well have seemed like the start of it. Only it wasn't.

I began saying sheepishly and considerably more naturally, 'Do people ever lease a business? I thought they did but now I've said it, the idea sounds a bit off-kilter. What I mean to say, Uncle George, is that I gather that you keep thinking about retiring, but as it stands you can't actually do anything about it until you've got the business into a state where you can reclaim some of that lost capital?'

'In a manner of speaking, yes. But that doesn't mean that you—'

I saw the movement as my aunt put her hand upon her husband's arm to discourage him from correcting me. I experienced a sudden memory of being quizzed as a child on my spellings as my uncle sat there on his deep settee, fingers pinching the stem of a small port glass – the only size suitable for his lethal brews – while my aunt urged leniency upon an affectionate man whose angular frame was clad in a pale blue jumper that was fine enough for his braces to show through.

Blinking through the force of the memory, I repeated seriously, 'You could lease out the business, couldn't you? You could lease it to me or Robert, and I ... we ... or Robert or I could muddle our way through one job at a time until things were more robust once more. Whichever of us did it, you'd certainly stand a reasonable chance of getting some form of pension.'

I knew I didn't sound sensible. I could feel Robert's attention on my profile, like a touch from his mind. He at least had noticed the way I had drawn his name into this scheme. I didn't know whether he liked it. And I could feel the counterargument brewing in the older couple sitting upon the settee where they would explain that the business couldn't support three salaries – mine, my uncle's and Robert's.

There was no way it could support a pension if the workforce were to be reduced to just the two of us. And aside from that I had the tangle of knowing that everyone here had expected Robert to take the lead, and yet I didn't seem to be leaving much room for him to talk.

I found myself hoping vehemently that they could at least see that this was different from the last meeting I'd shared with the two men; that this was being inspired by more than a stubborn refusal to sit quietly while my uncle and Robert sorted it out between them.

My attention was drawn by the brief and private flare of Robert's own brand of seriousness as he leaned forwards to prop his elbows upon his knees. He meant to speak to me.

But his gaze was drawn across the room by my aunt's brisk query. 'Do you mean, Lucy, that we should pass the shortfall along the line?'

She always did hide a very precise nature behind the homeliness. I suppose it was what made her equally a fearsomely capable cook, typist, telephonist and draughtswoman.

A bauble from the tree lightly brushed my shoulder as I stirred to say carefully, 'I mean to say that by working at it piecemeal, time isn't on Uncle George's side. It'll take too long to save up again.' I heard my uncle sniff and I added, 'I'm sorry, Uncle, this isn't a terribly tactful thing to say. But you *have* been talking about retirement.'

I added, 'If you lease the business to me – or Robert – we can agree a fixed income, or at least I think we can. We still have to work out if the business would be able to pay you enough to make it feasible. But the main point is that if we do it this way, it won't be you who spends the next run of years reclaiming that lost capital, and there won't be such a fearsome deadline. It might take ages to break even; it might not even be possible. But all the same it won't matter any more, because we'll be meeting the work. And you'll be getting your pension.'

From my place on my little footstool between the watchful scrutiny of Robert, the tree and my relatives, I felt the force of all the assumptions I was making about Robert's involvement.

'Why would you do this for us?' This was from Uncle George. This was like that meeting I had joined in his office, when I had suggested that he and Robert had been wrong to pursue a certain course. There was a grimness here that rang painfully like disapproval and a hint that I was overlooking some of the harder arguments.

It was then that I was suddenly struck on a very faint but doubtful note by the memory of all those ill-founded comments from the doctor about my upbringing and the question of an inheritance. I had the excruciating suspicion that this sounded like I was undertaking the sort of manoeuvrings that would force these people to put my name very specifically into their Will.

I tried not to fidget upon my footstool. This was not why my aunt and uncle had sent Robert to bring me here. I hadn't even let them speak. I was rubbing my hand upon my arm as I reached for a better excuse than a mildly apologetic, 'I think my solution suits your nature better than the one you were going to suggest.'

My uncle sniffed his disapproval again. 'I was going to explain how we might work quickly to pursue more new authors.'

I countered him gently, knowing I was straying from kindness into going too far. I sensed Robert's stillness in his armchair as I said, 'Yours is a policy which depends on growth. The pursuit of new customers is a natural strategy for any decent businessman, I know that. But how are you even going to achieve growth, when legally you're only permitted to buy enough paper to output the same volume of books as you did eight years ago at the outbreak of war?'

I saw my uncle stir. He believed I had just tried to scold him about the purchase of that blasted Nuneham's paper yet again.

But it was then that Robert surprised me by speaking from his armchair. 'You don't need to invent arguments here, Mr Kathay. You don't need to protect Lucy from her own generosity. Because she isn't acting entirely selflessly.'

Robert eyes didn't stray from their steady gaze across the room when I turned my head, but I saw the flicker as he registered my look all the same. He told the older man, 'She's pursuing the course that is most likely to lead to her success. You don't even have to retire here. Under her terms, this can simply count as an insurance policy.'

'Insurance?' This was a question from my aunt.

'For all of you. Because she isn't even offering to buy the business on instalments as any normal person might. And you don't have to retire, Mr Kathay. You can lead this business for as long as you like. It remains your business. But you can at least rest safe in the knowledge that if you *do* take Lucy's proffered pension, you'll be helping her too.'

He paused before adding, 'She might be committing herself to a lease she can barely afford. But at the same time, she'll also be tying her name to your business's reputation. She'll use it to build an increasing list of published works of her own. This isn't a simple act of self-sacrifice, Mr Kathay.'

I wasn't entirely sure I liked his summary of my motivation. But I certainly noticed that he had excluded himself from this plan. He was smoothing out the potential for misunderstanding between me and my relatives, when he might have used their confusion to introduce an offer of his own.

I told him before I had thought, 'I haven't forgotten the promise you asked of me, you know.'

I saw him jump and then blink his way into the memory. He understood what I was saying about letting him join me in my future work, but he didn't exactly like the way I was reminding him of his request now. That made something stronger than embarrassment drag my mind down to the glass in my hand.

The partially consumed contents were swirling and glittering gold in the depths. Dandelion wine was delicious but fierce, like water mixed delicately with a musky kind of fire.

Miss Prichard had plenty to say about this drink. A number of ancient records existed for its use as a health tonic. And all the while the man who had given me her manuscript was sitting very near to me. I thought he was studying what little he could see of my face while I turned my head away. Even the thought of it made me feel exposed. In fact, it was the same feeling that had struck me when he had left me in the office after that last bus ride. It had been like being met by the very deepest kind of care, except that he always retained certain boundaries.

I had a horrible feeling then that the doctor had been entirely wrong when he had listed friendship amongst Robert's reasons for deciding to stay. So wrong in fact, that I ought to have been perceiving that every one of Robert's generous efforts on my uncle's behalf with the paper – and now for my sake in this room – were all meant as a gift before saying farewell.

Chapter 19

It was two hours later and about nine o'clock when I stepped into the hall to put on my coat.

My aunt was there to help me. She was warm and pink from the wine and the general energy of the evening's party after that serious discussion. I expect I was too. It hadn't all been deeply thoughtful. There had been laughter and my uncle's idea of witty puns.

Now Aunt Mabel was passing me my hat. She was pretending to be fussing about whether or not I needed walking home, which I most definitely did not. The comfort that had been batted about her living room was almost more intoxicating than the wine. It was certainly heating enough to make me relieved that I was going alone into a confrontation with the teeth of the dark wind outside.

Robert was in his armchair anyway, still talking to my uncle. My uncle was fiddling about tuning the wireless for the nine o'clock news.

I tipped my head at the wall as I wound my scarf about my neck. 'Is that a routine they've enjoyed before?'

I expected her to smile. My aunt had turned her head to

the sound of male companionship as well. Then she caught me watching, gave me one of those energetic beams where affection, worry and denial met all in one place, and finally buried it all by thrusting a second unnecessary scarf at me.

She said, coiling it around my neck, 'You didn't mind having Rob here tonight, did you?'

She was patting my hand where it had paused in helping her to smooth the bulky fabric. For a moment, this was all too close to sounding like a continuation of the conversation I'd had with the doctor, where people misunderstood the things I said.

Then my aunt betrayed that she hadn't really meant to ask me that anyway. She asked instead, 'It wasn't too much for him, was it?'

I experienced a sensation that was like a cold breeze passing over the skin on the back of my neck.

Because she was nervous, seeking reassurance, and then her attention returned to me in time to catch the dismay on my face. 'Aunt Mabel?'

I didn't think that such instant sympathy was the reaction my aunt expected. 'Oh,' she said, blinking as if she'd made a mistake. 'I shouldn't have said that. I'm not trying to complicate things. I was just thinking out loud, so don't mind me. Anyway,' she added brightly, sweeping onwards, 'it was nice getting the decorations up, wasn't it? I must ask Rob whether this means he'll join us now for Christmas dinner. We'll have one of the chickens from next-door's garden, as always. You know the form, don't you? There's a reason why we give them all our scraps.'

It was her chatter that made me brave. I found that I was folding my fingers gently around the worried knot of her hand. I pitched my voice to fall below the murmur of the wireless next door to say on a very odd note, 'You believe that Robert's leaving too, don't you?'

Aunt Mabel froze.

I added in that same undertone, 'I *thought* it strange that Uncle George was happy to sit by while Robert dashed about visiting Nuneham's. All this business of hiding the paper from me and keeping Robert at home while I took the attic; it wasn't about protecting me, it was about him. You've been keeping Robert busy until he can't help but forget his urge to wander. And now I've thrust my way in, and you're terribly afraid that I've made him notice that you've been working hard all this time to keep him here.'

'Yes,' she confessed desperately.

My aunt wasn't frozen any more. She had been returning the pressure of my hand. Now she was clasping my hand between both of hers and adding equally desperately, 'And yet no.'

Her voice was an urgent whisper, 'We won't blame *you* if he goes away. I mean, you're right about the attic and our desperate wish that he'll stay. But the rest ... you've got it all the wrong way round. Your uncle and I aren't keeping him tied down with work. We're so afraid that we've been asking too much of him.'

She was staring at her old hands as they enclosed mine. She was tilting her head as though the thought hurt as she told the tangled grip, 'The wretched purchase of that paper is only the end of it. Without that young man's help, we'd have been ruined months ago. Rob's arrival in the spring came at just the right moment to help your uncle. I was in a very bad way back then. It was all falling apart. Deadlines were being missed catastrophically.'

Her hands were moving ceaselessly, wringing mine as she admitted, 'We were going to have to tell you about it and beg you to come back from Bristol, only we didn't want to do it because it wasn't fair. But then Rob landed in a heap at our feet.'

She drew breath and added on a courageous note, 'Your uncle picked him up and gave him a job and he was good at it. We knew we shouldn't learn to lean on him, but he turned out to be so reliable. We should never have allowed it to get to the point of letting him take over the job of chasing about after that ridiculous paper.'

Her hands stilled. 'But your uncle couldn't manage it. He was just getting cheated. And you know why we didn't tell you. You had enough to deal with. Rob made us believe that this was what he wanted.'

I couldn't help the way my mouth tightened to a line. This was a fresh brush with the wrench of the many heartfelt discussions I'd shared with Robert, where he had acknowledged the strain he'd been under, and yet still he'd been very clear that he was willing to do it anyway.

Eventually, I said, 'Has he ever explained *why* he's been so ready to help?'

She didn't fully understand my question. She only confided sadly, 'I've realised that Rob's dependable quality is the part of him that his wretchedly unbending parents try to prey on. You won't know this but he went abroad with some of his young friends from his university. He was captured with one of them. And then the lad ended up on the floor of the camp with a bullet in his lung.'

'I know,' I admitted with a cautious glance towards the wall between us and the other room. The wireless was masking anything we said. 'Robert told me about it. At least, in part.'

I saw her blink, and her surprise. 'Did he?'

And then I saw acceptance and the gradual change to her thoughts. Her next words were deeper, harder and pitched perfectly to raise the hairs on the back of my neck. 'In that case I think I'm free to tell you that I have no doubt the prison guard very nearly put a bullet in Rob for it too. But by far the worst part it for me is the way his family must have seized upon it as soon as he came home. They harped on about it as if he'd led those boys there – as if those bright young men didn't all go in for the adventure together.'

She faltered for a moment.

Then the rage bubbled. 'Rob doesn't say it, but between you and me, I think his parents believe they have a duty to make him admit the mistake he made. They actually lectured him on getting down to work in his medical career and bearing up a little better in the face of his *responsibilities*.'

My hand was almost being crushed by hers but I was hardly going to mention it. I didn't want disturb her as she remarked fiercely, 'Personally, I've always admired how Rob seems quietly purposeful in his way.'

I saw her chin lift with a certain degree of defiance. But

then she had to blink very rapidly as she added, 'Recently, though, I've begun to be afraid that he really might be pushed into leaving us. I've had to consider whether or not we're behaving as his parents do. I'm afraid that we're exploiting him too.'

'Surely not. I—'

But she was already plunging into admitting, 'You see, I know we've been asking too much, just like they did. He's been so wearied sometimes after he's come back from one of his trips, but still we've let him go again.'

Her voice fractured. 'We need him and we love having him here ... But we aren't noticing that we're hurting him.'

Through the wall, I could hear that Uncle George had turned his attention to the wireless and was cheerfully disagreeing with everything the newsreader said. In this hallway, the yellow and brown wallpaper was clashing horribly with my aunt's vivid blue frock.

I heard my voice in the midst of this flood to the senses like it was something remote saying, 'But, surely, Robert must have told you how he feels about staying here?'

'He says everything is fine.'

'Well then.'

My practical note only went skin-deep, but I wasn't expecting it to make her react in the way that it did. She extricated one of her hands to give a very motherly pat to my cheek.

She said gently, 'Bless you, Lucy. But don't you know you say that all the time too?'

She actually made me laugh.

No sooner had I been shocked back into the fullest sense of being the child of this house, than she abandoned her concerns about Robert for the sake of turning her mind to me.

Suddenly, she was my strong, indomitable aunt. I knew she was going dig deeper into that idea she and my uncle had that I hadn't been fit to bear their troubles when I had first returned home. She was going to ask me about Archie.

It had, after all, happened often enough lately that I thought I ought to be able to recognise the signs.

She was already saying, 'It really was all right, wasn't it, having Rob here tonight?'

I'd been wrong. The turn of her care wasn't what I had thought. I felt half a bewildered smile form upon my lips. Because we were back to this question again and I wasn't sure how deep it ran.

I said cautiously, 'Of course?'

My aunt was flushing. She was beaming at me like she was sure we understood each other. She was saying earnestly, 'I mean, you mustn't mind him, must you? Not if you already know him well enough that he could share all that about his past? I wasn't sure. I'm so relieved. I couldn't be certain you'd let us know if you were feeling uncomfortable. And I could hardly ask, could I, because I wasn't confident that you were ready to think like that about anyone, and what if your uncle and I made everything complicated just by putting the thought in your mind?'

'Put what in my mind?' I blundered, stupefied, and yet at the same time I was feeling the headlong dive into something appallingly like fear just because of the lurch of daring to guess.

As it was though, I didn't get to define what I was guessing at. She must have thought she had made another mistake. The change came with the same swiftness she had used before, when she had veered into speaking about Christmas chickens.

In the next moment I found that she was asking briskly, 'Where would you have lived, do you think, if he'd come home?'

'*Archie?*'

It was impossible to leap from one man to the other. She did it like this was an easier turn. Whereas I was crashing into admitting clumsily, 'I have absolutely no idea where I would have lived. I suppose if I had ever dared to think that far ahead, I must have assumed that Archie's passion for steam would sweep me along with him to somewhere busy and industrial. It would have been an adventure.'

My aunt was nodding. We all knew he would never have picked the quiet country town of Moreton. She was saying cheerfully, 'I always told myself that at least we had the comfort of knowing you hadn't married a man who would fix you in some rustic idyll.'

This was a return to that old joke about my dislike of farming. And it changed my understanding of every giddy current in this conversation.

Because the truly important detail I should share here, is that the entire joke was founded upon a lie.

I had never hated farming. I had no particular aversion to sheep or mud or country things. And if I bore any scars at all from that childhood move from my parents' house, it was probably the weight of this endless charade.

I had been brought up to feel loved by both places, the farmhouse and this printworks, but I hated the urge everyone had to explain away my move as if it had somehow been my choice. They made me suspect that they were doing it to hide something cruel. They made it impossible to ever fully escape the belief that at some point I was going to have to accept the simple truth that none of these people had ever wanted me, and it was just convenient to pretend that I had brought it upon myself.

That wasn't true either, though. The charade was another mark of care. How could anyone explain to a child that she had been considered surplus to requirements at the age of four? My parents couldn't, and Aunt Mabel certainly couldn't.

If I had forced the issue, my aunt would probably have admitted the ugly, unhealthy part; that if she blamed Robert's parents for working to keep him close, she also could never quite forgive my parents for being willing to let me go. And that sort of truth would have injured all of us – me, my parents and everyone – because at some point the rift would have cut too deep.

So we maintained the falsehood. And tonight, in this hallway, my aunt used the same joke to conceal a different emotional pitfall.

I thought that in the midst of all those disjointed questions, she had been asking if I would mind sharing her Christmas dinner with Robert.

So, first of all, I told her as if it didn't hurt me, 'I'd like to do this again. With the four of us, I mean. I don't want him to go either.'

Then I reached out a hand to lift a stray fragment of crepe paper from Aunt Mabel's hair, handed it to her and said seriously, 'I love you.'

'We know, dear,' she replied calmly. 'But after all you've said this evening about the survival of our business, please don't do anything reckless like work too hard, or try to make up your uncle's losses by working for a pittance, or anything silly like that, would you? We need to improve your wages as it is, and, besides, I may not be at the office any more but I still check the accounts each month. So don't imagine we wouldn't notice anything untoward.'

I asked, aghast, before I had thought, 'Did Robert tell you that I planned to do that?'

'No, dear,' she said gently. I had surprised her again but this time she chose not to remark on the news that the second editor and I had confided in each other. She merely told me kindly, 'I just guessed.'

Then she sent me home.

Chapter 20

The street outside was practically black. In the distance, the distinctive shape of the Curfew Tower was a single block of whitened stone near a streetlamp. A few shops and hotels showed light behind their curtains, and that was all the glimpse I had of this old familiar town.

I had gone away from this life because of the war. And stayed away afterwards because I hadn't been quite ready to think of what else to do.

Now the adjustment in my mind came gently like the settling of a cloud of dust. I had been wondering for a while if I had to remember I was a woman. At last I could see that the change was more magnificent and yet more solitary than that. It was a new sense of being fixed in this body, and walking with these two feet through this darkened night towards my own future here.

Which was why it was such a powerful endnote to the thought when I was stopped about twenty yards beyond my aunt's front door by a call of my name.

He called the name that was solely me, I mean – the one that spanned all the years of my life.

261

'Lucy.'

Robert had barely taken the time to snatch his coat from its hook. He was sliding his arms into its sleeves. I had turned in the middle of the wintered line of trees that marched down towards the market hall. He was nothing more than a faint shape of a man in this freezing night, moving closer amongst the black sky, the road and the town. I could barely see the shadow of his eyes.

I faltered there in the midst of experiencing a peculiar urge to forget all those wise thoughts about walking my own path through life, and repeated instead that old test of whether this was real or fantasy. He drew nearer. I said foolishly through a fog of my racing heartbeat, 'Do you know, I don't think my uncle has any idea at all of retiring.'

'No,' Robert's shadow agreed. His hands were straightening the collar behind his neck. 'I suspect Mr Kathay just wanted some assurances that he isn't facing this alone. And got them, I think, along with a few surprises.'

'Such as hearing my ambitious plans for stepping into his shoes, you mean? He must believe he raised a shark.'

Robert had come to a halt before me. He was taller than I was, and close enough that I could just make out the features of his face, but I couldn't quite recognise the expression I found there. There was a steadiness to it that was nothing like that former barrier of reserve, because I think the serious-ness was in me rather than him. He was merely finishing tiding his collar.

His hands dropped. The movement was a marker of the end of one conversation and the beginning of the next.

All of a sudden I wasn't quite ready to hear the opening line, or give it myself.

I said impulsively before he could speak, 'I saw Doctor Bates today, by the way. He was convinced that he had to break the news to me that we're losing Amy Briar. They're getting married.'

I sensed the change in him.

Robert's body stiffened. So did his voice to match when he asked, 'Why would you tell me that now? And in that way – as if we're only speaking about trivial matters?'

'I don't know.' It was another hasty lie. Because I knew perfectly well why I had told him.

It was because every other thought in my head was rattling around that feeling of being very alive in this body. I could feel the tightness of the belt about my waist and the depth of the pockets that held my hands. I could definitely feel the ground beneath the soles of my shoes. He was making me nervous and I was betraying every unhappy doubt in my head.

I admitted sheepishly, 'Doctor Bates came to see me today and quizzed me about your plans. I didn't want it to be a secret that I'd met him, so I told you. Are you planning to leave us?'

There was something very raw for me in the way he took a moment to answer the question. The slight movement of his head gave a negative. He said, 'You've asked that before and the answer's still no. Not that I'm aware of.'

The pavement behind him was being touched by the marbled gleam from a nearby inn. Its shutters were slightly parted so that it was possible to see the empty bar inside.

And now my mouth was moving on rapidly – to say what, I have no idea. Some mindless nothing, I imagine, directed at that thin chink of light because I could feel the tug of the cheery part I usually played at the office.

But he was already saying, 'Lucy, please. Be clear. Don't make this an endless dance around the edge of misunderstanding. Just tell me – after everything you said tonight about working with me, are you trying to explain that you don't want more from me after all? You don't even want me as a friend? Just as a colleague?'

'What? No! Of course not.'

My bewilderment shattered the night.

I blundered into life; into touching a hand to him. I suppose it conveyed my disbelief. It showed him that I had thought the reverse – that he didn't want me.

My body felt almost feverish. I was moving like I was still expecting him to recoil, even when the moment of contact from my reaching fingertips acted upon him like a firebrand.

Because my hand was met. Gripped. He drew me sharply closer. The hard crush of the way he took hold of me rivalled the way the night air closed around us in the lull between fierce gusts.

At first, the lift of my mouth to meet his was clumsy. There was so much of my need in it. And I didn't know why any of us had been so afraid we were hurting him. He didn't believe either I or my aunt or uncle had ever caused harm by leaning on him. Now I felt the tide-rush in my mind as I glimpsed the truth.

It was some time later that Robert drew back enough to permit a dizzying descent into release; into the madness of racing to catch my breath. He turned his head aside a little. I plunged headlong into breathing in the scent of him only to find that every nerve was aching. I hadn't prepared for this.

'Don't be afraid.' I felt his whisper against my forehead. There was the faintest hint of a laugh. His arms still crushed me.

He added softly, 'I think I understand at last why you keep accusing me of being about to go away.'

It took me a moment to find my voice. 'Do you?'

'I think so. But believe me when I say there is, at the very least, no present state of war that could carry me from this place.'

I didn't know at what point in the past minutes he had discovered his confidence, because I was more shaken than ever.

Now my pulse began to run in a lighter race. I kept my eyes closed to feel the gentle drift of his jaw against my temple while I tried to find an explanation for my nervousness that didn't depend so much upon my history. When I spoke, my voice was less giddy, more ready to sound like my own. 'After our latest bus ride, when you left me, you said—'

The silent touch of his smile interrupted me. It was a fresh introduction to my habit of confusing his words with everyone else's version of him, and was in itself a final answer to the manner of his farewell those few days ago. The gentleness of his departure hadn't been inaction in the face of the hint I had given, but the opposite of it.

In the wake of that appalling day, his simple use of my name had been a very decisive action indeed. Because I'd made him free to use it. And after a day of extreme emotions when it might have hurt us both to react too swiftly to the better feelings I'd shared – for him the use of my name had been a promise of the value he placed on getting to know me.

A car slunk past in a blaze of light and a choir was practicing its carols in the very distant memorial hall beyond the Curfew Tower – which was as stark and still as it ever was because no bell tolled an end of things in this town tonight.

He didn't let me go. Beneath the intermittent drift of that distant song, I confessed, 'All the same, I still don't understand why you made me wait so long before letting me meet you at home. I felt so cut off.'

'I promise I didn't mean it like that,' he said gently, 'and the choice wasn't all mine. But I suppose your past was sufficiently matched by my own to make me sure you needed the room to settle in on your own terms. I thought you needed to do it without the pressure of finding a strange man crowding every footstep. Didn't you?'

He didn't require an answer. This wasn't another remark on that slight discrepancy between how resilient I thought I was, and everyone else's idea of me.

Because he was already sharing this piece of his own history when he admitted, 'In truth, I believe I've spent a lot of time worrying about you, one way or another. When you met me that time on the landing outside your aunt's bathroom with

266

your hands full of childhood treasures, it came after the latest of many hellish visits to failing publishers. All of a sudden there you were. There was no camouflage at that moment – for either of us.'

I felt his grip tighten on the memory as he added, 'So then I had to worry about what it should mean, and consider the way your aunt and uncle and I were all teetering on the brink of lying to you horribly. And with that in mind, I should tell you that I wasn't under orders when I met you at Bourton. It was my choice, and I was painfully nervous about what your reaction would be.'

'I'm sorry.'

I sensed the warmth that grew in the dark. 'Lucy, I'm trying to say that I like worrying about you. You make it so harmless. And I don't have to feel ashamed.'

No one had ever said anything like that to me before. And I didn't think I had ever heard anything quite so brave. Framed somewhere within that last part was another tentative attempt to explain that there had never really been any doubt that he would stay, or that he would do what he could at Nuneham's.

Sometime later we were stepping out into the deserted road. I asked very gently indeed, 'What did happen to your friend who was shot? Did he die?'

Robert took the question as it was meant: a quiet continuation of what had been shared just before.

We were passing the Curfew Tower and I didn't know why I had been convinced that a choir was working its way through

267

its Christmas repertoire. The meeting room was black and silent when Robert told me with some relief, 'Fergus didn't die.'

He added, 'The better German prisoner-of-war camps tended to avoid having a British soldier's death on their hands, if they could help it; just as we did here with our prisoners. Both sides had a system of medical exchange, where we'd attempt to return the patients who were in most danger. I managed to galvanise the warden into getting him evacuated. Fergus lost a lung but he's living in Bognor Regis these days. He's well enough.'

We were at the shop door. Without fully knowing what I was doing, I hesitated in the recess of the doorframe so that he turned to face me. Then I reached up and kissed him.

And then in the next moment, I was shyly ducking my head for the sake of rummaging in my handbag for my key.

My shoulder was lightly resting against him as I searched. He didn't move away. It was a powerful feeling, understanding how the simple, everyday ordinariness of this contact mattered too.

Suddenly, every confused emotion in me was vivid and warm, and my probing fingers couldn't find that key beneath the usual clutter of purse and diary and other nonsense. Tonight, I could immediately lay a hand upon my handkerchief, which was no use at all.

Still searching, I asked without thinking, 'Unless you've got your set to hand?'

Then my skin burned when I realised how much that sounded like an invitation. Robert's reply above my bent head left some ambiguity about which question he was answering. 'Not tonight.'

I lifted my head. I asked on a strangely uncertain note, 'You're going?'

It wasn't that I was trying to rush this. Or returning to that old fear of loss. Suddenly and without being able to fully define why, I didn't want to end this by stepping back in there myself.

He understood, at least in part. His hand lifted to leave the smallest trace of fire upon my cheek.

He told me, 'Goodbye is only until tomorrow, isn't it?'

Chapter 21

A storm blew in during the small hours of the night. By about seven o'clock in the morning, the attic was cold and groaning and sleet was hammering against that loose square of glass in the widow. The little table that turned this bedroom into something of a living room was strewn with the wide sheets of the test print for Jacqueline's book.

The edits were all marked out with pencil at long last, so I did what I would probably regret once Mr Lock found out. I wrapped myself in warm clothes and a blanket and took a cup of tea and the papers down to the print room.

The linotype machine struggled into life beneath the roar of a downpour on the tin roof above. The long run of glass up there was still cast to that impossible depth of black that could only happen in December, when sunrise was an hour or more away and would only present itself as a short burst of grey anyway.

I knew what I was doing would disturb Mr Lock. No one was supposed to understand this machine of his. He wouldn't realise that a childhood spent roaming these buildings had left me with more than a simple love of books.

The machine worked by transferring letters from a deeply complicated keyboard into a molten alloy of lead and tin. There were far more keys here beneath my fingertips than I would find on my typewriter. As I worked, the machine was pressing out the letters in a complete line – a slug – in reverse, so that once it had been added to all the other slugs that made up that particular page, and inked and printed onto paper, the text would read the correct way round once more.

The gas burner took a while to heat the metal so I filled the time by slipping back up to the darkened office to open the overlooked drawers in my advent calendar.

There were more sweets for Larry, so the mystery leaver-of-dried-herbs must have added his own ration too.

But to my collection, I was able to add a small packet of rhubarb seeds and a single white mistletoe berry. I couldn't quite remember what treasures of my own he'd taken as payment. A set of miniature pencils, perhaps, and a neat square of cloth.

Several hours later, I was in the icy space of the workshop, some lightness had come to the heavy skies and I was recoiling from the pattern that was forming in the corrections I had made.

I couldn't seem to spell the Ashbrook name either, but unlike Mr Lock, there were no variations in my efforts. The freshly printed ink swam upon the white paper, reading the same name time and time again.

Ashbroke.

I stepped back from the press. In fact I retreated from it like it was poison.

Logically speaking, it was my own fault. I was an amateur at this and this was a very early morning after a particularly distracting night. Mr Lock would probably cry when he saw how many lines of type I'd scrapped. The slugs would be melted down and re-used of course, but still he would resent the waste.

But none of that mattered when the error, this room, this day, all felt dark and wrong. Because the same word ran broken across the pages. And then they were accompanied by that feeling again, like sea-sickness where the senses tilted.

It grew out of the cold dawn. It was the absence of any sound other than my own breathing that did it. The still air carried a burden of meaning because this house always moved and now the creaking timbers were waiting on bated breath.

It was an echo of the stillness that had met me in Jacqueline's hotel.

That incident had been, I admitted now, not entirely without precedent. It had followed in the wake of the many strangely hushed months of my life in Bristol after the bombs had stopped falling.

At the time, I had deduced that the feeling was a product of shock and perhaps grief. I had decided that the dreadful impulse to shatter the peace by crashing about finding fresh noise might be soothed simply by turning to my aunt and uncle. Robert didn't know it but I had valued him for months now for the steadiness of his presence in their office.

Lately, though, it had seemed as if nothing had changed for me in the months since; and not even after last night. And yet I couldn't have sworn any more that this was the same persistent unease, or that it stemmed from the deeper workings of my own mind.

Because I had begun this day with the simple businesslike practicality that comes from hope.

Nothing moved in the workshop. The stillness was absolute. But all the while, the dark type that ran through lines of chatter about giraffes was punctuated here and there by the misspelled word: *Ashbroke*.

It ran like a message.

The contradiction to it stepped into the office building behind me. I didn't catch a sound, but this time I felt the change as a breath of damp air on my cheek. It might have been a draught from someone trespassing through the great coach doors in the archway, except that they were barred and bolted today. I'd made sure of that.

It was hard to trace the origin of that change in the air. I moved quickly but my body was strangely leaden. I clumsily worked my way from anchor to anchor towards the shop door like wading through a racing current. The change was in the front door into the shop from the street outside. The door was locked with the key in its place. But the key wasn't mine.

Mine was upstairs in my handbag. This key had been left as a courtesy by a person coming quietly into the office on a Sunday when the shop was shut, and he didn't want me to think he was invading my home.

I shot drunkenly for the stairs. Robert was there by my desk. He had my advent calendar in his hands and he was setting it down again. He'd had about three seconds of warning before I opened the door from the stairs, thanks to the telltale groans of the bare boards.

Robert turned there by my desk, lit by my lamp and looking slightly ruffled by the day outside.

In fact, he looked rather like a man who had seen me at work in the print room and had hoped he could slip upstairs and down again unnoticed, but didn't really mind that he had been caught. It was, I realised, only about nine o'clock.

I arrived in the doorway and stopped there with both my hands outstretched upon the handle for support, and demanded in the midst of a battle to catch my breath, 'What are you doing?'

And then the feeling of life running slightly out of kilter with time stumbled to a dizzying halt, so that my thoughts abruptly came to a stop as well. I discovered that I had stepped into a mystery I had already tentatively solved.

He was setting the advent calendar down as I moved a little closer to say, 'You lied to me. You're the person who has been leaving me the little cuttings of herbs.'

He was entirely unapologetic. 'It wasn't really a lie. You accused me of tampering. This is a recipe. And I had to come this morning because the ingredients have changed.'

'Oh?'

I was distracted but something very lovely plucked at the corners of his mouth. 'No, Lucy. I can't tell you what it is. You still have to wait until the drawers have run their course and see if you can work it out.'

He had no idea, of course, that the concept of secret messages would send a shockwave through me. It was like an invitation to the oppressive thing that had chased me from the printworks. Now I actually turned my head to look for it on the stairs but found nothing, of course. Silence didn't take solid form. I stepped smartly in and shut the door.

'Good morning,' I said at last. I couldn't quite get my mouth in order. Half my mind was shaken. The other half was swooping into a memory of the power of his farewell last night. I was aware that trust was supposed to mean that I was safe to show this man the quirkiness that shadowed my steps, but I was reasonably confident that this confession would sound like madness.

I said, 'Have you been here long? I woke early and got to work on the giraffe book but it's cold down there in the print room.'

'Yes?'

'Aunt Mabel believes this winter will be the kind that rushes in before Christmas and sweeps away into a mild and damp new year.'

'Famous last words,' he said. Then, 'Is something the matter? And don't,' he added quickly, 'say you're fine.'

The remark was designed to jolt me into concentrating on him. And it worked.

It made me give a shy laugh, too. In a way, I don't think I had ever looked at him properly until that moment. He was the same man he always was, of course; tallish with a poised kind of energy that went hand in hand with the expression in his eyes.

But I knew now how easily that mouth might move from seriousness into a smile and back again, and then a different kind of truth broke out of me with a lurch. 'I was coming to find you.'

I put up a hand to sweep the hair from my face and was surprised to find it unsteady. I repeated, 'I felt the air change and I realised you were here. I was coming to find you.'

I didn't know what he was seeing in me. I saw his posture change to something stronger as I moved away from the door and stepped closer. Then I faltered because the hand that had been tidying my hair was black with ink. The sight of it checked me. That sense of being crowded hadn't swept in after me at the top of the stairs because it had stalled when it had seen Robert, and then I had shut the door. But part of it was in here with me and on my skin all the same.

I was staring at my left hand as if the smudges were a curse as I said on a distracted note, 'This is like the difficulty I had speaking Archie's name. I've been battling with it for a long time, and I thought you were making it worse because you were making me admit all the parts of me that hurt. Then I found it was good to learn to talk to you because I caught a glimpse of a way out if I would just learn that I can tell you anything.'

I added in a rush, 'Only I haven't shaken off the past at all. This isn't purely a shadow of the war. This is something else instead. Suddenly it's here and it's stronger. It's as if last night with you has finally weakened my defences against it.'

I didn't think I was making much sense. If I had been, I might have found room to be afraid that he would think I was trying to explain that I had changed my mind. But I didn't grasp that danger just then.

I dropped my hand. I told him, 'A different kind of grief dwells in that Ashbrook house, and I've brought it home with me. First it led me on that mad race about graveyards and now it's taken up residence in the printworks. It's in Jacqueline's book and in the gaps between the creaks on the stairs. The test print is riddled with mistakes and I feel as if the dead have decided that if I won't reach out to them, they'll find their own way of coaxing me into listening.'

Abruptly, I approached the desk and claimed the support of the cool wood by settling back against the rim with my hands on either side of my hips. I couldn't quite meet his eyes. But I had seen the way his body had jerked once in a single uncontrollable start as I had moved closer, and I knew he had watched me when I had sought this place against the desk as a compromise between distance and reaching for him.

This felt very close to him anyway, because he was just there beside me and he still had his fingertips out upon the desktop after returning my advent calendar to its place.

Now he said in a very strange voice, 'Archie is talking to you through Jacqueline's book?'

The hard wood of the desk was running in a line behind my thighs and beneath my hands. I gave a hasty shake of my head. 'No. I'm confusing you. I don't know what this is. Archie wouldn't try to keep hold of me like this. It's too cruel. And I'm not speaking about the sort of conversations my mother and grandmother have in a darkened room with a few shattered souls either.'

I drew breath and found it steadier than I had thought. I was able to say firmly, 'This is too close to being internal. I only say I don't know what *they* want from me because I haven't got a better word for what this is.'

'You think you have to do something?'

There was a sudden twist of a deeper kind of puzzlement in Robert's voice.

He made the room stretch into focus where before I had only been aware of him, myself and the stairs. That was the moment when I vividly recalled what he had said about conflict and his lack of fitness to bear it.

I found I was turning my gaze to him to tell him quite plainly, 'Until this moment I hadn't grasped how I could prove this experience, even to myself. But it occurs to me that while Mr Lock was doing the typesetting, the misspelling on the printed pages said all sorts of things. Now I've put my hand to the task, the error has clarified to say one thing and one thing only. *Ashbroke.*'

I waited for a strangely stretched run of seconds while he turned something over in his mind. The sudden sense of space between us was emphasised by the coldness of this wood-lined office on a Sunday when I hadn't lit any of the fires. And what was it he had said last night? That he was growing to believe that he ought to be allowed to worry about me without feeling ashamed?

Well, unexpectedly, when he finally spoke, it wasn't to retract that generous statement. It was to touch something deeper inside me that rippled into certainty.

He remarked, 'It just so happens that when I took the proof copy of Jacqueline's book home the other night, it was to do my own research. That quote the family used on the uncle's epitaph – "A man dies not while his world, his monument remains" – I've read it somewhere before.'

'On a grave?' I found that, suddenly, my heart was beating very rapidly.

For the second time in as many days, I was powerfully aware again of every inch of the contact between my body and this dark furniture and the floor beneath my feet. And he was still standing near to me, with his fingertips touching the desk barely inches from my left hand so that the wood became the link that connected me to him in one staggering experience.

He told me swiftly, 'I found the original words for that memorial in a book; in a novel, in fact.'

'A novel? Which novel?'

'*King Solomon's Mines* – the wild Victorian adventure in Africa by a man named H Rider Haggard. It turns out, after much thought, that the family memorial misquotes a line that ought to read, "Yet man dies not whilst the world, at once his mother and his monument, remains".'

There was something very beautiful about Robert's sincerity when he added, 'The original version is, you'll notice, a little less about bricks and mortar than the Ashbrook interpretation. It better befits a hero who is braving untold dangers with an entirely Colonial mixture of romanticism and a tendency for shooting exotic animals first and then admiring them afterwards. Have you ever read it?'

For once, I was actually able to say that I had. 'A long time ago. But clearly not thoroughly enough to be able to hunt out the quotation at a moment's notice. My uncle has a copy on his shelves at home, doesn't he?'

Robert gave a nod. 'I dredged the idea from my memory late on Friday, borrowed the book yesterday and finally found the exact line very early today. It seems you aren't the only one who rose early to work this morning.'

'Oh?'

'Yes. It must be something to do with all the excitement of last night.'

I caught his swift sideways glance. Then he said rather more seriously, 'I can tell you that the original passage doesn't stop with that line. The original text goes on to say something very meaningful about the way a man's name becomes lost as time marches on, but the air he breathed and the words he spoke still exist. The author was writing about the parts of human life that transcend the physical limitations of what we can control or fix into living memory.'

'A man's name becomes lost?'

He caught my emphasis on the particular kind of loss. 'Does that mean something to you?'

And then I was shaking my head. 'Not really,' I said, because it was the truth, and yet at the same time I was feeling again the weight of that odd and formless pursuit, both up the stairs just now, and previously on my own hunt through those graveyards.

My hands were gripping the lip of the desk when I conceded, 'It doesn't really mean anything that you can quote the original book. The Ashbrook people clearly didn't retain much of the principle of the passage you read. Their monument declares that Walter's legacy was physical and real and continues to dwell in the material things that he and his father created.'

'But?'

'All right,' I agreed. 'But all the same, names do matter, because even though his children are recorded, his orphaned niece Harriet is emphatically missing from the epitaph that was inscribed for him.'

At that moment, I was conscious of many things – Robert's eyes upon my profile, the polished wood bearing my weight, his nearness and my seriousness. He watched me as I in my turn watched my left hand gingerly ease its grip upon the tabletop. I had been holding the wood tightly enough to turn the knuckles white.

I added, 'Last Friday, the morning after my obsessive but futile race around churchyards, I finally did the intelligent thing and asked Jacqueline where Harriet's parents were buried. They're somewhere in Norfolk; in or around King's Lynn. Presumably, Harriet's body was returned to them.'

He didn't make the obvious remark about being able to guess where my next bus trip would take me. I found I had no choice but to lift my head and ask at long last, 'Is that what this is? Am I supposed to find Harriet's grave and finally correct the uncle's neglect to the point of satisfying even an Ashbrook's idea of permanence in this world?'

'Is that what you think?'

Abruptly, I was amused. 'I have absolutely no idea. I doubt it.'

I drew breath and stretched a little to ease the stiffness in my shoulders. Suddenly, it was as if all the time since my early start had been passed in a clouded dream and this was my first moment of waking.

I admitted in a better voice, 'This isn't what you deserved from me this morning, is it? You wanted to creep in to rearrange my advent calendar while I remained oblivious in the print room. Then you were going to stage your arrival with a knock at the door and follow it by hinting that you ought to be invited in for a cup of tea and a happy chat about the future.'

'Well, in actual fact,' he replied steadily, 'when it comes to cups of tea, I've been meaning to talk to you about that. I presume you realise that your aunt used to do both your job and mine? She's set a high bar for both of us. Today, I'll make the tea.'

There was something very dry there. It was the comfort of being teased. Then I put my hand out to cover his where he still reached to touch the tabletop.

He didn't move much but every nerve of mine was sensitive to his concentration upon my touch. There was a temptation to ask why he was helping me to discuss this madness. But I knew why. Because I needed him to.

I told him simply, 'I love you.'

And those three words should serve as a sufficient explanation for why, a short while later, I returned alone to the print room to collect the test print.

It wasn't entirely a question of courage that made me do it while he went to set the kettle upon the hob. It was also a sense that he had acted just now to shield me from the oppressive feeling I had left stranded on the stairs. I didn't intend to test his protection by steering him directly into its path.

Chapter 22

The kitchen occupied the space at the head of the stairs between my bedroom and the storeroom. We were higher now than the ribbed roof of the printworks, which meant that the narrow windows on this floor hadn't been bricked up. While I laid out the printed sheets on the wide table, Robert drifted along to the partially open door for my bedroom.

It amused me to watch the way he lingered on the threshold and used the lightest of pressure to ease the door ajar just enough to peer in at the clutter and books and general home-liness. He must have sensed the drift in my attention. He turned his head and I raised an eyebrow at him.

'What?' I said. 'Did you imagine I'd be living up here in forlorn squalor while you revelled in the comfort of my uncle's house?'

The attic room had changed a lot since he had last seen it. The mattress still lay on the floor beneath the front window, where he and my uncle had placed it, but I had added a rug and the small round table where my handbag rested at night. The thin partition wall was hung with pictures and there were a few pretty ornaments and vases on the mantelpiece. After a moment of thought, Robert drew something out of his pocket and stepped in to set it carefully beside the tallest vase.

'What was that?' I asked, as he rejoined me.

'A tiny ceramic hedgehog that was once yours, but has lately come to me by way of a drawer in your advent calendar. I thought I should return it.'

For a moment I thought he was making the point that he didn't want his own mantelpiece cluttering with idiotic trinkets. Then I grasped a small hint of a gentler truth. After all this talk about lasting monuments, he had thought I might appreciate the return of a few harmless tokens of my own. He knew that the little hedgehog, all of half an inch high, had been a childhood treasure.

Now, although he didn't mean it to, the gift forever carried the memory of his presence here on this day too.

Robert was studying the printed sheets I had spread across the table. If I had ever wondered about his fitness to do this job, I only needed to observe his concentration now. It was some time before his eyes flicked up to catch me watching.

Oblivious to the way he had made my heart miss a beat, he said, 'You are aware that there are other errors in this text beyond the misspelling of the name Ashbrook?'

He didn't require an answer to that. Instead he returned his attention to the test print while I took up my teacup and retired to a place against the wall.

His finger lightly tapped a line of text. 'There's the epitaph on the family memorial.'

After moment he added, 'Do you know, I'd love to understand how those few lines from a Victorian adventure story came to hold such special importance for this Walter fellow that his children should have very specifically chosen to adapt it for his memorial.'

'Well,' I said, straightening from my lean against the wall. 'It's simple enough to observe that the book has a good deal to say about Africa. Perhaps Walter liked it, or knew the author or something. It was published during Walter's lifetime, wasn't it?'

'But after Harriet's, I believe.'

'And what does that mean?'

I saw his mouth give a little downturn at the corners. 'Nothing, probably.'

'So are you trying to tell me that the African connection means that I'm actually being called to restore Walter's name? Perhaps I'm meant to prove that his memorial is dedicated to the herd of diminutive giraffes? Jacqueline will be delighted.' My voice didn't need to convey my disbelief.

After a pause he began very tentatively, 'Lucy, don't take this the wrong way, but Archie doesn't have a grave, does he?'

I set my teacup down on the kitchen sideboard with very careful precision to show that I was prepared to accept the question. 'No grave. He was lost with his ship. It went down with about half the crew so technically he's buried at sea. His name will be listed on a war memorial at some point.'

'More memorials?' Robert had straightened from his bend over the papers. He reached out a hand to stem my instinctive protest before telling me, 'No. I'm not trying to accuse you of creating this urgency for finding Harriet's grave out of the loss of Archie. I'm trying to suggest that you might be interpreting the pressure you feel in a certain way because of your own history.'

'Doesn't that amount to the same thing?'

'Not really.'

Robert's reach across the table had just barely touched my sleeve. Now he let his hand fall. He stood there, very much focussed upon this methodical process of unpicking my thoughts. It was an odd experience, seeing him work with me like this. It showed how much he had kept away from me before.

His attention returned to the papers. He was marking up the few errors I had missed with a pencil. Because above it all, and regardless of how many complications I thought I was finding within the pages of Jacqueline's book, it was undeniable that we were also swiftly approaching the deadline for publishing it. And I knew now just how much it mattered to Jacqueline that we helped her to achieve her goal.

I told him this. And then, as his hand marked a circle around another misspelled variant of Ashbrook, he remarked quite as if it didn't matter, 'Every turn of yours keeps bringing us back to the issue of Harriet's loss, doesn't it, even when these misspellings by your own hand clearly mention *Ashbroke*.

If it were me, I might truly begin to think that my errors referred to an Ashbrook, not Harriet Clare.'

He added thoughtfully, 'But you've had all these conversations with Jacqueline. You know how much your last visit to that house left you preoccupied with the issue of the child's neglected name. And now it has spread to this building too, and the depth of your reaction frightens you, doesn't it?'

His uncompromising question made me fold my arms. I told him, 'Frightened seems a strong word to use.'

'It seemed to be a strong feeling just now. So?'

After a moment when I still didn't have an explanation, he said simply, 'Listen, Lucy, I have to admit that I know what I saw in your eyes as I lifted you from your fall on the stairs at the Ashbrook house. It was there again today when you stepped into your office and I know that look. I've seen it before, and it is not one I would ever have expected to find in you.'

Now he had shocked me. He was speaking about the experiences of his fellows in the prison camp again, I knew he was. A chill ran over my skin like a breath of air.

I whispered, 'The dead aren't ghouls who can stalk us on a whim, I know that. If they were, I needn't have worried so much about accepting the balance in my mind between living this life and remembering those who have left me. This isn't about reaching out.'

I struggled to find a better explanation. I told him, 'Perhaps this feeling I have is the effect of war and loss and being forced into a closer acquaintance with my own mortality or something like that, but my world is nothing like my mother's or my grandmother's. When they extend a hand to a wandering soul, they do it kindly and generously and in the fullness of their faith. But this isn't a conversation. This feels invasive. The darkness is in my mind and it already knows my thoughts. It feels dangerous.'

I bit my lip defensively as if, despite my better words, I were summoning it after all.

But nothing danced about on the stairs outside my kitchen door.

After a moment while Robert's gaze followed mine to the head of the stairs, he quoted softly, 'Truly, the universe is full of ghosts, not sheeted churchyard spectres, but the inextinguishable elements of individual life which can never die.'

I felt my muscles adjust into puzzlement. 'What's that?'

'Nothing really. Another misquote from that African adventure, worthy of our friend Walter. It suggests that the ghosts of this world are all around us in the words and actions of those who have gone before. You don't need to reach out. Because the air Harriet breathed is still here.' He turned back to me and straightened.

'And that, by the way,' he added as I sharply stopped my intake of breath, 'is meant as a word of comfort. There are things she will have left behind for us to find, even if she didn't mean to.'

I let out my air with a faintly guilty smile and he reached out that hand again to lightly give a reassuring touch to my elbow.

The touch steadied against my arm when he stepped around

the corner of the table to move nearer. He said seriously, 'I know you aren't about to take off on a madcap journey across one hundred and fifty miles and four changes of train into Norfolk without exhausting a few local possibilities first, so what *are* you going to do? Will you ask Jacqueline's vicar to let you take a look at the parish registers?'

I shook my head. We already knew that Harriet wasn't buried in either of the nearby churchyards. I admitted, 'I thought I might begin with the newspaper. For the death notice.' Then on an entirely different note, 'Robert?'

His attention had strayed to the crease between his thumb and forefinger on his free hand where, in the moment before, his palm had run against a sharp edge of one of the sheets of paper. A thin line had been scored there. Now I was close enough to share his examination of the mark. He found the cut had barely broken the surface, dismissed it and then returned his attention to me. 'Sorry? Yes, of course. I will have time to help you tomorrow, Lucy.'

His readiness made a mockery of the faint tension that remained in me. 'Actually,' I said, working hard to lift my gaze from his hand. 'I wasn't thinking about my uncle's pressing deadlines, or his despair when we both abscond from yet another day of work on the Willerson archive. I was going to ask a question on a somewhat different but related theme about the rhubarb seeds.'

He repeated blankly, 'The rhubarb seeds?'

'In my advent calendar,' I said. 'I thought you wanted me to unpick the clues from Miss Prichard's manuscript but she seems to have omitted rhubarb entirely. What are they for?'

I saw an eyebrow twitch. 'Medicinally? Rhubarb is a mild purgative.'

Robert was teasing me. I remarked dryly, 'In that case, your choice of ingredients for my advent calendar is a bit immediate, isn't it? A plant that will rid the body of harmful things?'

That swept the humour clear from his face. He suddenly had his hands on both my arms.

'The present worry was not,' he said firmly, 'foremost in my mind when I first set about leaving you little gifts in your advent calendar.'

He explained, 'The rhubarb seeds belong to the original recipe. They bear no relation to Miss Prichard's manuscript, or this work, or in fact any book. They relate to you. And it must be said that you've made everything simpler, because yesterday I was still struggling to source the last two ingredients. Then you freed me. I found a new recipe. And, since it uses all the same ingredients bar two, it's a saving on many accounts because now I don't have to source sloe berries or the everlasting flower Xeranthemum.'

'Xeranthemum?'

His hands moved lightly on my sleeves as he met my slanting smile. 'Your aunt has a sprig of it in her wreath, as I learned yesterday, and I was going to have to perform a minor act of vandalism to get at it. And,' he added, 'if you're fishing for another hint, I have no idea about the plant's medicinal properties.'

There was a thrilling little pause after that – the sort that made me suddenly very conscious that he was holding me very still before him. Nothing moved except my pulse. Then he bent his head and kissed me.

It was some time later that Robert spoke. His arms had enfolded me very tightly and when I caught the quieter murmur of his voice against my hair, it seemed to be a seamless continuation of the reference he had made to my aunt's Christmas wreath.

He said, 'You did understand me, didn't you, when I said that it wasn't all my own choice to give you room to come home properly? You did understand that I'm reasonably certain that your aunt has guessed what I think of you?'

I said, 'I think you've just explained what she was trying to ask me about last night as I left her house. She seemed to be convinced that I would either be frightened away or work myself up into hurting you, if she said too much.'

I asked, 'Are you trying to tell me that she *told* you to keep your distance?'

'That isn't what I'm trying to say. Although, I believe that your Aunt Mabel foresaw the impact you would have on me. And immediately decided that she had no wish to experiment upon your feelings by thrusting us together over her family dinner table.'

It was very quiet up here in my attic. I thought he had noticed my interest in that vacant stairwell. And in that faint line of a cut on his hand.

That same hand was holding me very close. Nothing was stalking him from the shadows here, and he wasn't being my guardian either. He said almost fiercely, 'I'm trying to say that we're all so protective of each other's welfare that we might forget to simply live. When you're already pretty formidable, as I said, aren't you?'

He stayed with me that night. After many hours of work to find the errors, and get fresh blocks made up after dinner, what remained of this time was ours.

I woke to the cold air of a bedroom on a wintery Monday morning to find him sleeping on his side beside me, his back turned to me and his hair ruffled again, this time by my pillow. The weak light of a damp dawn was drifting in through a chink in the curtains to cast a soft line across his cheek and onto me. I had overslept if daylight was beginning to show.

Very gently, I touched my lips to his shoulder. There was a confidence that came from this kind of proximity. It awoke a thrill in me when his eyelashes lifted and his thoughts turned immediately to me; a new sense of determination that grew from being able to recall precisely how this place had felt last night after the building had grown dark; when the only silence had been the one that had fallen peacefully between us, while the sounds of the floorboards had gone on whispering to the shifting air outside my window.

Chapter 23

We found the newspaper office near the point where the bustle of the Cirencester shops gave way to the wide space of a country lane.

The reception was made of wood and more wood, and contained a very crisp young woman journalist who directed us back into the town again. The newspaper archives were held by the town library, a splendid Victorian affair with a front door that opened directly from the street.

Inside, a green-tiled stairwell led us into a room fitted with plasterwork ceilings. Tall bookcases crowded in ranks around heavy oak reading desks where a librarian guarded her drawers of index cards. It was hushed and terribly serious.

'I had thought,' remarked Robert in an undertone while the librarian bustled away, 'that your uncle's office was unique, but apparently not. Is it a rule do you think that places that house books must line the walls with wood?'

The newspaper archive was yet another Victorian creation. For over a hundred years, every edition had been thoroughly indexed by name or subject and recorded in these drawers of cards. There was no card conveniently marked for Harriet Clare, though.

Diphtheria, on the other hand, featured in thirty-one different articles.

'This must be the outbreak that claimed her.' My stilted murmur called Robert away from his own newspaper to examine mine. '"Tragic Loss of Church Boys" in March of that year – 1873 – but no mention of Harriet Clare. No mention of anything to do with Walter Ashbrook at all.'

This was the eighth newspaper I had examined, and now we would have to wait for the next in line to be brought out.

I propped myself upon my hands on the tabletop and muttered, 'I know the librarian is only permitted to bring out two newspapers at a time, one in each hand and dangling from its wooden bar. And I realise that it is fair that the library should wish to protect its historic collection. But I do think the rule is making things far more difficult for us than they need to be.'

I wasn't being entirely serious. We hadn't left Moreton until the second bus of the morning as it was, thanks to the complication of waking late and the responsibility of opening the office ready for my uncle. And somewhere in the midst of that morning rush, I had opened the next drawer on my advent calendar.

I had done it at just the moment when Robert had stepped quickly up the stairs from the print room. He had found me standing spellbound, with a packet of powdered yarrow laid in my palm. It had been accompanied by a dried spray of elderflowers and a fragment of paper that had been torn loosely into a question mark.

The ingredients formed an anagram.

The original run of clues, before he had decided to omit the dried flower beginning with an 'x' and the sloe berries, would have spelled MERRY XMAS. And the discovery of that detail in itself almost mattered as much as the shorter message ... almost.

Because his first effort had been a simple mark of friendship, and he had thought to do it for me long before I had learned how to speak to him.

At this moment, as he approached my side with the mutter of traffic rattling dully past outside, I felt a stirring of that same memory of piecing together the two messages. I could still feel the peacefulness of the office and the consciousness of the fragile question mark held between my fingers.

Here, I controlled the rush by turning my head to him to say quietly, 'That last article mentioned the village church. The outbreak was only reported at all because two of the little boys were new recruits to the choir, and that played sufficiently upon the heartstrings.'

The other newspapers I had read covered outbreaks at various boarding schools. Which showed how alarmingly commonplace the infection must have been, if the only time it deserved mentioning was when it wreaked an extra bit of devastation.

There was no article for Harriet though. Her death notice didn't appear in any of the newspapers that the librarian brought out next. I'd asked for those that fell around the date of the outbreak we'd uncovered.

But Harriet wasn't mentioned in any of the neighbouring

editions, even after allowing for the possibility that she had succumbed more quickly, or lingered. It took some time and the endlessness of it all made the high wooden features of this room feel considerably less like home.

I lifted a hand to my neck to ease the stiffness there and found that I had caught Robert's eye. He asked quietly, 'You're beginning to worry again?'

I smiled at him. 'Not in the way you mean. Miraculously, today, the thoughts are very definitely in my head, and not looming from the darker corners of the room. Do you know, I'm increasingly convinced that you were right to tackle me about the way I might be letting my own past influence this. This is beginning to feel like that afternoon I spent dragging you about graveyards. Misguided.'

In truth, the silence between these towering bookcases wasn't absolute. It was closer to tranquillity, as if the stresses of yesterday had abruptly decided to leave me alone, and I could guess why. Beside me, Robert bent to retrieve a fallen pencil from the floor.

On an impulse, I stepped to the drawer holding the index cards for 'A'. I stood there for some time in the light of a fierce little lamp while my fingers worked their way through the cards until I reached that familiar name. There was a clatter behind me. It was Robert knocking his shoulder against the table as he straightened from his reach beneath the desk. From the noise it made, I thought it might have hurt a little; the librarian simply looked severe.

'Sorry,' was all Robert said when he caught us watching.

Then the librarian scuttled off and someone else came in.

Robert watched this new person walk to the natural history section and then he waited for me to rejoin him at our desk before asking, 'What have you sent our tireless assistant to get now?'

Again, it took an infuriatingly long time to work through the references until the librarian brought out the newspapers I thought I wanted, but finally I had the article in my hands. I turned the sheet of newsprint towards him on the desk.

'What is it?' he asked, reaching to draw it closer. He had been idly examining the other paper the librarian had brought.

'Walter's obituary,' I told him and saw his eyebrows lift. I added, 'And, interestingly, the title implies it was written by his daughter.'

'The person who installed Walter's memorial in the village church?'

'The same,' I said.

'May I?' I asked as I drew the paper back again. Out of the corner of my eye I saw his concentration as I quoted out loud:

Our beloved Walter John Ashbrook will be forever remembered by the family as an inspiration, a tireless mind and a dedicated source of encouragement.

But here, for the benefit of those who knew him, near and far, I will lay out my respect in the terms of the greatest affection for a great man's work.

I shivered a little as I read that. I suppose I wasn't expecting to suddenly encounter this first real remnant of a voice from that time, particularly his daughter's. Walter was thought to have been a cold, remote father, so it was peculiar to go on to the next section and feel my own mouth speak of her affection in such terms as *kindness, generosity* and *devotion.*

I said on a note of wonder, 'I don't think she considered herself estranged from him at all. She says here that she admired Walter. She says that he spent his life working to further medical science, as his father did before him. It was their shared legacy.'

I faltered upon that word, legacy. Robert didn't notice. He was turning his attention back to the other paper. He asked, 'Walter was a doctor?'

I rescanned the crowded lines. 'No. I don't think so. No, here it is. She goes on to say that he edited and delivered the bulk of his father's research on fevers to one of the great London medical colleges.'

'London,' Robert repeated flatly. He was bending closer over his own paper as he remarked on a distracted note, 'Wasn't that where he was supposed to have gone while Harriet was lying neglected?'

I straightened as I grasped his meaning. I said on an uncertain laugh, 'It'd be funny, wouldn't it, if we've just found evidence that will redeem him in Jacqueline's eyes. She can't hate Walter if it turns out that when he went away during that fatal diphtheria outbreak, he was fulfilling his dedication to Graham Hanley Ashbrook's research.'

Then I corrected myself by shaking my head and saying, 'Actually, I don't know if she will like this. There's no mention of the giraffes, or of Harriet.'

Then my eyes caught upon the author's closing line. She'd signed herself '*His Daughter, Mrs David Murray*'.

Legacies and names stilled in my mind. Because the name Murray was familiar. It was more than familiar to me after that reckless hunt amongst gravestones. During his life, old Mr Sampson Murray had been the estate manager from the farm at Bramblemead, and in death, he had been buried by his son near that little sinking church.

His son had bought the farm later, Jacqueline had said. She believed it had been made possible by the terms of the last Ashbrook's Will. I thought that David Murray must have been much younger than Walter's children, if Jacqueline was convinced he had been young enough to have known Harriet as a boy.

'Lucy?' Robert's voice brought life back into my senses like sound being suddenly switched on. Outside, a bus was rattling past the window. Robert drew my attention to the paper beneath his hand.

His newspaper dated from many years before the obituary. It had been brought out by the librarian because it contained a paragraph about a visit to the Ashbrook house by children from the village school at Christmas in 1877. They had been welcomed and presented with their oranges by a young woman of seventeen, 'Miss Clare Ashbrok'.

'I—' My voice failed.

Misspellings of the surname notwithstanding, I knew that Clare could never have been an accidental misspelling of the daughter's name, Janet. And besides, by Jacqueline's idea of dates, Janet had been old enough to have been thoroughly installed in a home with her own family by the time these children would have been visiting the house.

In fact, Janet would have been so grown up that her husband couldn't have been David Murray either.

My incredulous whisper didn't sound like my own but it was mine all the same. 'Harriet didn't die.'

Robert's expression mirrored my bemusement. 'Yes. I mean, no. She didn't,' he said. 'And after all that strain.'

He made me straighten from my lean over the desk with a sudden little intake of breath.

It was ridiculous to be so shocked. And yet it was with me still as I said more warmly, 'That's why Walter's affection for his daughter suddenly became such a feature in the house-keeping diaries after Harriet disappeared. Walter didn't abandon the girl on her sickbed, or expunge her name from the record. She lived and he loved her. He adopted her.'

All of a sudden, it was hard not to give way to laughter. 'And why did she drop the name Harriet Clare to become Clare Ashbrook? Because it was a tribute to both her parents and her adoptive father?'

By way of a reply, Robert reached out to lightly touch the final line on the other paper. The name of the estate manager's son was there again.

He gave me a moment to reread the closing words of the obituary, then he remarked, 'Is David Murray the reason why Walter abruptly wrote that forlorn note about Miss Ashbrook leaving the house upon the day of her marriage?'

I stared at the lines of Harriet's tribute to the man who

had raised her. Robert added what I had already partially guessed, 'Walter would have known that she would have no need of a room in his house any more, if she'd married the estate manager's son.'

No wonder I had been feeling the relief of being left alone today. The obsession could never have sustained itself after the better peace of last night. This was the thrill of knowing that with this discovery, the giraffe book was free to be printed and it mattered that Robert was with me.

I suppose I ought to have felt a fool after making all that fuss. But the release of excitement hadn't reached that stage just yet.

Instead, I was experiencing that giddying sense of perception tilting once again. The disorientating rush of thinking my way through these past minutes was like that experience on the stairs in the Ashbrook house, where as ever the single dependable presence was Robert.

That time, I had been made blind by the confusion between a past and present grief. This time, the feeling was happy and there was very little I could grasp beyond the many changes of Harriet's name.

Her final name, her married one, wasn't in the telephone book, but then hardly anyone was. The electoral register was missing too. It hadn't been produced for the duration of the war and this library hadn't yet received a copy of the updated version.

Then the librarian appeared by my shoulder. She was bearing the last list the Commission had issued. Taking it, I said doubtfully, 'It's from 1939. It's nearly a decade old.'

She opened it for me at the right page.

Ten years ago, D. E. Murray and C. H. Murray had been registered voters. Their address was Bramblemead Cottage.

In the next blink, I was outside and getting damp again beneath a sky that was growing dusk-like already. Robert was turning up the collar on his coat.

We stepped off the kerb and took the direction that would lead us to the bus stop for Fairford. Robert was asking me, 'I gather you mean to go and visit this cottage?'

'Don't you?'

It was one of those questions which didn't really require an answer, although we could both remember Jacqueline's disappointment when she had found the farmstead ruinous.

I didn't know whether it was the sudden delightful lifting of the shadow of Walter's guilt, or the whine of tyres on a rain-drenched roadway, but every sound was being extraordinarily amplified. And the sensation was doubly unexpected because no part of the pressure to pursue my thoughts of Harriet had ever deafened me before.

It was like drowning in sound.

The clatter of a horse-drawn wagon squeezed rather too close to us and made Robert swiftly step in behind me against the wall of a shop as I heard myself say with abrupt honesty, 'I don't know what this means.'

I surprised myself. And that wagon really had come quite close to Robert. I paused to assure myself that he was unharmed before going on to say, 'I feel liberated, I suppose. And amazed. And yet I never believed I'd discover that I'd been misled by my own history quite to the extent of imagining all this.'

I resumed my course through the stream of busy shoppers before saying on a calmer note, 'And yesterday, when I raced up the stairs to you, I believe I would have told you quite bleakly that happiness wasn't likely to be my outcome from this.'

I felt Robert's hand check me. He stopped me and made me turn. He told me, 'We don't have to go, you know. We can just leave it at this little positive discovery and move on.'

He was doing more than curbing this impulsive dash towards the bus stop. In answer to my questioning look, he admitted carefully, 'I'm remembering the way you begged after that maddened race about graveyards never to be made to return there.'

He made my senses switch back to their normal levels.

People were hurrying along wet pavements and I was able to address his sudden undertone of caution. I studied him through the fading drizzle and saw him with unexpected clarity. I told him calmly, 'I was desperate to trace Harriet when the story of that place only existed within the delusion of her neglect. It would be far more in keeping with my own memory of childhood to go these few steps further knowing the real Harriet was loved, don't you think?'

'Good,' he said gently.

Some time later, after we had claimed our seats on a bus, I found myself asking, 'Do you remember what you said to me over dinner at Bourton?'

I felt every word of his reply. A rattle of traffic slid past unnoticed beyond the fogged window while he told me steadily, 'The old urge to keep moving has only really settled since meeting you. Well, here I am.'

I agreed with a flare somewhere deep inside, 'Here you are.'

I think it was the drone of the engine as the bus pulled away that gave me the room to realise what was running in the background of my senses.

It struck me with a wrench. It was the contradiction of secretly straining to catch the first hushed note of that strange oppressiveness, whilst knowing that at some point the lull would run on so long that I would probably have to learn that there had never been any real external influence on my mind at all.

I heard myself say with sudden urgency, 'Take care, Robert. And please don't leave me.'

I said it without even quite knowing why; beyond knowing it was something to do with my sense that the Ashbrook house still stood, and Walter's memorial had been installed by his loving adoptive daughter. Set in those terms, my discovery of their joint legacy ought to have been a symbol of freedom – for all of us.

But only yesterday, each new misspelling of her family name had seemed to bind me to a memory of loss.

Suddenly, I could vividly recall the quotation Robert had given me about a person leaving a trace behind in the things that they had touched and the air they had breathed.

It gave Walter's philosophy that he could never die while his world, his monument survived the substance of a darkening threat.

Chapter 24

Robert was slipping on the mud of the bank by the river. I was too, although my slight heel was helping me to fare a little better.

We'd been set down by the bus near that little church and now I was picking my way across the river using the narrow and crumbling footbridge. I was expecting Robert to say something about the rain running down his neck in a way that was reminiscent of the responsibility I had felt when I had brought him through this churchyard once before.

Robert didn't remark on the weather. He asked, 'Lucy? Why did your parents give you up, really?'

He had noticed my quip about being able to prove at last that my only material connection to Harriet was not loss or abandonment, but happiness in childhood. He waited until we'd reached the far bank before he added, 'I mean the full reason; not the edited version your aunt and uncle give. I presume you do know?'

I did know. And I didn't mind the question. We were slithering along a particularly greasy path through trees and rotting bulrushes beside an overflowing river. Normally we would have left the river behind by turning left towards that high ridge with the lime avenue and the Ashbrook house. Instead, we'd taken a filthy old path to the right, and now a general decay of leaf mulch was leaving dark spatters on Robert's skin and clothes. Probably, there were splatters on me too.

We ducked under a low bough from a willow that had toppled but not died, and stepped out onto a wider path and into better air.

I said, 'I do know. I frightened my mum and dad by asking when I was about fifteen, and the truth is profoundly ordinary. They'd had a couple of fearsomely bad years – a lot of farms did in that time after the Great War. My parents were desperate to lighten their load. Quite simply, my older brothers might be useful on the farm, whereas out of all of us, it was probable that I would cope the most easily with the change.'

'And besides, everyone agrees you didn't like the animals.'

Robert supplied the line for me when I faltered after I'd led the way between straggling hawthorns. He added as he joined me, 'You don't want anyone to think they made the wrong choice, I know.'

Then he stopped beside me and uttered a faint sound under his breath.

The first thing that met us at Bramblemead was a flock of very aggressive geese. They raced white and grey out of the derelict farmyard where the moss grew.

This was the farmstead I had seen from our walk along the distant drive between Jacqueline's gatehouse and the Ashbrook house.

It was impossible to make out that great house. Even the elegant roofs of its stable yard were screened by the stand of trees that ranged damply beside the river and spread thickly uphill. In fact, there was no sign of light or occupation up there at all. Not even a distant church tower pierced the skyline. I wondered who farmed this sorry farmstead. Or, rather, I wondered who I ought to complain to.

This was because there were a few bullocks and a dairy cow in the most robust of the rotting sheds that ranged beneath the ancient stone walls. The light was poor by now so it wasn't exactly the best time to see this place but what house there had once been was without glass in the widows and its door had been widened so that the ground floor could provide summer shelter to livestock. Red paint was showing where the paper was peeling from the walls.

There was a hay store in an old barn but nowhere near the cattle. The dairy cow was ill from being left full of milk and the others were in hungry squalor. The place stank of muck and filth.

'The path we've just come along.' Robert was twisting to look behind us. 'Does that look like an overgrown trackway to you?'

I followed his gaze. There was perhaps a sign of old cart-ruts between the wintered hedgerows.

We retraced our steps and met the whisper of the river again as we reached that fallen willow. It looked impenetrable. To the right was the poorly marked footpath back to that little church. But somewhere ahead, a dove was crooning to its mate. With a word to Robert, I forced a path through the mess.

There was a small garden gate and a dirty bit of ground that might have been designed as a vegetable patch. The river was close and the same fate was befalling this ground as was claiming the graveyard beside the small church. Everything was sinking, even my feet.

A ramshackle sprawl of sheds emerged from the net of a tangled bramble. The first had a wooden floor set on saddle-stones in an effort to keep out the rats, but a partition wall had collapsed. It had left a great scar of damaged brickwork on one side.

This place was very different from the genteel dressed stone of the Ashbrook house or Jacqueline's gatehouse. This was a hovel of crude bricks and timber set beneath the spreading fingers of a vast old oak and a darkening sky. I thought the shed was meant to be a dovecot.

The floor inside ran to a wooden panel with a door set in it. Doves were rustling about in the rafters when I tentatively set a foot upon the floor and found it firm enough to bear my weight. It stank of bird mess. I had to cover my face with a handkerchief to bear it and Robert had to guard his face with his sleeve. The door was locked. Or, rather, when I gingerly lifted the corner of the disgusting net curtain that screened the glass, I found that the door led nowhere but was merely doing service as a roof support.

Robert had found a way past the back wall. I joined him, slithering, cursing and beginning to think we'd do better to turn tail and run straight up to Jacqueline's gatehouse to ask who owned those bullocks. But there was another shed ahead, darker than the dovecote because its walls were intact.

Robert's hand gripped my elbow when I slipped on the edge of a drainage gully. I nearly took him down into it with me but with a heave, he righted me. Then his hand pointed out the low opening. He didn't speak. Neither of us did. We stepped into the sort of darkness that had its own hush as it filled the air with more of that acid smell of bird dung.

There was a sharp clap overhead. A white shape swooped. I felt the air move as it passed close to my head. The birds weren't doves; they were pigeons and their mess hurt the lungs.

My fingers were knotting upon the fabric of Robert's sleeve. I was suddenly shaking my head. I was turning to steer him back. This didn't feel safe. This wasn't right. This stank of decay and the end of things.

'Robert? I—'

But speaking his name wasn't permitted. I had known all along that the danger was in my mind and in my thoughts. It knew I meant to retreat, to tell Robert to abandon this useless scramble into the dark.

In the space of a heartbeat, that familiar sense of desolation crashed in. It swallowed everything – light, hope and everything. Because suddenly I understood why I had felt such dread.

All this time I had been hoping that the easing of the dreadful pressure meant that it was going to leave me alone. But this wasn't like that at all. It had been with me all this time. It was simply that, from the moment yesterday of following me up the office stairs, it had abruptly fixed its gaze upon Robert.

It had watched me bring him here. It wasn't going to let me take him away now.

I felt the shadow move in my mind like wings spreading. It stemmed my flight. It was like drowning in panic when I had no idea I was capable of feeling so much desperation on my own.

The feeling was in me, but more than me. And this time, for the first time, the darkness showed itself.

It lunged, blacker than night, out of a corner. I thought at first it was human; a man's shape growing from floor level to chest height within a stride. But the mouth was too wide. It gaped as it leapt.

It wasn't silent either. It came with a roar. I was braced but it swept past me and went straight for Robert. I was caught anyway by the pressure as it passed. It sent me backwards with an agonising twist into Robert. I collided with him at the same time that it did. I heard Robert's breath get knocked out of him and felt his instinctive reach for me. Then his shoulder met the doorframe.

Wood splintered and took us down with it. The fall came with the hard shower of the wall collapsing, raining hard rubble like cement dust only fouler smelling and I crashed down onto my side. I had fallen half across Robert. I caught a brief glimpse of his face near to mine before he put his hand up to shield his head from the shower as batons and shingles from the roof came down. I began to scream.

A falling splinter had cut a hard line across his forehead. He was on his back beneath me. I thought he was dead, even though I knew he wasn't. I felt his arm tighten around me. But it wanted him.

I had begun to notice his little slips and injuries. I should have guessed that each of them was a warning that what had befallen Archie must befall Robert too.

Because I was the common connection here and yesterday morning in the office, when I had run to him, it had finally seen him. I should have known that this had been its purpose all along. This was my fault.

Now violence tugged and snatched at my coat and tried to tear past me to get at Robert amidst a flurry of filth and rotten timber, but I wouldn't let it.

Robert had fallen through the crumbling wall. The shed was made of brittle wood and mortar anyway. And I had twisted across him with my hands on his chest and I was screaming like I might defend him. I was sobbing out to the darkness both within me and moving on the edge of my sight, 'Leave him alone. Please. You can't take him.'

Only I wasn't even sure that the source of the violence wasn't me.

Robert was beneath me in a tangle of debris and struggling because I think he was fighting me too. He was trying to get up and get me behind him, but he couldn't do it with the weight of wood across his chest and me and the pressure of this other presence darting in.

I had my head turned towards it. My memory was full of the sheer recklessness last night of asking Robert to stay. I was crying out to anything that would listen and begging it to leave him because I couldn't bear to have the things he had said robbed from me. I gripped him and sobbed out, 'I won't do it. I wasn't rushing last night because I thought I would lose him too. It's simply that we were happy. I won't let him go. Just leave him alone. Please.'

This was like the madness of sometimes believing it was me who had died in the war. Perhaps we both had – Robert and I, I mean. And this was the moment when I realised it. His spirit would be torn from me, and I would finally be truly on my own in the eternity of the gathering night.

At the same time though, the snarl was beginning to clarify into the form of a dog. It was lean, lithe and moving about on the periphery of my vision like a black and white spectre of vengeance. Or like a living arrow; one of the farmyard sort who might live half wild on a diet of shepherding and scraps.

And Robert was taking advantage of the slackening of my fight to stir at last, hands pushing the wood away and getting a better grip on me even while I was distracted by the blur of the moving dog. I was conscious, suddenly, of the fierce heat of Robert's living body against mine in the midst of that wretched pattern of loss.

And the dog didn't bite and then Robert was saying something.

'What?' I asked faintly. My stumble out of blind panic into this single stupid word of a question met amusement. Of all things, there was a hint of a smile in his voice.

He told me, 'It matters that you would try to save me, but would you please stop for a second, and just listen?'

He had eased himself into a sitting position very close to me. I was sitting beside him but facing the other way – facing towards him with my legs curled uncomfortably to one side and my arm across his body where I presume I had imagined I was shielding him.

Now my eyes were fixed on his, while his own concentrated on the gentle task of lifting a shard of wood from my hair. He knew I had descended into the depths of my darkest nightmare, and barely come up gasping.

I fought my way out of the sickening giddiness into the effort of seeing the world steady. He was still here. There was a single dark bead of blood on his forehead but the rest of him was whole and streaked white with the foul dust of pigeon mess. We both were.

Then something dragged his mind to a place somewhere beyond me. I twisted with a fresh lurch of fear to follow his gaze. I saw nothing but the remains of the partition through which we had fallen and an awful lot of pieces of the shed door. I turned back.

He was gathering himself to gingerly pick himself up from the floor, only he needed me to untangle myself first.

'Did you hear that?' he asked. 'Someone called the dog off.'

It was as I settled back on my heels and he reached to lift one last encumbering length of wood aside from his leg that I heard it. A timorous voice – a woman's – calling out a fearful, 'Who's there?'

The dog had been recalled by her command.

When Robert climbed to his feet, he wasn't wearing any other expression than shaken curiosity. I wasn't sure for him this tumble through rotten wood had ever been more than a grim accident. That line I had seen drawn across his head hadn't run to a lot of blood.

Now I was standing beside him while he blankly touched the heel of his hand to his forehead. He seemed vaguely surprised when it came away darkened.

I searched for my handkerchief and gave it to him but he barely seemed to spare a thought for it, really, with his other hand steadying me while he focussed intently upon tracing the source of that sound.

He took a step past me, with a glance at me to ensure that I was ready to follow. He moved towards the back of the shed. He called through the panel, 'How do we get to you?'

His voice was serious and concentrated. There was a door with a hole at the bottom where presumably the dog had got through. The door stuck, but opened when he set his shoulder to it and we both gave a determined thrust. Beyond was a storeroom of furniture and rubbish. And beyond that was Bramblemead Cottage.

Chapter 25

'**M**rs Murray?' I asked.

The passage into the house was narrow and without the luxury of electric lighting or even gas. At this dusky hour, there was a single oil lamp at the end. It was bitterly cold and full of dark corners like a cellar.

Robert had his hand to his head again, dabbing at the fresh trickle of blood that had been gently building. Suddenly, the pain had struck him, I think. It bewildered him. He was staring at the stained handkerchief in his hand like it was a question he didn't know how to answer. Then I saw the moment his gaze lifted to focus once more upon the passage before us. His manner changed.

'Dear God,' he said on a hardened note I had never heard before.

There was a woman here in this house that smelled of damp. Mrs Murray was standing in a faded housecoat, with skin that was so translucent though age that she was almost as pale as silver.

She had hands where the fingers were all curled in, and she was, in fact, so tiny and hunched over two walking sticks that it was hard to perceive how she could walk. The dog was slinking at her heels like a wraith. He was the only thing that moved. Mrs Murray was staring at us from the heart of the passage. I could see the glitter of her eyes.

Then she spoke and made me jump. Her question was a husky breath of incomprehension and yet character burned within. 'What are you?'

She truly meant 'what', not who. And she had spoken with defiance in the face of fear.

The reason went through me with a shiver, even as I gave our names. We were crusted grey like ghosts, and then she admitted, 'My husband is ill.'

She'd thought we were death come to collect him.

Robert was already moving. Decisiveness had set the line of his mouth in a way that matched the depth that had come into his voice. His grim purpose was also a match for the smell of poor toileting that met us in the bedroom.

Mr Murray had the dark skin of the old man Jacqueline had encountered on a walk in the woods behind the Ashbrook house, but he was ashen to the point of seeming grey all over. He was lying in bed with one foot bruised and swollen, and an awful cough. I saw Robert touch his fingertips to the old man's hand. I could tell from the way Robert's fingers contracted that Mr Murray was utterly frozen.

This house was bringing Mrs Murray to the brink too. There were no stairs here, just a few doors opening off the passage to left and right into three rooms that did service as kitchen, sitting-room and bedroom. There were no fires in any of the grates, and not much light either, expect the faint cast from the lamp in the hallway.

Robert's voice broke into the gloom and this time it held a note I knew. I had encountered this part of him before, when he had instructed me how to test for a break in my hand.

He asked, 'What has happened here?'

There was a depth to his concentration that transfixed – I honestly wouldn't be able to find another word to describe that level of intense attention, or the kick of the heart it gave. Particularly when, today, I could see that he really had told the truth when he had said that I made things generally harmless.

When he had assessed my injury all those days ago, I had been puzzled by the ease with which he had overcome his supposed aversion to practising medicine. This time, he wasn't treating me and there was no doubt about how deep the memories ran.

I could sense that Robert's pulse was racing terribly when Mrs Murray replied to say, 'Influenza. And then he had a fall by the wardrobe five days ago.'

Mrs Murray spoke for her husband. He was lying under blankets and she was shuffling to the other side of the bed. Her voice was a dusty whisper when she added, 'David was managing quite well until then. He was getting better.'

I didn't believe her.

Robert had the handkerchief pressed to his forehead again. I saw the faintest of tremors there, quickly suppressed, as he asked, 'Mr Murray tends to do the bulk of the outdoor work?'

He meant things like chopping logs. Mrs Murray fidgeted in a way that drew attention to the walking stick in either hand. She admitted, 'I couldn't walk far enough to feed the cattle.'

Harriet Clare had survived childhood to become Clare Ashbrook, and now she was Clare Murray and living with her husband in a hovel which might as well have been an icehouse. I didn't know at what point they had surrendered the old farmhouse to the cattle. Probably when she had grown too frail to mount the farmhouse stairs. Regardless, this small woodsman's cottage was in a sorry state now and she couldn't even, with those hands, have taken up the job of wielding the heavy maul upon their woodpile.

Robert put the handkerchief away. It had come away dry from his cut this time. I saw him nod as he absorbed the conditions here. Then his eyes move to the open door into the hall like a man eyeing escape.

His body followed it. He slipped through the narrow gap between me and the wall without even a word.

Robert wasn't abandoning us.

While I turned my mind to practical things such as reaching for the unlit lamp on the bedside table, he went into the kitchen to wash his hands and face clear of the grime. Now he came back to drop his coat over the foot of the bed and moved to press his fingers to Mr Murray's wrist for a pulse.

He approached his patient in the manner of a man squaring his shoulders to face the inevitable. This was a routine he must have performed many times before and he was hating it, but he would do his duty anyway.

On the other side of the bed, Mrs Murray eased herself down into the old-fashioned armchair by the empty hearth, and told us both, 'There's no fire set because I burnt the last of the combustible stuff within reach yesterday. The picture frames, and so on.'

Then her eyes took in the state of my skirt and she asked me, 'Did the dog get you?'

I gave a firm negative. The beast had gone more for Robert than me, and at the time I had taken it as a sign of the terrible danger that had passed from me to him. Now I was able to slip behind Robert and past the foot of the bed towards the hallway, and ask more reasonably, 'The dog doesn't like strange men, does he?'

Mrs Murray's hands stirred in her lap. 'We don't often get visitors. The poor dog doesn't get many opportunities to practice.'

I carried the lamp out into the hall, lit it from the lamp out there and then carried it back in again. I asked, 'Doesn't anybody do your shopping? Would nobody call at all?'

'No, no one. The postman brings us a few bits and pieces by way of groceries now and then.' Mrs Murray's eyes were following the new light. She added, 'We don't need much beyond what the animals and the garden give us.'

'And how often does the postman come?'

'The postman comes roughly once a month when our grandson writes. We have a daughter but when you're as old as we are, your children can be pretty infirm as well.'

'Your daughter doesn't live locally?'

'No,' replied Mrs Murray. 'Well, in Weston-super-Mare. What I mean is that we're all waiting for the news to come in the post that our grandson has been demobbed. When he comes home, everything will be put to rights. We've just got to hold out.'

She was aware, I think, that I was only asking questions for the sake of introducing a little touch of normal conversation into this stark sickroom, and she was trying to help me. It certainly didn't seem to occur to her to be anything but open to these two strangers who had broken in with the dusk.

I reached behind Robert to return the lamp to its place and saw Mr Murray's face clearly for the first time. He must have been in his late eighties. He still looked grey.

He could speak, though, just. I heard the old man hoarsely mouth the word 'Doctor' as Robert bent over him. The old man said it with relief I thought. The pitch of hope in his voice alone spoke volumes about how desperate things were here.

I saw the slight turn of Robert's head as I retreated to the foot of the bed to give him room. The light seemed to help him too – more than the simple illumination of his work, I mean. I thought he was noticing, as I had, that the lack of a fire must have meant that these people had spent the past winter's night and day without a hot drink or a cooked meal in their stomachs. Equally, no one here would have been able to walk as far as the cattle shed since Mr Murray's fall. No wonder the cattle had looked ill. Everyone here looked ill.

But then, in the pause while Mr and Mrs Murray busied

themselves with trying to calculate certain details about the illness, Robert took the chance to turn his head me properly. And briefly claimed every thought from my mind in one powerful wrench.

He knew I was regretting bringing him here even more now. This place embodied his own shadow. I had been bracing to discover that the set of his mouth was that of a man who was learning that there was no freedom for him, even in a new life in a small country publishing house. Because how could there be, when it could still confront him with the past like this?

And perhaps he really had been feeling that, because his forehead was warm with sweat in this icy room.

But then, suddenly, he turned his head and looked at me. Afterwards, his serious way of dealing with old Mr Murray didn't seem so much like the manner a man might have if he were braving a return to that old life. Perhaps, in truth, he never had been. There really was a difference here.

When he had looked at me, he had found a young woman with her hands gripping the cold rail of the bedstead, acting as though she might start trying to save him again – which probably both alarmed and touched him in equal measures just as much as before.

And I, in that single glance, I saw the way he was sharing this hard responsibility with me; and found we had exchanged something vital and reassuring.

In the minutes that followed, my pulse grew oddly forceful but steady. Mr Murray's prone form was laid within a mess of sheets, but the bold light from the bedside table was also showing a man in homely flannel pyjamas. He had grey stubble on his chin. I could hear the precision as Robert asked Mr Murray to sit up and lift his shirt so that he might listen to the man's chest. Robert had no equipment, but a tin mug waiting beside the lamp-stand would suffice for a stethoscope.

I was ready to slip away myself now. I was accompanied across the passage into the kitchen by the light clack of dog claws on tiles. This room was a fresh shock. There was no mess because the poor dog got whatever was spare. But most of what was left in these cupboards was dried pulses or raw root vegetables and, to be honest, without heat, I doubted these people would have managed to find even one more digestible meal.

Most miserable of all, there was a can of something unappetising on the sideboard; only partially opened because Mrs Murray's hands couldn't work the tin opener.

I washed my face clear of the grime. It was odd to follow this simple act by stepping out through the kitchen door into the woodshed. It took some courage to go out into the dark, but nothing waited for me. And yet nothing was different either.

I kept expecting to feel the recent storm dissipating, in that way I imagined my mother and grandmother might sense the departure of a soul during one of their séances. I expected to feel the lurch, as if Walter – or the echo of his life – had really been guiding our steps; but now he felt his work here was done.

But this dark, unfamiliar woodshed didn't feel empty. It

didn't bring comfort. And it didn't feel as if I had imagined the whole thing either.

This place was desolate and silent and great logs needed hewing in two. And, all the while, the hush of night-time kept me company like a memory of the subtle undertone that had met me as I had first stepped into Walter's bedroom at the Ashrbook house, before a greater violence had chased me down the stairs.

When I reappeared in the bedroom, Robert was examining the swollen ankle and Mrs Murray was still sitting in the armchair by her husband's bed. Her hoarse repetition of an earlier question was stronger now and addressed to me as soon as I moved into the room. She asked, 'Who are you?'

She had our names already, of course. She watched me as I approached her chair and knelt in the space before the vacant hearth. I began laying out split logs, a hatchet and a few strips of paper as I said to her, 'A friend of ours is writing a book about your old family home. We found you because she wanted to dedicate it to a girl named Harriet.'

'Harriet?'

The name went across her face like a ripple on a pond. Her face was lit by the distant oil lamp. She was, as I have said, a shrunken old woman, but it was possible at that moment to trace the features of the dark-haired girl in Jacqueline's photograph.

I had begun knocking slivers of kindling off a length of wood by tapping it against the hearth with the hatchet before she murmured, 'It's a long time since I've been called Harriet.'

'Well,' I remarked flatly, hesitating with the hatchet hanging from my hand, 'what did your uncle call you?'

'Love, usually,' she replied with a sudden smile.

She didn't seem to find it odd that I should immediately ask about Walter John Ashbrook. Whereas I was suddenly feeling that nervousness I had felt a long time ago, when I had first rediscovered the courage to speak my husband's name. But, truly, nothing moved here to answer me.

Only the living were being cast into vivid perspective by the hard lamplight; Robert, his patient and Mrs Murray, who was adding, 'What is this book? And why should someone I've never met dedicate it to me?'

'The author is Mrs Jacqueline Dunn. Your husband probably bumped into her about nine months ago in the woods nearby. She has written a children's history of the house, and is particularly interested in Graham Hanley Ashbrook's life there. Whereas you're—' I stopped while I laid out the kindling in a little stack on the grate.

I took a breath, then added in a rush, 'You see, the book is dedicated to you because we couldn't find any trace of you in the housekeeper's diaries after you reached the age of about thirteen, and Jacqueline found that distressing. We, well ... we thought you'd caught diphtheria as a child and you'd died.'

'I'd *died*?' Mrs Murray seemed perplexed. Her hands were fidgeting in her lap again and she was tilting her head like it was an alien question. Perhaps she hadn't caught anything at all.

Or perhaps the reference to illness and death was just a

touch too close to the bone here. I said swiftly, 'Out of interest, what were you doing when you were thirteen?'

'Travelling with Uncle Walter? Glowering at my governess?' She happily accepted my change of tack. She told me, 'I couldn't say without a bit of time to think, because the possibilities are endless. But I didn't get ill. Surely you've noticed that my name isn't on the monument in the church?'

'Just your flowers laid at the base?' I asked with a slight smile.

'Oh? Are they still there? They must be very dry. They've been there for the whole winter. The postman took them from my garden last summer, since I can't get there myself.' She showed me her slippered feet, as if I needed proof.

'And the inscription?' I asked. '"*A man dies not while his world, his monument remains*"? We found the line in that popular novel. Am I to understand that you're Walter's world? Or was it for the giraffes?'

I don't know why the reference to the giraffes slipped out. This was Jacqueline's influence. Her passion for Graham Hanley Ashbrook's supposed obsession had worked its way into my brain. But I saw Mrs Murray blink as I struck a match.

Then an inward kind of amusement followed. I heard her say thoughtfully, 'I like your summary of my relationship with my uncle. His world, indeed.'

In her smile was the sudden unshakeable evidence that we'd all been beyond wrong about Walter.

I glanced at her as flames began licking at the twist of

paper in the hearth. Her eyes had glazed a little upon the increasing glow. In her face, I could see that his legacy wasn't built in cold stone and old houses. His lasting influence dwelled here in the memory of the upbringing he had given to a little girl called Harriet.

I got the impression that she was revisiting those memories now. The feeling was so strong, I was almost walking with her through the corridors and bright, sunny rooms of the Ashrbook house.

If I was, she didn't wish me to trespass there.

With a little inward shake, the grown woman before me abruptly returned to the present day. She said with startlingly energy, 'We wrote his inscription – his children and I, I mean – because it symbolised his unceasing drive. He swept us along. Bore us up. We planned it for years before I finally installed it. And the quotation from that book allowed us to privately reference Africa.'

'For the giraffes?' I repeated stupidly. I know I was looking doubtful. 'We saw your photograph.'

'Which photograph?' Mrs Murray was nonplussed. 'Was it taken at London Zoo?'

Then, while I reached for an answer, she leaned in to confide, 'By the way, you have noticed, haven't you dear, while you're searching for meaning behind our affection for Africa, that my husband is descended from a Kenyan man?'

Unexpectedly, we made Mr Murray laugh.

I thought the old man was reviving purely from the relief of being tended. When I turned, Robert had straightened to watch us. They both had. I had the sense that this time it was my features that were being cast into living warmth as the fire grew in the hearth beside me.

I could feel it flickering against my skin while Mr Murray drew breath to say, 'Did you know that my father came here to manage the farm when old Mr Graham Ashbrook retired and gave up his foreign life?'

I nodded. I told him gently, 'We found your father's grave. I thought he would have been buried with the family in the village church.'

Mrs Murray laughed. 'Did you think he was segregated? The boundary of the smaller parish runs very close to Bramblemead, and David's father particularly asked us to bury him near the home he loved. He said it would be like being amongst friends again, being in the churchyard where most of the farmhands were laid.'

I suppose it should have occurred to me to realise that it didn't actually mean anything that I hadn't recognised the names on the other gravestones, when the old estate manager might have known them.

It was with a slightly humbled air that I turned to Mr Murray when he spoke. The old man had the wonderfully indistinct intonation of the South Cotswolds as he told me, 'I was very small when we came here, just a baby, really. My mother had died of the yellow fever, and so did my father, very nearly. But he recovered.'

I said on a soft note of realisation, 'Was your father working closely with Graham Hanley Ashbrook in Kenya? I mean, was he involved in the old man's research?'

Mr Murray nodded.

I added more precisely, 'They were friends?'

He told me, 'My parents assisted old Mr Graham in everything. Mr Graham was devastated when my mother died and my father was ill. He always gave my father the credit for inspiring him to push on with his research. And when we came here and Mr Graham grew too old, the friendship and the work passed down the generations to Walter. That's what the memorial is for. It's for all us.'

The fire cackled beside me while he added hoarsely, 'No one will remember our names – not my father's, nor Uncle Walter's, nor even Graham Hanley Ashbrook, because they were all far too quiet in their work – but what does that matter? Science has its own memory. And for me, my wife, the life of this farm and all of Walter's children – we remember that Old Graham Ashbrook brought us all together, and that Uncle Walter's unswerving purpose kept us close.'

After a moment's peaceable contemplation of this room's growing heat, Mrs Murray drew breath as though she were drawing order to a conversation that had become temporarily waylaid.

She asked me, 'So this Mrs Dunn is writing a book about my Great-Uncle Graham? For people to read? Can she do that? She ought to have asked me first.'

I shook my head helplessly. 'She didn't know you were here. She asked at the village about Mr Murray but didn't understand the details of where he lived. She certainly didn't grasp that Miss Clare Ashbrook was Mrs Murray. I don't know that anyone even mentioned it.'

'My dear girl, who would remember a detail like that?' Mr Murray's reply was spoken through a grimace of internal discomfort. 'You're speaking as if the marriage between the adopted daughter of the local gentry and the black farmer from Bramblemead should rank as a fresh novelty, but most of our nearest neighbours weren't even born over sixty-five years ago. And it barely caused a ripple back then. If our grandson were home, things might be different. He's the one they talk about, but he isn't a Murray or an Ashbrook. He has his father's name. I told you the Ashbrook people were private.'

'Your Mrs Dunn doesn't want to write half-baked nonsense gleaned from old photographs,' remarked Mrs Murray. She was suddenly looking a little pink in the new light of the fire. 'She can't make up stories about what Great-Uncle Graham did with that house, or what his son achieved afterwards. She can't publish the book. That's all there is to it. This Mrs Dunn will have to see me first.'

She was suddenly brimming with determination. Which was wonderful, except for the minor complication that my mind was filling with the waste of my uncle's stock of paper and the realisation that Mr Murray had really been making a powerful point when he had been telling me that no one would remember Graham Hanley Ashbrook's name.

I had probably just been informed that the giraffe book would soon be withdrawn completely.

Robert's voice drew my head to the doorway. I found that he had crossed the room and he was lingering there. 'Lucy? Could I speak to you?'

I rose and went to him. As we passed out into the hallway I could hear Mrs Murray whispering across the room to her husband about what they each had said.

Robert led me into the kitchen and turned there behind the screen of the doorway so that we might speak without being overheard. I could feel the energy flowing in him; constrained as always beneath his usual sense of purpose, but still running steadily towards that old urge to roam. We were lit by the distant light of the oil lamp in the hall.

'They can't stay here,' he said.

'No,' I agreed. It was good to feel close to him. He was the one consistent note within all the strangeness of being here.

My hand had gone instinctively to his arm where he had lightly rolled his sleeves back to examine Mr Murray. With my mind upon the heat that lay beneath my fingers, I asked gently, 'How bad is it?'

'As far as I can tell, it isn't as bad as it might be. Mr Murray may be teetering on the brink of pneumonia, but might just escape it if we can get him fed and warm. He's probably fractured some of the bones in his foot. But I haven't got enough equipment to tell for sure, and I'm not his doctor.'

I asked, 'And what about you? How is your head?'

'Sore, but I'll live.'

It was then that I saw that Robert had brought his coat through into this icy kitchen with him. I watched him set it down to one side upon the sideboard. He straightened his sleeves, and then he was free to turn back to me. After a momentary consideration, he moved to draw me to him. It felt very natural, even though I could feel the very faint current of that energy passing from him to me.

He said, 'We're both feeling the strain of finding these people, aren't we?'

I confessed, 'I can't help thinking that if I was right; that if the pressure that drove me really did relate to the history of the Ashbrook house; and if I truly did feel the moment its focus moved from me to you ... that old title of yours – doctor – is why.'

He said, 'Mine were the skills it recognised?'

I didn't say it, but there was the strangeness of wondering if it would permit him to leave now.

Very determinedly, I said, 'Someone needs to make them a strong cup of tea, and someone needs to go for help. It would be quickest if you went to Jacqueline.'

He noted my directness. Briefly, there was a whisper of gratitude there. He knew I was aware of how much he needed the room to move, to walk, to shake this off.

Then the change in his attention built an ache in me. He focussed on me and me alone. He asked, 'Do you trust me to leave you here while I go for the real doctor?'

Now it was my turn to reveal my restlessness. His sudden tenderness sent a shiver straight through me. Intensely. Because his question passed through the mess of our care for these people and my fears for him, and ran straight to the bruise that dwelled in my mind.

'Oh, Robert,' I said helplessly, 'of course I do.' Because I didn't want to think like this any more. I wanted to remember how much I was growing to know him.

And I suppose I might have tried to turn away from him and the pressure to answer his question more honestly except that he still had his hands at my waist and they steadied me, quite firmly.

I'd been a fool to try to turn away. The confidence that had been built between us this morning over my advent calendar was rippling back and forth between us like a wave. He knew me too. The thought was followed after a moment by the gentlest of pressures under my chin to bring my mouth up to his.

Then, in the seconds afterwards, he told me, 'I love you.'

I couldn't help softening then. I think he was beginning to smile when he let me go. I didn't see. He was turning his head aside to look for his coat and I was letting out my breath in one extraordinary release of tension while I stepped aside to seek the support of the sideboard. Standing before me now, he worked his way into his dirtied raincoat.

As he straightened his collar, he said altogether more briskly, 'Do you think Jacqueline is going to cope with all this? She's about to have her evening filled with the trouble of taking me to the various houses of people who can be summoned to help, before descending upon this place with food and blankets, and plans for the evacuation.'

The features of his face caught the light from the distant oil lamp as he turned his head to catch some sound from the other room. They were fine, just talking.

Suddenly, I was experiencing a powerful sense of the value of this man who could treat every detail with such care.

All the same, I managed to say with an incredulous laugh,

'You're asking whether Jacqueline will cope? Truly? She'll be delighted, of course. You've just found her the first of her guests, and she's about to discover that Walter's role in that house was even more splendid than that of her darling Graham Hanley Ashbrook.'

His attention dropped to me. 'And what about you? Will you cope on your own for a few hours? What about those animals? Can you manage to get hay to them?'

'Robert,' I told him quite flatly. 'You've already guessed that I keep up the pretence about the animals for the sake of my aunt and uncle and for my parents, so I don't see why we should have to sustain the lie between us too. I'm not afraid of those poor beasts.'

I was speaking defiantly but I couldn't help the way doubt crept in with the silence that fell briefly between us. To my right was the beckoning shape of the kitchen door.

His head briefly turned to follow the stray in my attention. He knew at that moment that I was waging a battle between good sense and a violent urge to beg him to come back to me.

His promise was given freely anyway in the form of a reply so quiet that even the ghosts might not hear.

'Here you are,' he told me softly. 'And I don't like leaving you.'

It was some time later, after he had gone – without anything moving out of the dark to stop him, and after I had done what I could for the pathetic beasts in the cattle shed – that I turned my thoughts at last to the other silence that was waiting in the corners of this house.

I wasn't even alone. I was kneeling by the hearth and waiting for a simple pan of soup to cook through. But I wasn't reaching for Walter or this idea I had that some part of me had been sensitive to the force of the man's life.

This was something that dwelled deeper, enduring beyond the immediate plight of an old couple. It resided in the part of me that had been harnessed by my grief. And it lay in the knowledge that I had to consider the larger question here, which was framed around the puzzle of why it had been my search, and not Jacqueline's, that had discovered this last relic of the Ashbrook family.

Perhaps their desperate need for help had already reached out to Jacqueline, but found the connection between them too vague to sustain on its own.

On an impulse, in the full light of the fire in the hearth, I turned my head as if listening, and found something very peaceful. I spoke for the first and only time clearly into the void.

I said, 'I always did say that you were focussed on the bigger things. If it was you who taught them how to reach me, Archie – thank you.'

Marjoram
Arrowroot
Rosemary
Rhubarb
Yarrow
Mistletoe
Elderflower

A note on the text

The unscripted misspellings of Ashbrook within this book were entirely accidental and, out of respect for the ghost, were allowed to remain.

Author's Note

Thank you so much for reading *Mrs P's Book of Secrets*. I hope you've loved Lucy's determined account of her effort to begin her life again within the quiet rooms of the Kershaw and Kathay Book Press. I certainly loved helping her to discover love and friendship there.

This is a book about the echoes of the past. It is a ghost story without white shrouded spectres, or wailing ghouls. The fading notes of those who have passed are simply a steady part of Lucy's struggle to discover the healing freedom of her newfound life in the Cotswolds.

This is also a book about belonging. Lucy is feeling a bit unsure of her place now that she has come home. She doesn't know it, but Robert is facing a similar struggle. He is a man who has endlessly had to stand firm for what he truly wants instead of resuming his high-flying career in medicine, particularly when every part of the past is touched by so many memories of his life as a POW. For me there is something wonderful in the way he assembles plants and oddments for Lucy's advent calendar. The final collection forms an anagram for his proposal, but his first message, the anagram of MERRY XMAS, is almost more important.

He decides to extend a little gesture of friendship to Lucy after their first brief meeting on the stairs in her aunt's house. He isn't asking anything of her, but he wants to find a harmless means of showing her how important she is. And he does it long before she has learned how to talk to him about her past, or learned that he and her aunt and uncle conspired to bring her home – or even told him how much she values the simple kindness of his presence in the office.

Friendship touches every part of their lives in that old building. Books are a vital theme too. They almost rank as a character in their own right. The books in Lucy's life certainly have a personality. They link the past to the present, and forge connections between people too. Lucy herself describes books as a wonderful monument to unity. And they are – not least because they play such a crucial role in the search for the old couple.

Personally, I find it incredible to comprehend how many people have been involved in the creation of this book. The book within your hands, whether digital or print, is formed of the words that have grown in my mind, but, beyond that, so many people have played their part.

My editor at One More Chapter made vital suggestions about the text. Then other people in the team took the finished work and formatted it, and made it ready to meet the world. Someone cared to design the cover. Someone engineered the e-reader app, or operated the machine that printed the book too. And someone, often many people, were involved in getting the book to the person who will read it. There is something truly uplifting in that.

Lucy's story unfolds in 1946. When I research a book, I am usually drawing on oral history from the time, so in a way my characters borrow from real voices. Perhaps it is my background in archaeology, but I am the sort of person for whom the traces of the past are ever present in the world I see around me. In this book, Lucy takes an intensely personal journey into the heartfelt connection she feels between herself and those who have gone before her. I find it quite strange to consider that, by now, at the present year of writing this, Lucy's first discovery of trust and healing with Robert in that old creaking office would in itself count as history.

I can't help wondering where life has taken them since then. I know they will have been happy.

With love,

Lorna

Acknowledgements

I have been helped and supported by so many people in the course of writing this book. I am particularly grateful to Stuart Samuel for allowing me to borrow his invaluable expertise as I researched bus travel in the area. Many thanks also to Alan Brookes for helping me to uncover the terminology and technology of a 1940s printworks.

My family and friends have been as ever an invaluable support, and my eternal gratitude and affection goes to my husband Jeremy for being endlessly by my side.

Finally, I'd like to thank the team at One More Chapter, but particularly my editor Charlotte Ledger, whose clear and insightful advice has proved so inspiring. Thank you.